DEMON BETRAYED

DEMON ENFORCERS, BOOK 5

JENN STARK

Katana Midland can't catch a break.

She finally sells her first big graphic novel—complete with the scorching hot guardian angel who's been haunting her dreams—only to have her apocalyptic tale come to life.

Now there are magic bombs dropping on New York, demons running through the streets, and a deadly cabal of sorcerers gunning for her and her angel. Has she finally met the perfect hero only to lose him?

Hugh of the Syx, the most devious demon of an elite squad of brutal enforcers, has a problem. His one shot at redemption is to convince a human female that he's—wait for it—an *angel*, because she's more psychic than a box of Magic 8 Balls and the Syx's only chance at fixing a world gone mad.

From the moment Hugh jumps off the page and into Kat's life, she triggers emotions he didn't know he could feel—and desires he wants more than anything to be real. But every step they get closer to the end of Katana's twisted tale is one step closer to their story ending, forever.

The truth will never set you free when you're a *Demon Betrayed*.

For those who see things other people don't.

PROLOGUE

Jerusalem, Israel

This section of the ancient city lay in smoking ruin. Fires burned in hollowed-out buildings; embers floated in the air. The bodies of charred and blood-soaked humans lined the streets, streaked with the black ichor of demons. Some of these mortals had understood who and what they'd been fighting against. Most hadn't. Demons were a singularly uniting force, but they weren't the true enemy here.

Michael the Archangel watched as the human sorceress stalked through the streets of Jerusalem, her slender, weathered hands drifting over the bodies of the fallen, ushering souls to their reward. She was a long, lean woman who could have passed for thirty or fifty, her pale eyes now focused on her charges, her fair cheeks flushed with the day's exertion. Her short, spiky, platinum hair was wild with smoke. Blood and soot stained her long-sleeved shirt and tattered jeans. She carried no weapon. That wasn't her place on this battlefield.

It wasn't his either.

The woman had been known by many names throughout her long life, but currently, she went by Blue. And she *was* still human, despite the fact that she had become immortal in service to the arcane power running through her. Immortal, but not unkillable. An ancient Celtic priestess who served lesser gods, she was a heretic by the rules of the Church, though neither she nor the Father paid as much attention to such things as most humans needed to believe.

Michael fully understood that, by rights, he should let Blue take the path the Father had mapped out with her before she entered this life...but he couldn't.

It wasn't her time to die.

The world still needed her.

For all the long buildup to today's epic battle, the attack of human sorcerers against their own kind had come swiftly, in the end. The Shadow Court psychics had attempted to subjugate the remainder of the world's psychically gifted by detonating a terrifying array of psychic weapons across the globe. It had taken the combined might of another, even smaller, faction of magicians to stop the Shadow Court, but their success had come at a terrible cost to Earth.

Fortunately, most humans would neither see nor truly understand that cost...only those with psychic ability running through their veins.

Michael set his jaw. How many times had he seen it? The petty battles of mortals for dominion over each other were doomed to fail. The death and pain they caused rippled across decades, sometimes centuries. But this attempt was deeper and more devastating than anyone yet realized.

The human priestess trudged toward him, distracted, then stopped abruptly as he stepped in front of her. Blue narrowed her eyes against the brightness of his form, but he wouldn't hide himself from her, not here. Not for these few brief moments.

She settled herself on her heels, not afraid of him, but not quite sure of him either. She was one of the ones responsible for saving humanity—technically, so was he. But they couldn't be less alike.

When he didn't move, just looked at her, she squinted. "I figured you'd be back in your tower, praying for the salvation of everyone left and the sanctity of those who've passed on."

"I should be," Michael agreed easily, but he couldn't mask the quiver of desperation in his voice, the fear. The irony wasn't lost on him, that she should be so certain and he so shaken with doubt.

"Do not..." He swallowed, then continued, his words slow and resolute. "Do not continue your work here this day, Blue."

Her brows leapt at his use of her name. Michael wasn't surprised. Of all the members of the Arcana Council, he kept himself the most apart from his human brethren.

Partly because he wasn't human.

As an angel of the Most High, Michael had been given long-sighted jurisdiction to aid and support this flawed and fragile race. No one had fully understood his decision to join the Arcana Council at the fall of Atlantis nearly six thousand years earlier, but he had no real choice. He was compelled to do what he must to aid God's children. It was the same reason why he had also taken command of the Syx, an elite squad of demons who yearned for forgiveness, even if they wouldn't—couldn't—admit it. From their rage-filled leader, Warrick, to the wisecracking Finn, the witch-defying Stefan, and the empathic Gregori, four of his Demon Enforcers had secured their redemption. Now it was Hugh's chance—a one-time Fallen angel who had misled God's children with a deception so casually issued, and ultimately deadly, the humans had begged God to destroy him.

And so the Father had.

Hugh had suffered a thousand torments for his sin, but he still possessed an unparalleled ability to deceive. He'd better, because to redeem himself and his fellow Enforcers, the demon was about to be forced to sell the lie of his life—to a human fated to betray him.

At least Hugh's path had been made clear to Michael. The test of the final demon, Raum...that was blocked to him.

Which could only mean that Michael wouldn't be around to see it. Undoubtedly, that was all part of the Father's larger plan. A plan that, up to now, he had willingly followed.

But now...

The archangel tightened his jaw as Blue lifted a hand to rub her temple. Her fingers grazed the shaved portion of her skull where the hair lay flat and straight, then raked through the thick platinum shock of it that draped across her brow. "Why shouldn't I work here?"

"Because that path..." Michael abruptly shuddered, fighting the transformation that swept over him at his surging panic. His skin grew warm and healthy, his wings spread above him in an iridescent rainbow, while deep within him, his heart beat. In this moment, the Father knew his innermost fear, fed it. Nurtured it. Allowed Michael to see all that he could be—a Fallen angel, a true part of this world—if only he was strong enough to withstand the temptation that role brought with it.

He wasn't.

Death blinked, and he read the confusion on her face. She was thinking that angels didn't have hearts, not in the way humans did. So how—

Michael exhaled slowly, forcing himself to return to his ghostly pallor, and Death released a breath he suspected she hadn't realized she'd been holding.

"That path leads to your death," he told her.

He didn't miss the immediate denial on her face, the certainty that almost bordered on smugness. It was always this way with humans. Even though they knew—*knew*—that they could be killed with the barest of efforts, they ran headlong into the fire.

Once again, Michael felt the kindling of that strange and unwanted force within him, the quickening of a life not his to claim. Power. Heat. A passion to fight—to feel. To truly live.

"It is not my place," he continued, his words little more than a growl as the hourglass tipped. He had no more time. She had to understand! "It is not my duty. It is not my freedom to choose one life over another. But I would choose your life, Blue. I would—"

And then it was too late.

The movement came so swiftly, Death never saw it. She stared at Michael as he shifted again into the form that taunted him with its forbidden strength. He knew what she saw—his face warm, tan, lined with wrinkles from laughter and squinting into the sun, his hands calloused by the weight of hard work, and his wings bursting forth with radiant color. So engrossed was she in the miracle of Michael's transformation from Angel of the Lord to something not quite human, but no longer fully angelic, she didn't notice the thin, wiry assailant leap from the shadows of the alley, didn't see the cruel, curving blade slash down toward her chest, angling for her heart.

"*No*," the archangel cried. He turned and flung his hand out, a fiery blast incinerating the human where he stood.

Time stopped.

He heard Blue shout his name as the heavens opened around them and a thousand winds roared in their ears. Michael had killed a human. He had committed the most grievous sin any angel ever could—and he knew it. He gave her a smile that he hoped, somehow, could convey what he felt for her, all the words of admiration and honor he could never speak.

"Humans are our weakness," he said instead, whispering into the raging storm. "But you shall not die this day."

"*Michael*—" Death cried, and he held on to that word, the tone and tenor of it, the grace and strength, even as it was snatched from her throat and the earth and sky seemed to fall away from them. A horde of demons burst up out of nothing and swarmed Michael, pulling him away from Blue with howls of pure, otherworldly glee.

Michael filled his whole mind with this last image of Blue, even as his wings were shredded and his robes were torn. He had defied the Father, himself, and his path. Now he would be punished with an endless cycle of torture and pain, an eternity of agony befitting the condemned. His only shot at redemption was now in the hands of the final two demons of the Syx.

The irony of this moment wasn't lost on him.

Then a yawning pit opened wide, and Michael the Archangel was ripped away into darkness, the sky and earth rushing back into place as if he'd never been there at all.

1
_____

Hoboken, New Jersey
Three hours earlier

The lights flickered ten minutes into Jeremy Bolling's Master of Miniatures presentation. There was a slight murmur of interest through the room, a few glances to the ceiling, but most of the small crowd at Gotham City Games & Magic kept their eyes trained on the maestro on the small stage in the corner.

Dressed in a Jets jersey and cargo pants lined with uniformly overfilled pockets, Jeremy was the star attraction of the day-long RPG and Fantasy Fest at the bookstore. Kat was happy to let him bask in the limelight. She'd talk about her graphic novels that afternoon for anyone who was still around. But she'd only come to this event to justify the cost of the real reason why she'd flown to the city: to hand-deliver a manuscript to her first official New York editor.

Her agent had told Kat that she worried way too much,

that she could have easily emailed the *Dead End* file and it would've been perfectly safe. But her agent didn't understand how much all this meant to Kat—to finally be chosen, to be the one whose dream was coming true. No more doors getting slammed in her face, no more sucking it up and biding her time, no more paths turning into, well, dead ends. She'd *made* it.

And it was magic.

Her editor, a Princess Leia-bunned, Birkenstock-and-socks-loving nerd named Emily, had indulged her earlier that morning, solemnly accepting the Hello Kitty thumb drive from Kat as if it wasn't a glorified children's toy. She'd given it a place of honor alongside her collection of other whimsical paraphernalia that lined her real live New York editor's desk.

Kat didn't care how silly she seemed to either woman. This new graphic novel had been something special from the very beginning. Though she had been dinking around with pieces of the story for years, the final idea for *Dead End* had come to her in a flash about nine months ago. It'd been so fully formed and perfect that Kat had stopped cold in the middle of designing the mind-numbingly boring email she'd promised to one of her best clients and had spent the next two hours sketching out possibilities. The story was the perfect combination of high stakes action and richly energetic artwork, with just enough emotion to keep the whole thing bouncing along.

She'd thought that would be enough for a sale—a legit sale to a big shiny publishing house—and it *had* been enough for her to secure representation for the book. But her new agent had strongly suggested she make some changes to the early going of *Dead End*, mainly because she'd killed off the love interest and blown up half of New

York by page thirty. Kat had argued, cajoled, and finally outright whined at the changes, but by the time she was finished with the updated story, she had to admit her agent was right.

Now the story started with a much smaller cataclysm—and in Chicago, not New York—then took off into a twisting, crazy race through a world filled with chaos and magic, pitting the plucky heroine against some evil magicians who'd created a shadowy court in a citadel she'd named Sorcerer City. The heroine—with the help of a powerful, charismatic, and, this time, very much alive love interest, at least for several more chapters in the book—traced a perilous, adventure-filled path to said city, unlocked the citadel to let in the good guys, confronted the evil magicians, and saved the day. Confetti and magic all around, each step perfectly laid out in gorgeous, full-color, easy-to-follow panels.

Kat grimaced. At least, she hoped the panels were easy to follow. They had to be, because she didn't have all the words for them yet.

It'd always been that way for her. Images first, words later. Even now, six years after she'd self-published her first graphic novel short, and despite the modest indie success she'd had up to this new book, the words came way too slow. She knew, roughly, what should be conveyed in every one of her panels, but crafting that message down to a handful of sentences was an art she hadn't quite mastered. She used too many words or not enough at the critical points, always rushing on to the next panel unfolding in her mind. The story was like a house with too many intersecting hallways, each one a possible dead end.

Her lips twisted. *Dead End* had been the working title for this graphic novel longer than it should have. She'd grown attached to it. She didn't harbor any hope that Emily would keep it, of course. It would get shifted to something that would sell more books, maybe even catch the interest of a content streamer looking for a new animation or live-action urban fantasy.

That extra sale could happen, her agent had assured Kat after she'd seen the first few chapters of the novel. It was the whole reason why they'd held back those rights, even though Kat would've been equally happy to sell everything all at once. She'd been on the fringes of the business long enough to know you didn't often get a second chance.

"And now for the big show," Jeremy announced, his voice loud enough that Kat refocused on him. "This baby's my pride and joy. You gotta let me know if you like it."

He brought the small figurine under the lights, and Kat jolted.

"Who is it?" someone deeper in the room asked excitedly. "One of the Mystic Warrior line?"

"Birds of Prey?" someone else demanded, while Kat could only stare.

Jeremy grinned, turning the figurine under the camera, but looking up at the screen like the rest of the room, his face radiating pure, unfiltered joy. "It's a whole new line, guys. The idea hit me a couple of weeks ago like a ton of bricks, filled me up with so much fire, I couldn't stop working on it. It made me hopeful, you know? The idea that something— someone—was out there waiting to stand up for us, to help us fix the mess we've gotten ourselves into. And we're the ones who'll see that someone coming first. You, me, all of us —we're standing on holy ground here at Gotham City Games and Magic. We see things other people don't."

The crowd murmured an approval that sounded a little

too earnest, too loud. Kat tore her gaze away from the figurine to scan the group, blinking quickly at the shift of energy in the room. Jeremy's words were bold, but this wasn't some crazed cabal of wannabe psychics. Half of them were gamers who never grew up, the other half maybe-probably believed in magic, but that really didn't get them very far in the real world. Still...there was no denying the fervent expression on too many faces, the gleam in several sets of eyes.

They believed in—something. What, she didn't know, but something bigger than themselves. Even if they'd never gotten a chance to express it.

Jeremy sighed down at the figurine he held so reverently.

"This is the first one, a prototype never before seen before today, and I've still got some kinks to work out. I'm calling it the Guardian Angels line. Whattya think?"

A hushed "Ohhhh" of appreciation rippled through the room, and it was deserved. The image on the screen that focused on the figurine no larger than the palm of Jeremy's slender-fingered hand was hyper-specific in its detail. The wings, spread in a canopy of heavy gray-and-white feathers, opened in anticipation of flight. The male beneath them was human in his features, but even in miniature, he looked built to a larger scale, with bulky arms, broad chest, and heavy thighs.

The most arresting thing about him, though, was his face. Jeremy angled the figurine toward the camera to give everyone a better view. The guardian angel's eyes smoked with a deep, wickedly purple gleam, and his mouth was pulled back in a snarl that managed to convey a feral glee. He looked dangerous and not entirely stable...and he was also devastatingly gorgeous, something you couldn't say about most figurines.

He was also completely familiar to Kat, and not just in a general wicked-cool superhero kind of way. She knew those eyes, that face. She knew the way the angel's thick black hair flowed back from his head. She knew the wings that crested far over his head, and how much strength and power rolled out from him when he leapt into the sky, those great, feathered limbs propelling him upward. In contrast, she knew that when he landed, when his feet first touched the earth, he made no sound at all. He could as easily be a single feather dropping to the ground before surging forward, shaking the earth with his pounding boots.

She knew all these things because they'd been part of her original download of inspiration for *Dead End*—at least the version of the story that had ended up with the beautiful angel getting betrayed by her heroine and slaughtered on the streets of New York—but how the *fuck* did Jeremy know about her angel?

"Is it a commissioned piece?" She was surprised at the question, mostly because she was the one who asked it.

Jeremy looked up, brows lifting. He was a medium-tall guy with sandy brown hair, shrewd brown eyes, and an easy smile—and even for a demonstration such as this, he never dressed up. That jersey and those cargo pants had made an appearance at every con they'd attended together. Jeremy wasn't heavy, but he was skinny soft, his arms and legs as thin as spaghetti while his stomach rounded like an oversized meatball.

They knew each other, of course. There weren't that many sci-fi and fantasy cons in the northeast, and Kat had always understood that her particular style of artwork played better in bigger cities—New York, Chicago, LA. But she lived in a tiny little town in North Carolina, lucky enough to eke out a living as a graphic designer while she worked on her urban fantasy graphic novels. She'd met Jeremy maybe six years ago when she was still in college and dreaming of the big time, and he was a thirty-five-year-old living in his mother's basement, and they hadn't progressed all that far since then.

He grinned at her, waggling his brows. "It could be commissioned, for the right buyer," he said. "I've got other orders, but this baby was too eager to be first. He's done now, at least in prototype, but I haven't shopped the series yet."

"How many will there be?" someone else asked as Kat's mind jumped to her own meager bank account. The sale of *Dead End* had promised her a windfall. But she'd signed that contract months ago, and no money had shown up yet. The nature of publishing, everyone said, but that platitude didn't pay the bills.

"Six, I think," Jeremy said, scratching his chin. "I haven't quite got a fix on the other five, but I know they're all a set together. Six avenging angels, setting the world to rights. Came to me in a vision, you could say."

There was a murmur of approval from the room, while Kat nodded at Jeremy. "Let me know when you set a price."

Jeremy grinned back at her, looking pleased. She couldn't press him too hard, or he'd jack up the number. They might be nodding acquaintances at the cons, but this was a business. Artists had to eat.

A crack of lightning streaked across the sky, so bright that everyone jumped.

"What the hell?" Jeremy asked, squinting towards the windows. "Why is it so dark outside?"

A few fantasy enthusiasts stood, straining toward the

windows as the proprietor of Gotham City Games and Magic, Gable Sizemore, stepped onto the sidewalk.

"Holy shit, it's cold," he reported, sounding shocked. "It's probably dropped twenty degrees."

Another flash of lightning sparked, this one blanketing the room in white light. And Kat suddenly realized what was wrong with this picture.

"There's no thunder," she blurted. And in her mind's eye, she saw a tower thrusting up out of the ground made of nothing but electrical currents and sparking light. It had been a fantastical structure, ominous and awesome, and it had graced the original opening pages of *Dead End*. But she'd made that up—she'd made all of it up. The guardian angel, the electrical tower, the green smoke...the bombs.

"Electrical storm?" somebody asked, and now everyone was on their feet. The following questions came fast and furious. "Should we go out? Should we block the door? Does this place have a basement?"

"We do have a basement." Gable spoke the words in almost a shout to carry over the hubbub. "But it's a little cramped down there. The storm seems pretty far off. I'd hate to tell you to go home, but..."

He didn't have a chance to finish his sentence. There was a general stampede toward the door, everyone jostling. Most of these people lived within an hour of the city, and most of them relied on public transpo. If the subway shut down, it was going to be hell getting home.

Kat grabbed her backpack and shouldered it, then bounded up to where Jeremy was hastily replacing his figurines into foam-lined boxes. "Need a hand?"

He jerked a narrow-eyed glance at her. "Don't try anything funny. They're all chipped. You steal one, and I'll know it."

The warning was snapped, both serious and urgent, then Jeremy ruined the effect by sliding into a grin.

"Pretty cool, huh?" he said, not pausing in his packing routine. "A lightning storm breaks out the moment I unleash Hugh the Destroyer, guardian angel numero uno. I'd say someone upstairs is taking note."

"Someone definitely is." Kat picked up another of his figurines and slotted it into its foam case. *Hugh. His name is Hugh.* She hadn't known that, because once again: words. In *Dead End*, she'd always simply called him Angel. "How long have you been working on him? A while now?"

"Not that long. Like I said, it came to me a couple of weeks ago. I had to stop everything else and make it. That ever happen to you?"

"Yeah." Kat recalled the fugue state that had gripped her for weeks every time she turned to *Dead End*, the high-energy euphoria that had slipped away the moment she'd finished the last panel. She'd delivered the opening chapters to an agent she'd wanted to represent her since she'd first started looking into publishing and had gotten the response within a week.

Then came the sale, an honest-to-God *sale*. It'd seemed like a dream come true at the time, and she'd immediately begun planning for the life she'd lead next—a new apartment. A car that actually ran most days. Maybe a move to a real city.

That high-speed train to the promised land had slowed way down in the months that followed, but Kat was still riding high. Only, there was no way Jeremy could've known about her work. Which meant Hugh the Destroyer, the winged warrior angel of her wildest bookish fantasies, existed in only three places: Kat's laptop, currently safe in her pack, on a Hello Kitty thumb drive in downtown

Manhattan...and at Gotham City Games & Magic, cradled in Jeremy's pale-fingered grip.

She whipped her head around at a high-pitched whistling noise. A firebolt shot across the front windows of the gaming store and exploded. Green smoke erupted into the street. Lights flashed, Kat's ears popped, and then a wave of heat blasted through the building, shoving her back into a low bookcase.

Her last thought before losing consciousness was that she'd seen this all before.

2

Jerusalem, Israel
North of the city

"*H*ugh!"

This particular shout wasn't all that helpful since it was just his name. But when spoken in the heavenly choir-caliber voice of Raum of the Syx, it conveyed everything necessary to Hugh. Specifically, duck and roll or you were gonna become demon chow.

Hugh dove to the side, releasing his shuriken blades to do their worst. The weapons had been a gift of the witches, his fellow demon enforcer Stefan had said—and at this point, the Syx needed all the help they could get.

The blades delivered on their promise of quick, decisive death. The demons charging him fell like a curtain dropped from its rod, all of them dissolving into the black spew that made up their kind.

The Syx had been fighting alongside human warriors

for what felt like days now, but was, in reality, only a couple of hours. Still, the battle would never have taken this long if anything were normal about this godforsaken demon puke fest. Unfortunately, as the Syx had come to realize, this particular crypt in the heart of Jerusalem was the closest he'd ever seen to a hellmouth since the Middle Ages. If they could hold this portal, they could fully assess the damage that the psychic assholes known as the Shadow Court had wrought across the earth.

There was no question that someone had lit a fire under the collective ass of the horde today. Except whether the spawn were operating in collusion with the humans or simply taking advantage of the chaos that the Shadow Court had sown with their psychic blastapalooza, Hugh didn't know. Still, the Syx were allowed to kill demons. Humans were another matter altogether, damn their blessed souls.

"Report." A new voice thundered in his head, clipped but not exceptionally stressed. Warrick, leader of the Syx, rarely got stressed. Bulky, dark, and amber-eyed, looking like he was permanently pissed off, Warrick lived to fight. They all did. It wasn't like they had much choice, but at least they were well suited to the job.

Through circumstances that had thankfully faded into the mists of time, unless he thought really hard about them —which he didn't—Hugh had long ago been conscripted into the most elite fighting group of his despicable kind. The charter of the Syx was simple: kill the worst of the worst of demon horde, and follow the orders of their leader, none other than the Right Hand of God^{TM}, Michael the Archangel. The killing part was easy. Bowing and scraping to the so-fair-he-was-almost-invisible archangel was more tedious, but there was one hell of a carrot Michael dangled, for all of them.

If the Syx were good little demons and killed enough assholes while making the world safer for God's children, they'd be freed of their condemnation and returned to their former states. They wouldn't climb back up the ladder all the way to angelhood, but they'd at least regain their status as the Fallen.

That was fine with Hugh. Full-on angels were assholes, always had been. He was well rid of their kind.

"I said, *report*," growled Warrick again, this time sounding slightly more irritated. He *was* a demon, after all. They weren't known for their patience.

"What do you think report is?" A new voice joined the fray—blue-eyed Finn, the youngest of their team, though that wasn't saying much since they all had existed before the dawn of recorded history. Still, Finn was light on his feet and sharp-witted, and never shy about speaking his mind. "This battle fucking sucks. Everything sucks. We're being fed a steady diet of rancid demon ass, and it sucks."

"The outer guard is holding," Gregori put in, the voice of the big demon ringing with the pain he was picking up from the humans who fought all around them—his empathic nature was both his gift and his curse. He was the largest of their number, but in some ways the most gentle...not that he cut any of the horde any slack. "The human warriors are strong, and the witches are stronger. But they tire. They are not made for war such as this."

"They'll hold," Stefan countered, and Hugh supposed that he would know. Of all the Syx, the lean, red-eyed Stefan was most attuned to the covens of witches that still, after all these generations, had proven to be the only humans who could exercise some control over the demons.

Most normal witches used that skill to keep the world safe from the bastards, but some had been lured over to the small group of dickhead Shadow Court psychics to help them with their dark designs. Lured, or pressed into service, either way. Stefan had been captured by witches on his own twisted path to redemption while under the careful eye of Michael the Archangel, who was conspicuously MIA now that the fighting had turned dirty. The archangel never did like to get his feathers dusty.

This time, Hugh didn't need Raum's warning. He could feel the pressure of the attack to his left. A new wave of demons spilled out of the crypt.

God's teeth, these assholes were as ugly as angels were beautiful, and Hugh's lips curled. He could no longer remember his time as an angel, of course—those memories had been blasted from him along with any desire to give a fuck. All that was left for him was an endless charter to throw himself, body and absent soul, into the fire.

He might be able to be killed by demons, but he wasn't about to be taken out by these particular lame asses. He turned back to the battle, and the day wore on.

Even when a curious lightness filled the air around him, signaling that the worst of the psychic attack of the humans was ending, the demons kept coming. It was like someone had jammed the faucet of evil to full, causing all the scum of the earth to rush through, bubbling out to spread across the land.

There'd long been rumblings among the horde about that kind of unleashing. The Syx had already gotten a taste of it with the magic of the planet hiking up over the past several months—and it had only gotten worse when certain factions of mortals had gotten it into their heads that they could control the horde as well as their fellow psychics.

Both situations had proven disastrous. Humans weren't ready for magic. They weren't ready to have their psychic abilities, gifts from the Father on High or not, stretched to their breaking point. The free will He set such store by put His children at risk of making deadly choices. The strong would always oppress the weak. The strong would never cease in their desire to be stronger still. And when the blood finally dried from this day, there'd be hell to—

A masculine cry of utter, soul-wrenching anguish ripped through the air.

Pulverizing the demons directly in front of him, Hugh watched as the rest of the horde turned tail and dove back into the hole from which they were spilling. As one, Stefan, Hugh, and Raum raced after them, but Warrick's voice once more cut across their minds.

"No," Warrick bellowed. "To the archangel. Now."

A moment later, they materialized across the city in one of the harder hit sections of Jerusalem. Fires still raged in the darkened streets, but the only humans remaining were lifeless bodies. At least the stench of demons had receded here, though the sharp smell of sulfur was undeniable.

Hugh hadn't felt a summons from the archangel, though there was nothing that Michael enjoyed more than crooking his little finger and yanking his minions back from whatever blasted corner of the world he'd sent them to do his bidding.

To his surprise, the nearly translucent figure of the archangel, so pale that he seemed little more than a puff of smoke in pristine robes, was nowhere to be found. Instead, the human priestess who went by the name of Blue now stood looking as broken as he'd ever seen her, her face wild with rage, grief, and guilt.

Hugh felt his nerves prick up. Of all the human emotions, guilt was the most dangerous. This could be interesting.

"What happened?" he demanded before the last of their number had fully formed.

Blue turned, her eyes far older than her appearance of middling years. They also brimmed over with power. She belonged to a council of sorcerers who strove to keep the balance of magic on the earth, and who had worked tirelessly to that end since the Great Flood had first driven the pagan gods from this land and sent them back behind the veil. During that cataclysm, Atlantis had sunk, the gods had fled, the Arcana Council had risen up to take care of their people, and the Creator had laughed.

By then, the archangel had already put his team of the Syx to work for him, while he had taken a six-thousand-year sabbatical in Hell to get away from it all. He'd returned only a few short years ago. The reunion hadn't been a happy one, but since he'd come back, Michael had been living up to his end of the bargain he'd struck with the Syx all those years ago.

Four of their number had followed his instructions and achieved redemption. Only two were left—though all six demons needed to succeed for them all to reach the promised land. Hugh wasn't going to be the one to let them down. But where was their fearless leader?

"He's gone," Blue said as if he had voiced the question aloud. He blinked, and she waved at the empty street in front of her.

"What do you mean, gone?" Warrick demanded. He wasn't the biggest of their number—that honor went to Gregori—but Warrick was powerfully built, his skin streaked with dirt and demon blood and his brown hair plastered to his scalp. There was something tight in his voice that Hugh didn't like, a note of desperation that arrowed through him. "The Father would not have suffered his death."

"Well, he certainly was willing to let him suffer the agony of getting his wings ripped off and then being hauled away by demons," Blue said flatly. She shoved a hand through her spiky white hair. "Is that enough suffering for you?"

"What?" Finn blurted, his usual grin wiped away by shock. Raum stepped forward, looking equally stricken. He was the most beautiful of all the demons—the closest to what they had looked like as Fallen angels, once upon a long ago age. But now his soft green eyes were haunted with remembered pain.

"He killed," he said, his voice a dirge of seraphs. "He killed a human."

"Fried the guy's ass right into the ground, yup," Blue confirmed, her jaw clenched. "Saving my life, as it happened, not that it earned him any brownie points. I don't follow your god, and he knows it. This latest move isn't winning me over, for the record."

"But…" Stefan spread his elegant hands. "What does that mean? If he's dead—"

"He's not dead," both Blue and Warrick cut in. Another voice confirmed the same—Gregori, the empath of the group, stood at the edge of their small group, looking despondent. He held something shimmery aloft, and when Hugh squinted, he could see it. One of the archangel's translucent feathers.

"I will get him back," Blue said, her glare narrowing on the feather. "In the meantime, you have to carry on with the work he gave you. Much as you did before, when he consigned himself to Hell."

Warrick scowled at her. "What do you know of that? Do you know where he is?"

She shook her head. "I came down this path looking for the dead. There are too many souls who are refusing to leave this plane, especially these last few hours. Great magic has been unleashed. You can't tell me you don't feel it."

Warrick shrugged. "There has always been great magic in this world, for those who can see it."

"Well, that's a whole shit ton more people now, and what they're seeing is a lot more dangerous," Blue snapped. "I'm not just talking demons, I'm talking the filth of humanity rising up against itself *and* demons. You two are what's left of the Syx's redemption tour." She fixed Raum and Hugh with a hard gaze. "You need to finish the cycle. It might help get the archangel back."

Raum's face darkened, and Hugh looked at him with new speculation. He knew his own sin, of course. He'd been steeped in the pain of it for millennia. And he knew nearly all the others' sins as well. Warrick had been condemned to eternal demonhood because of his rage, Stefan, not surprisingly, because of his pride. Finn had been turned through his lack of faith, Gregori because he'd told God to fuck off.

Hugh always did like that sin the best.

As for Hugh himself, his transgression was a cosmic joke. He, the most silver-tongued of the golden host, had been duped by the very children he'd been created to serve. Granted, he'd lied to them first—but come on. They'd had it coming. When they turned the tables on him, he'd been blindsided. Straight up betrayed by humans, and too stupid to recognize it before it was too late. His first clue that he'd been screwed had only hit him the moment his wings were ripped from his body and his blood began to boil. Heaven's biggest dumbass, hurtling to earth to pay the eternal price.

Never again.

After all these millennia, though, Hugh didn't know Raum's sin—though it was clear the beautiful demon was still carrying hella baggage. When all that pain came rolling out, it wasn't going to be pretty.

"Well, there's one big problem with your plan, Blue," Hugh said, if only to get the others' attention off Raum. "Namely, if the archangel isn't here, then we don't know what his assigned missions are. We don't—"

"We do," Gregori interrupted with uncharacteristic firmness. He turned to Hugh and lifted the feather. It looked ridiculous in his massive hand. "The path for Raum isn't clear, but for you, the archangel had a plan. There is a woman in danger."

Hugh lifted a brow. "Show me a woman who's not in danger with the shit that's been going down the last twenty-four hours."

"This one merits particular attention." Gregori's chin now tilted up, his green eyes distant, and he practically quivered with intensity as the feather shimmered in his hand. Had the archangel known that this was a breadcrumb Gregori would be able to pick up? Had Michael suspected he was going to die this day, or at least wish he was dead?

Hugh grimaced, trying to work through the angles. God may rock his role as the benevolent Father of all humanity, but he didn't play favorites. If Michael had in truth killed a human, if he had given in to that base need to destroy, God wouldn't be merciful. Michael had to have known that and simply hadn't given a shit in the end.

But why?

Even as Gregori droned on, Hugh slanted a glance to

where Blue stood glowering, her arms crossed tight across her chest. Was the archangel capable of actual feelings? Fallen angels were, at least those who consigned themselves to work with humans. It was a hazard of the job. And Michael had been back on this earth for several months now, not to mention the time he'd spent in the bowels of Hell. Had those experiences changed him, made him weak? Susceptible to falling for a human?

But of all the humans to choose...why Blue? She didn't even believe in God. She didn't believe in anything, so far as Hugh could see. As the immortal Death of the Arcana Council, she gave everything in service to the dead. She didn't care what they believed either—she helped their souls get to wherever they were supposed to go, to find whatever peace remained for them.

Now she turned to him, her eyes narrowing dangerously. "Gregori asked you a question. Are you up for it?"

The harshness of her rebuke didn't faze him, of course. Blue was showing her humanity, even if she thought she'd long outgrown it. But Hugh had no idea what Gregori had asked him, so he shrugged.

"Sorry, wasn't paying attention. I was too interested in trying to figure out why the archangel would trust *you* to save his ass."

Blue snorted. "He wasn't expecting to commit murder."

"Wasn't he, though?" murmured Raum beside them.

Gregori pointed the feather at Hugh. "What I asked is, can you act a very particular role without breaking character?"

Hugh grinned. "Story of my very long life, my friend. I'm the OG of bullshit."

"You'll have to play this part perfectly." Gregori's eyes went slightly unfocused again as he concentrated on the archangel's feather. "This woman, Katana Midland, has created some sort of visual record charting the next few days after the attack of the Shadow Court. She knows where they're holed up and how to get to them. More than that, she's created a map that navigates to where the highest concentrations of magic are. She knows where the raw materials exist that sorcerers can use to augment their powers, and she's chronicled some of the fell denizens that have drifted up from the bowels of the earth to walk beneath the sun once more. She has recorded it in vivid pictures as if..." He frowned. "As if for children."

"Oh, for fuck's sake." Hugh rolled his eyes. "What does a kid's story get us?"

"No, not a kid's story," Gregori corrected himself, clearly still trying to work out what he was seeing in his mind's eye. "It's a guide to life on earth from this moment forward, but... mostly in pictures. Vivid squares of imagery, very few words."

"Like a comic book?" Blue asked, her sharply angled brows lifting. "Is that what you're talking about? She draws comic books?"

"Who the hell cares?" Warrick cut in. "If she has this guide and if the archangel believes it's important, then we need it. If it's a look forward into the next few weeks, maybe he's revealed in those pages. If he is, we can find him and bring him back."

Gregori nodded, his eyes still fixed on a distant horizon. "I can't see the archangel, specifically, but you are definitely in this book, Hugh. She has seen you, but not as you truly are."

"So there you go." Finn clapped his hands together, grinning at Hugh. "If she's seen the future, and you're in it, then boom. Go get her and her kid's book and we can get back to the business of kicking demon ass. Because business is good, my friend. And it's gonna stay good."

"Works for me," Hugh agreed, rocking back on his heels and settling his hands on his hips. As missions went, this one sounded pretty straightforward. "What else do I need?"

Gregori lifted the strange translucent feather. "Only this. You must present yourself as an angel to this woman to gain her trust."

"What?" Both Hugh and Raum barked the question at the same time, but only Hugh reared back, genuine horror ripping through him. Angels were right and true, blessed by God and open to every thought, wish, and whim of His children. They were the tuning forks of mortals and had to work like hell to blunt the chaos of human emotions at every turn. Some angels were more sensitive than others, but all of them could feel the pull of humanity. And that pull could get under your *skin*.

They were also the dickheads of the cosmos. "No," he stated flatly. "I've got no business being an angel. I gave that shit up a long, long time ago—and I was clearly no good at it then."

He'd been worse than no good. He'd been stupid. Naïve. The Father's holy messenger, betrayed by the humans he'd been sent to protect and nurture. He'd screwed up, made himself too vulnerable at exactly the wrong time...and God's children had destroyed him.

Never again.

Blue's laugh was harsh, even bitter. "Then you should plan on doing what you do best, deceiver. You lie. Only this time, maybe watch your back a little bit better."

3

*K*at choked on a ragged breath as she clawed her way toward consciousness, too disoriented to do much more than wriggle out from underneath the bookcase that had toppled over onto her.

She stared around blindly. It was still weirdly dark outside—the greenish dark of a storm, not true night—but there weren't any lights on in Gotham City Games & Magic, nor on the street outside. In fact, a thick, dark green fog had rolled in, as heavy as a blackout curtain. Nothing moved in it, and as far as she could tell, nothing crackled in the city beyond. What had happened here? Some sort of strange weather event? That might explain the lightning in the sky, but...

She froze, her brain coming fully back online.

Dead End. This was all uncomfortably close to the original opening to her story. The attack on New York, where her ex-mercenary, obscenely rich heroine was forced by a guardian angel to leave her tony Central Park West apartment and go on a quest to save the day. The bombs, the smoke, the greenouts—it'd all been there. The fact that Kat had cut two-thirds of that original opening and changed it to a mad dash from Chicago to New York and then into the magical *Dead End* maze didn't matter. She'd seen this. All of it.

And she'd laid out the whole thing on the thumb drive she'd handed over to her shiny new editor, who'd given the drive a place of honor on her desk.

Which meant anyone could find what Kat had written and drawn.

Find it and follow its clues to the dark and twisted creatures hidden in the smoke-filled hollows of bombed-out city streets. From there, slip into the airless corridors that followed ancient pathways of magic spread across the world. Hell, maybe they would travel all the way to Sorcerer City and open the gates for the angelic force to take out the enemy's citadel of power. Someone else could do that as easily as her. Anyone else, really.

Fuck. That.

Anger erupted in the pit of Kat's stomach and shot outward in all directions, so powerful that it bordered on hysteria. Her blood pounded in her ears, her heart leapt, her skin practically crackled. *No!* She wasn't going to let someone else follow her story, dammit. She was the one who'd written it, she was the one who'd dreamed it up—or if not dreamed it up, then received it as a direct download from the angels. It was *her* story. Her adventure.

Her *turn.*

She'd never been anyone's first choice, not once in her life. She'd been given up for adoption at three, maybe four years old, then passed around from foster to foster for six more *years* until someone had finally taken pity on her and given her a permanent home. Then even that had been taken away from her when she'd least expected it.

She'd been lucky enough—she hadn't gotten destroyed by that process—but her entire existence had been about biding her time, keeping her head down, staying out of the limelight. Taking whatever was left over from the rest of the world. But she'd made it now! It was her *time*.

No one was going to take this from her. No one was going to steal...

Kat pulled up short, her breath stopping in her throat as her thoughts leapt back to her thumb drive—and to the woman who'd treated it with such reverence, even if she was only humoring her newest, greenest author. She'd been sweet and appropriately solemn, and now...

"Emily?" Kat whispered, squinting outside again as panic knifed through her.

Had Emily been hurt in the attack of...whatever this was? In the original story, the temporary caretaker of the map to Sorcerer City had been killed, the map stolen. Had someone already found Emily, killed her, and stolen Kat's thumb drive? And why had the attack happened here in New York and not Chicago? Kat had *changed* all that.

Oh, my God. Should Kat have warned Emily that this might happen? But how could Kat have warned her? She hadn't expected any of her story to actually happen—and she'd *changed* all of it!

Hadn't she?

She fished in her pocket for her cell phone, brought it out. Dead. She wasn't surprised, wasn't even as panicked as she should have been, since this was all so eerily familiar. Electricity wouldn't work anywhere in the world after the psychic bombs had detonated. Not for a while, anyway.

That meant...that meant she had time. To find that fucking thumb drive—her, not anyone else. Time to fix this. Fix everything.

Kat flopped to her left, flinching when she encountered a warm body. Her hands skimmed along cargo pants overstuffed with tools and detritus.

"Jeremy?" she guessed, heartened when he groaned in response. She worked her way up his body, stopping only when her questing fingers made him cry out.

"Shoulder," he grunted. "Hurts."

She edged alongside him, trying unsuccessfully to peer through the weird fog that seeped into the room. "Where are the others? " she asked. "I can't believe they all made it out before those things exploded."

"You went down with the first bang. By the time I reached you, all hell was breaking loose," Jeremy corrected her, still not moving from his position on the floor. "There were at least another three bombs that went off in this section of town alone. More we could hear landing everywhere else. People lost their phones—and then they lost their minds. Then the electricity went out. Everybody was shouting, trying to run, half of them running inside, half of them trying to get out, and then there was a clap, almost like a clap of thunder, but it didn't sound like it. More like a belly flop into a pool. It was the damnedest sound... and then there was nothing."

He drifted off a little, and Kat jostled him, wincing as he groaned.

"I'm sorry, I'm sorry," she said, sounding a little squeaky. But she hadn't pictured Jeremy in her story. Not once. How was he hurt? How was anyone hurt like this? "But I need you to stay with me for a second. Are people dead? Did that explosion *kill* anybody?"

God, how was this happening?

Jeremy huffed a short laugh. "I don't know, but my shit sure went flying. I don't think I'll ever be able to find all those figurines again, especially if people got grabby. They're all fakes except for the Destroyer, but they're my best fakes, if that makes sense."

"It does," she assured him, though she had no idea what he was talking about. How was it possible to make a good fake? Jeremy was the original artist. If he made it, it wasn't a fake.

"I can't see a damn thing," she muttered, squinting over the tumbled bookcases. "This sucks."

"Right leg, below the knee. Flashlight. Solar powered."

"Of course you would have a solar flashlight." She laughed, but when she reached for his pocket, she discovered something else. Blood. "Jeremy, you're hurt."

"Pretty bad, yeah," he said, and for the first time, Kat picked up on the unusual strain in his voice.

"I tend to bleed really easily." He groaned and shifted a little beside her. "That'd be why I don't go on adventures, I paint miniatures of people who do. Usually, I can kind of tell when bad shit's gonna happen, but this...yeah. I didn't expect all this. I must've blacked out after that weird belly flop sound."

Kat made a face, but she pulled out the flashlight and flipped it on. Only then did she see the spreading dark stain on his pants.

"Jesus! We've got to get you to a hospital. We need to..."

Her voice faded, and Jeremy chuckled. "We've got no lights, no electricity, no cars—you hear that? That would be silence out there. Silence, this close to New York City. How the hell is that even possible?"

"Maybe I'll be able to see more when I get outside." Kat shivered a little, remembering what she'd drawn in those roiling clouds of green smoke—the hints of creatures and sparks of magical power. Was all that seriously waiting for her? The adventure she'd dreamed up?

"Well, if you do make it out okay, send me back any guardian angels you can find. Wings optional, but highly recommended."

The image of Hugh the Destroyer shot across Kat's vision, and her heart rate jacked. Surely he didn't exist. Not in real life. That couldn't be possible...

She forced a grin into her voice for Jeremy's benefit. "You got it. Now let me find something to clean you up."

It took her a minute with the flashlight to find the bathroom, and beside it a storage closet. She tried the lock, surprised almost out of her skin when someone hissed behind the door.

"Is it over?"

She blinked, then realized who it had to be. She swept the flashlight over the hallway, then back to the closet. She hesitated, then leaned close to the door. "Gable? Is that you? What are you doing?"

"Trying not to piss myself."

She stood back as the door opened, and the small bookish proprietor of Gotham City Games and Magic peered out, his face cut and his clothes ragged. He was thin, wiry, and balding, and he peered at her through square glasses that miraculously hadn't shattered. "I thought everyone got out," he groaned. "I locked the front door, barricaded myself in here, and started alpha meditating, determined to go down with the ship. Only the ship didn't go down."

"Neither did all of its crew, but Jeremy's beat up bad. You got anything back here to stop bleeding? And any more flashlights, while you're at it?"

"Jeremy?" Gable said, straightening, concern widening

his eyes behind his heavy glasses. "Holy shit, he said he was leaving."

"Yeah well, I think he came back to get me. I took a header with the first bomb or whatever, and I was down for the count."

"Shit, I had no idea. It was broad daylight, or it had been. Then it got so damn dark and everything went out, and there was all the screaming and..." He glanced away, and shivered hard, but didn't say anything more. "I programmed for the safety of everyone who was here today. I don't think it worked, but I tried."

"You did good. We're still standing, right?" She awkwardly patted his shoulder. She'd had no idea that Gable was into meditation, but she supposed it made sense. Everyone at the con today probably leaned a little woo. "But stay with me, okay? Jeremy needs your help."

"Jeremy," Gable echoed, nodding vigorously. He lifted both hands to pass them over his thinning, close-cropped hair. "What about you? Are you okay?"

"I'm great," she said drily. "But I've got to get downtown."

"What? Are you *nuts*? There's no way. Nothing's moving out there."

"I know, but..." Kat swallowed. She had *Dead End* stored on her own laptop, which was a good thing. Already she couldn't remember how it all had gone down—where the heroine had specifically found the doorways into the passages between cities and what was waiting for her when she did. But hers wasn't the only copy of the story. And if someone else knew it was out there...

She had to get that thumb drive. And she needed to make sure Emily was okay.

Kat swallowed, her stomach twisting. If she'd somehow gotten Emily hurt, she'd never forgive herself. "Um, do you have a bike or something? Like, maybe if there's no traffic, it won't be so bad?"

He stared at her. "You're going to try to *bike* to Manhattan? There's probably giant lobsters guarding the Lincoln Tunnel at this point. Have you *seen* how thick that smoke is? And it's green! Nothing good ever came of green smoke. Why in the fuck would you do that?"

Kat winced, but she couldn't tell him the truth. "You do have a bike, don't you? There's no way you drive here every day, and the subway..."

"I do." He squeezed the bridge of his nose beneath his glasses. "You're seriously going to do it. Bike through Lincoln Tunnel. On a bike."

"You said that part already."

"It bears repeating. Jesus, what time..." He scowled down at his watch, which was analog, its hands glowing iridescent. "It's almost the lunch rush."

"Not today, it isn't."

Gable's shaky laugh made her grin, but the glow of his watch caught her attention. "How is that thing working? My phone is flat dead."

"Solar," he explained, angling it toward her. "Same as that flashlight you got there. It's coming up on one o'clock. We've been out—the whole city maybe has been out—for close to three hours, looks like. Is that possible?"

She winced. It *had* been possible, at least to her. Her agent had made her cut all the seriously crazy stuff out, not believing anything could bring New York completely to its knees—not even bombs and energy-zapping smoke. But Kat had imagined it exactly like this. And had imagined what'd happened next too.

There were a lot of seriously screwed-up people about to come out of the woodwork. And in the book, they knew about the librarian with the map to Sorcerer City. Knew it and had come looking for her.

"It sure does look like it's possible," she said, as steadily as she could. "But it, um, probably won't last much longer. The lights will begin flickering on. Cars will start. People will wake up too. We did, right?" Her voice faltered. Why *had* the three of them woken up so quickly when the whole world seemed dead around them?

The answer came to her, unbidden and unwanted: *because we're different. We can see things.*

A headache started thrumming at her temples. The story of *Dead End* that had first downloaded into her brain was like a dream. Maybe it had been a dream, a vision. And like most of those, she hadn't seen every last part of it. She sure as hell hadn't remembered all of it.

But she'd remembered enough to create a story, dammit. She'd brought it to life on her computer. If everything she had imagined was coming true...

She swallowed, panic ripping through her. She needed to understand what she'd drawn, follow the steps she'd mapped out to get to Sorcerer City. If she could follow the story as she'd laid it out, get to the city, unlock the gates, and defeat the evil sorcerers, it would all be okay.

If she didn't—or someone else beat her to it—*Dead End.*

She knew it as sure as she was staring at Gable in his broom closet.

She waved the flashlight at him. "All right. I'm heading out. I'll also try to get someone to come back here for Jeremy, and maybe you too? Are you injured?"

Gable jolted, then looked a little sheepish. "No, no—I'm fine. I guess I had help, yeah?"

He lifted his hands, unclasping them, and Kat realized he must've had them folded together in prayer. She flashed her light over them and picked out the brightly painted three-inch figurine nestled in his palm. Hugh the Destroyer, guardian angel extraordinaire.

"Jeremy gave this to me after the first bomb hit, just picked it up and chucked it my way and told me to keep everyone safe. If you're going out there into that mess, you need him more than I do. The bike's right down the hall from here. You can go out the side door. You, uh, know the way?"

Kat gave him a grim smile. She had imagined her heroine running through Manhattan, yes. Right along with the pages that had ended up with Hugh the Destroyer bleeding out on Sixth Avenue. She hadn't specified where her heroine had been running *from*, but...Hoboken seemed a reasonable place to start. "Yeah. I do. And I've got a flashlight."

"Oh, like that's gonna help you a lot against the giant lobsters."

"This too." Kat held up the figurine. "I'll send help, okay? As soon as I find some. So maybe you should go keep Jeremy from dying all over your floor."

Gable snorted, and she turned down the hallway, doing all she could to hold herself together when her flashlight illuminated Gable's beat-up bike. Her heroine hadn't needed a stupid bike. She'd found a doorway from downtown Chicago to downtown Manhattan in a blur of smoke and chaos. Kat couldn't wait around for that to happen for her.

She opened the door, hesitating as the fog rolled into the building. Gable and her agent had been right—how was it possible to shut down New York City for going on three hours?

You know how. She pushed the door open farther, then

wrangled the bike through it. The fog was dark as pitch and sickly green, but as the light hit it, it seemed to fall away just enough to show her the sidewalk, then the street. As Gable had predicted, nothing was moving, the same as it hadn't been moving in *Dead End*.

Kat threw her leg over the bike, grateful it was an old-time cruising model, not something built for speed. Even more of a bonus, it had a headlight. She flipped it on, not sure if she should be relieved or more nervous when the thin stream of illumination leaked out over the street. There was no way Gable's bike light was solar. Had batteries worked when the bombs had gone off in the original draft of her story? She didn't think so. She'd glossed over that, sacrificing detail for the chaos of explosions and smoke, but she was pretty sure everything had shut down to start. Then, after the world had forever changed, batteries had started working first, then electricity.

Which meant she didn't have much time.

Kat took off, riding hard. She figured it was a little over five miles on a bike, which meant she had less than an hour given that there was no traffic. Then again, if there was something moving around out there...

A wave of fear washed through her. She bent over her handlebars, flipping off the light. She had a vision of zombies shuffling out of the darkness—granted, she hadn't written zombies into this story, but she hadn't written Gable's store in there either! And there were other things she'd glimpsed in the shadows where the earth had opened up and allowed access to the passages between dimensions, stuff she hadn't put into *Dead End*. What were they? And *where* were they, exactly?

The smoke had been concentrated in areas she'd called hell blocks—sections of the city that had been given over to unleashed magic, and within them were the doorways to other cities, other places. Kat grimaced, realizing she hadn't worked out her own world nearly well enough. There was too much she didn't *know*. Her editor was going to throttle her...if she was still alive.

Kat whimpered at that thought, trying desperately to remember how the story had gone. Her mercenary badass heroine, Sorcia Steele, had been able to navigate the passages between cities by going into the smoke-filled hell blocks and searching for a specific building to enter. It was always the same-looking building, no matter the city. Some of the byways between hell blocks took only a moment to cross, some seemed to take days—and some did end up as, well, dead ends. But which was which?

Kat had gone over the story so many times, made so many changes—but were the changes what was important, or the original download?

She leaned more tightly to her handlebars, gradually able to pick out details farther ahead. The smoke was clearing at least a little bit as she rode on, block after block. Still, there was something totally surreal about taking the ramp down into the Lincoln Tunnel, passing all the stopped cars.

Nobody moved within them, drivers remaining draped over steering wheels, passengers slumped against car doors. Why wasn't anyone moving? The smoke was thicker here, to be sure, but Jeremy had woken up and so had Gable. Did that mean these people would start waking up soon too? Wake up and see her—try to restart their cars and, when that didn't work, jump out and try to take her bike?

"Go, go, go," she ordered herself, speeding up past the motionless cars as an emergency light flipped on above her. "Shit!" She was already running out of time. Her heart pounding, she reached the far end of the tunnel and about choked up a lung as she added another burst of speed to the pedals, pumping her legs up and down. Sweat streamed down her face and snaked between her shoulder blades.

And then she was up and through. In Manhattan, oddly, the smoke seemed thicker again, heavier. The streets were still quiet, the buildings dark—and strangely familiar.

She knew she shouldn't be surprised at that. She'd used Google Earth to map this section of Manhattan, not only for the purpose of the story, but to help her locate her editor's office that morning. She'd taken an Uber, of course, but she still liked to know where she was going.

Kat wanted to slow down, to look around and get her bearings, but she didn't dare. As she rolled through an intersection, she spied another light flickering on several lights down. How long had the city been struck down? Three hours? Now maybe four? What happened to the hospitals during that time? Airplanes flying overhead? And was the whole *world* like this?

The truth hit her so hard, she almost rolled into a parked car, jerking the handlebars of her bike at the last second to avoid a head-on collision.

She *had* worked this out. She'd then cut most of the explanation, replacing it with a few lines in the final draft, but she'd worked this out. Everything had simply...stopped. An unseen force, allies her heroine hadn't yet met at the opening of the story, had stepped in at the last minute to keep the damage minimal. People still died, buildings had been destroyed, but where life could be spared, it had been. Earth would go on.

Kat scowled, her mind racing. She'd ended *Dead End* with the arrival of those allies to help her fight the bad guys in Sorcerer City. Said allies hadn't shown up until the very last pages, and she only had some hazy images in her mind about what they looked like. She hadn't named them yet, and the pages she'd sent to her editor hadn't named them either. Because, as usual, the words wouldn't come.

"Fuck," she muttered, trying to pick out faces from her memory, faces she'd naturally distorted and sharpened for the purposes of her illustrations. Nobody looked as good as their comic rendering, after all.

She gritted her teeth. No one except her guardian angel, who had apparently appeared as vividly to her as he had to Jeremy Bolling, so vividly that Jeremy had been able to paint a figurine in the guy's exact likeness. Guy? Creature? Celestial being? Kat didn't know, but she sent a prayer up to him anyway as she finally dragged herself onto Sixth Avenue, her lungs bursting. She squinted through the rolling green fog. Something was definitely moving in it, but she didn't know what. She hadn't drawn that far.

"Okay, Hugh the Destroyer," she whispered. "If you're out there, please keep me safe. Please keep all of us safe."

---

4

*G*reen fog rolled through New York City like a disease. There were no lights, and no vehicles moved. Three hours after the Shadow Court's attack, the city still held its breath. The sound-deadening fog kept even the cries of the sick, wounded, or fearful from reaching his ears.

Hugh's hands curled into fists as he stalked through the silent streets—silent, but not empty. He passed hundreds of people slumped over their steering wheels in stopped cars, others collapsed on the sidewalk. There'd be more inside the buildings, and hundreds if not thousands in the subway.

Before he'd left the Syx, they'd barricaded themselves into a hotel suite in Vienna, Austria—an establishment Blue had favored—and gathered all the intel they could on the new world order.

The Arcana Council's gambit to stop the Shadow Court had worked, more or less. Led by the two most powerful members of the Council, the Magician and Justice, they'd pulled great magic from alternate dimensions to negate the energy of the Court's psychic bombs—stopping the world in its tracks along the way.

For three hours or so afterward, demons had been vomited out of the bowels of the planet in a few, select spots, battled back by those willing to stand in the breach for humanity. While that conflict raged, only those worthy souls engaged in battle against the Shadow Court or critical to its success had remained awake.

The rest of the world had simply...stopped. Electricity had shut down. Gas-powered engines had ceased functioning. Planes had dropped from the sky, buffeted and buoyed by unexpected wind currents until they could safely land. Generators had stopped functioning and emergency backups had failed. Those humans who relied on both for their survival were held in stasis, their bodies preserved for the duration of the shutdown, safely in the palms of the mighty sorcerers of the Arcana Council who had orchestrated the resistance against the Shadow Court.

All other humans had collapsed where they stood, the electrical currents of their nervous systems overloaded. A mere handful of psychics worldwide had stirred early, waking up to the nightmare of their new reality. Most had not.

Now, however, the world was about to come back online. Bolstered by intel planted by the Arcana Council as the conflict had started, today's global blackout would be called an "an anomalous EMP event" triggered by a completely unpredicted and unheralded solar storm aimed directly at Earth. The event hadn't been tracked; it hadn't been recorded. Everything had been shut down—for everyone.

And those mortals who had died in the demon conflict? They'd be written off as victims of terrorist attacks that had been stopped mid-conflict. The survivors wouldn't say otherwise, that was for sure.

Granted, there would be hundreds of casualties in the bigger cities, Hugh suspected, even if the fog itself wasn't deadly. Fear was sometimes enough to break the frail tether that humanity held on life. But something still moved in the fog ahead of him. The drugged, maybe, since their sense of reality was already so altered, they didn't know when to stay put. Demons, he had no doubt. He could smell them. Something else too. Creatures he couldn't identify. A new plague to assail God's children, served up by their own kind?

Looters, strangely enough, were not part of those slinking along the city streets. If they were coherent enough to be aware of the fog, they were coherent enough to fear it. Which left one bobbing flashlight that flickered on erratically every twenty or thirty feet.

This had to be the woman Gregori had sent him to find, but what the fuck was the human doing? And was she being hunted by whatever was in the churning green fog?

He gripped the feather from the archangel's wing in his hand, its tip edged in blood.

That disturbed him too. Blood was a human construct, which meant that it was the blood of his murdered victim that had splattered on Michael's wings right before they had been wrenched out of his body by the horde.

Hugh shuddered. His own wings had burned away from his body as he fell to Earth. It had left him broken and paralyzed—for how long, he couldn't say. He missed them still, which was stupid in the extreme. The archangel had called him into service when he'd been little more than a curled-up wreck of a demon, more horns and fangs than brains, but holding Michael's feather in his grip brought back too many memories of the time right after his fall. None of them good.

The smoky mist rolled around him, suddenly heavier, and he crept forward. Eventually, he could pick out the woman approaching the doors of one of the smooth stone-and-glass buildings that graced this boulevard. These streets were almost deserted. Anyone who could scrape themselves off the sidewalk had long since hastened away, and those who remained lay where they'd first fallen, sprawled in disarray.

This fog wouldn't last, though. In another hour, maybe less, it would break, the work of the Arcana Council's magic complete. A distant part of him wondered how the humans would talk themselves into the idea of a solar flare as the culprit for this calamity, but only a distant part. He'd long since stopped caring about any lies other than his own.

"Fuck." The low, exasperated word reached his ear. He sensed other creatures stirring down the street. He was not the only otherworldly creature in this place. The human needed to be more careful.

Another sound from above drew his attention. A grunt. A dragging thump.

Hugh stepped forward, peering through the fog. Not a human, thank the Father for small favors. But there was something tracking the woman as she crept closer to the building.

A second later, he had no doubt what it was. Crouching atop a section of the building that stood out farther than the rest, providing it with the perfect perch to assess his victim, a demon loomed. Hugh could practically hear the clicking of its teeth as it leaned over, still a good thirty feet above where the woman edged forward, but already eager for the kill.

No. No, the spawn wasn't here to kill the woman, Hugh decided. If it was, it would have already swooped down and taken her out. It would have seen her coming from three hundred yards out—and leapt, mindlessly screaming its triumph as it rent the human from limb to limb. Instead it had watched, waited. Continued waiting even now, as if it was trying to determine if she was the right quarry.

Since when was a demon that particular?

Hugh scowled, then stiffened in surprise as the demon flicked its paw at its neck, a flare of blue light cutting through the smoke. What the fuck was *that*? A collar on a demon?

Gregori had told them all about the humans who'd sought to control demons, believing that their computers and artificial intelligence would succeed where before, only the witches had been able to make inroads. In fact, some witches were part of the human cabal that sought to control the demons—whether by their choice or otherwise.

It was a fool's game. You couldn't manage a demon any more than you could collar a typhoon. The best you could hope for was to direct the spawn's chaos and destruction for long enough to cause maximum damage, then get out before they turned on you.

Maybe that was the Shadow Court's plan. Or maybe demons were convenient cannon fodder. There sure were enough of the horde to go around these days.

But what was this demon doing here? How far ahead of the Syx were the Shadow Court that they already had someone in place to capture the female? Or, perhaps better stated, how long had the archangel known about Katana Midland prior to his untimely departure?

Anger flickered through Hugh. It would be just like Michael to hold back critical information on a human until he deemed it the appropriate time for action. Judging by the quivering energy of the demon hunched atop the outcropping of concrete and glass, this time, he'd cut it a little close.

The demon struck.

Howling with a feral cry of rage and glee, it rocketed toward the female, who spun in horror as Hugh rushed forward. Flailing back against the door, she choked on her own scream as Hugh tackled the creature, knocking it into the plate glass window about fifteen feet above the concrete sidewalk, then throwing it to the street below. The creature landed on all four limbs and jumped skyward, colliding again with Hugh as a flurry of sparks shot from its claws. What in the hell?

The demon fought and tore with surprising strength, its collar lighting up, along with a shiny metallic camera on a circlet around its head. Its eyes were wild, its screeching unhinged, and it was clearly well past anything but whatever orders had brought it to this place. Hugh could hear those orders, echoing over and over, even above the demon's howl. *Capture do not kill. Capture do not kill. Capture do not kill.*

So what the *fuck* was this asshole going to do with the woman after it captured her?

"Who sent you?" Hugh growled, but the demon only shrieked at him. Then it barreled into Hugh, giving him no option but to decapitate the dickhead.

The demon screamed one last time, then burst into a spatter of black ichor, disappearing back into whatever hole it'd crawled out of. Killing demons was never pretty. But this one was sloppier than usual.

Hugh stood back, avoiding most of the spray, then turned as the woman standing by the door gurgled a half sob, half curse. Something about her poked at him, but he wasn't sure what. He didn't think he'd ever seen her before. She wasn't the prettiest human he'd ever encountered, and she looked like she hadn't had a very good day. Her black hair was plastered to her face, sweat darkened her T-shirt, and her gray eyes were huge and haggard in her face. She watched him with eye-rolling panic—but not the terror he expected. More with...recognition?

Still, she didn't speak, and after a moment, Hugh remembered himself. With a long, heavy sigh, he shifted his glamour slightly. Wings unfurled behind him, their peaked tips stretching high.

The woman, if anything, grew paler.

"Do you need help?" Hugh asked her, his voice as even as he could make it.

She swallowed, her throat working for a long moment before she finally answered. "You're Hugh the Destroyer." It wasn't a question. The woman's voice was thicker, rougher than he'd expected, carrying a low, resonant energy that practically made Hugh's bones vibrate. "You're a guardian angel, and you're going to help me get to Sorcerer City."

His brows leapt, though she averted her gaze as she spoke, apparently unwilling or unable to look at him any longer. He rumbled an agreement, and she squinted past him toward the street. Nothing remained of the demon on the sidewalk but an oily black spot, which was how Hugh preferred his demons.

"Ah...what exactly was that thing you killed?" she asked.

"Demon."

Her tongue darted out to moisten her lips. Hugh jolted at the movement, suddenly too aware of how close she was to him, how critical to his mission. And, worst of all, how frail.

"Right," she muttered. "A demon. Those are real now."

He snorted. He couldn't help it. "They've always been real."

"Yeah, but—" She scowled, her gaze still fixed on the sidewalk. "This is the first time I've seen them in, um, person. I didn't know if they were...like, I don't want *everything* that I imagined to be real, you know? I mean... other than you. Seriously, thank you for coming. I didn't know if you would."

It should have been odd having a conversation with someone who couldn't look at him, but after so many centuries in service, Hugh was used to it. Still, there was something different about this woman. She wasn't avoiding his gaze because she was afraid of him...no. She thought she *knew* him. Knew him, and knew things about him that she believed to be true.

He forced himself to speak slowly and patiently. "You summoned me to protect you from a demon. That's what I do. That's what I will always do. Remember that."

"Okay." She choked out a cough. "Are there more of them out there? The demons?"

Hugh curled his lips back from his teeth. "More than you can possibly imagine."

She winced. "Oh, don't say that. I can imagine a lot."

Before he could respond to that, she turned back to the door, reached out to pull it open, then drew her hand back.

"It's locked. It's not supposed to be locked."

She spoke with such assurance that it caught Hugh's attention. "Are all your predictions so accurate?"

"That's...a good question," she acknowledged, her voice steady yet thin, quiet, the sound of a human barely holding on to sanity when she would rather give into hysteria. "A lot has come true, but things have also happened that I didn't predict. And I would suggest that I'm not predicting anything. It's more like I'm receiving information, maybe. Received. Months ago, not anymore. But I still didn't expect the door to be locked."

"What else have you foreseen?"

As he spoke, he drew yet closer, surprised she didn't have the good sense to run off. She was a woman alone without apparent weapons in a city shut down by fog and fear. He was a stranger. Even if she believed she knew him, believed he was on her side, she should be warier than this.

"I've seen enough." She grimaced. "The electrical storm, the firebombs out of nowhere, the green fog. In my book, the heroine returns to her, um, apartment to get her map to Sorcerer City. But I didn't leave the map in any apartment. I left it here. And now, I can't get in."

"Then you're in luck." Hugh stepped forward, and only then did she jostle off to the side, not looking at him, but staring resolutely ahead. He laid his hand on the bolted and reinforced door. Fortunately, the barriers of humanity proved poor sport for demons, especially after six thousand years. Energy crackled, and the door swung open. He turned back to the woman, seeing her now fully for the first time. "There. Now it's open."

She only stared straight ahead. Gregori had filled in only the barest minimum of Katana Midland's appearance—long dark hair, pale skin, light eyes. Medium height, about average for a human female in this century, medium build. The epitome of nondescript, Hugh supposed, except for her smudged and haunted pale gray eyes. And it was her eyes that were giving him pause. They glowed with an infernal fire that until now, he'd only seen among the Syx. Had this human always burned so bright, or was she reacting to his presence? Or possibly to the effects of the unleashed magic in this place?

Nah. Had to be because of him.

"You really are Hugh the Destroyer." As she spoke, Katana's eyes didn't quite meet his, but settled on his mouth, as if it was far too much effort for her to lift her head any higher. "Jeremy's guardian angel."

Hugh smirked. "I've been called worse. Are you going inside or did I just jam a perfectly good security system for no reason?"

"I..." She swallowed, still not moving. "It's just that, I changed all this. I'm not supposed to meet you until after the library...even though this isn't a library. You showed up later in the new version."

"Does me being early cause a problem I should know about?"

"Yes—well, no. I changed all that." She broke off abruptly and looked away. "But you still shouldn't be here."

Hugh didn't miss the way she'd started to tremble. She might think he was an angel, but her body knew differently. There was something indefinably wrong about a demon to a human. Even a demon as well behaved as he was most of the time. They reacted to his eyes, his size, his walk. Nothing he could do about that now. "You shouldn't be here at all," he told her. "Who's looking for you?"

"No one." She finally looked at him. "Nobody knows anything about me."

Something ignited deep within him as he studied her, a prickling of warning he recognized all too well. Katana Midland practically reeked of deception—and she sucked at trying to hide it. "Well, you're lying about something. What is it?"

His words were calm and unruffled, but the human

stiffened as if he'd poked her with a live wire. "I'm not."

"You are." He allowed his lips to curve. "I'm an angel. I know things."

He didn't feel even a little ashamed at his gambit as her jaw dropped. She snapped it shut, her cheeks flaming now while she worked with obvious effort to answer him honestly. "I'm not lying. You *shouldn't* be here. It's not safe."

"And it's safe for you? Alone, with demons hunting you?"

"Yeah, well, the demons are why you shouldn't be here." She made a face. "I...I sort of planned for you to die in my original story. My heroine met you, didn't believe the story you told her, and abandoned you to die at the hands of demons. She betrayed you."

Hugh lifted a brow, even as the old, familiar outrage spiked. "I get that a lot."

She blanched. "I didn't *mean* anything by it, I swear. I didn't know you existed, and I sure as hell didn't expect any of this to become real. Beyond all that, I changed everything around in edits. Now you're my boyfriend. My heroine's boyfriend. Whatever. I changed it. But there's too much happening that I didn't expressly write, and way too much happening that I *did* write. Either way, well...even in the revised story, things don't end up all that great for you. So you should probably go, like, right now. Thanks for opening the door."

Squaring her shoulders, Katana brushed by him with renewed energy. As she passed, Hugh took in the scent of her. A light, lavender soap, then ink and wood polish. Fresh oranges. Fear. She was any woman, every woman, foreign and untouchable. She'd also already given him more than enough reason not to trust her or the story she had woven around him. Same betrayal, different human.

At least this time, he knew it going in.

5

He's following you, and he's not scared. Does he know something you don't? Of course he does. He's an angel. He knows everything.

Kat tried not to whimper with relief as Hugh stalked behind her into the building. She'd tried her best to get him to flee—but she'd been desperately afraid he'd take her advice. She would've never been able to get in this place by herself, and who knows what she'd find in Emily's office? For the moment, she was grateful for the company.

She just hoped she wasn't going to watch this beautiful supernatural being die for his troubles. She really had drawn out his demise a dozen different ways—all of them currently scrapped at her agent's request, sure, but the story was called *Dead End* for a reason. People died. So had one really hot angel.

Stop thinking about that. You might make it real.

Oh, God.

Kat bit her lip as she watched Hugh more or less reset the door, then peered beyond him into the fog, her mind skittering off her own neuroses and back to the danger at hand. "Something's changed out there. They're gone."

The smoky mist still flowed around the building, but it was empty now. Everything she'd felt following her had vanished—except her guardian angel.

"Who's gone? Who else is following you?" The angel turned to stare at her, the sharpness of his tone catching her up again. Were angels supposed to be so curt? She didn't think so. Then again—how were they supposed to act? Humans had depicted angels as warriors, healers, even fluffy little cloud hoppers. But had any of them ever seen an angel up close and personal?

Doubtful. Not one who looked like this, anyway. Her guardian angel stood over six feet tall, with thick dark hair, eyes a vivid purple, and a jaw chiseled enough he could've recruited an entire platoon of marines. With every step, different sets of muscles bunched and shuddered beneath his black T-shirt and black jeans, and his black shit-kickers looked like they could stomp a legion of demons into the pavement. His breathtaking gray-and-white wings had unfurled in full-feathered splendor for half a second as she'd watched him rocket up toward the demon, then they'd disappeared.

Had she really even seen them?

He huffed impatiently, and she realized she'd waited too long to answer.

"Nothing. No one's following me," she said quickly, swinging back around to peer more deeply into the room. "I —I thought I saw things in the fog. But of course, I wrote it that way, so maybe they were there in my head, but only my head, you know? I don't remember right this second what I kept from the original version anymore. I've got to—I've got to get something up on the third floor."

Still babbling, she hurried forward, stepping around a security podium to crawl beneath the turnstile. Then she was on the other side, squinting into the darkened hallway. "There have to be stairs. The elevator won't work yet. Or at least I hope it isn't working yet."

"This way." He moved beside her, and she risked another glance toward him, but his wings were definitely gone. He walked by her almost as if he was an ordinary man...an ordinary man who could see in the dark.

Then again, angel. "Right," she said, nodding to his back. *Hugh*, she thought. His name is Hugh. Not the angel of her story. Not the heavenly creature her heroine had ended up betraying to the bad guys before she fully understood what was going on. Kat had fixed all that in the newest version of *Dead End*, and she hadn't written the latest death scene for the guy yet. That meant Hugh was safe.

Right?

"What are you here for, specifically?" Hugh asked as they moved down the hallway. "The entire city is asleep except you."

"And you. And Jeremy and Gable." She tensed, but he didn't react. "They were with me when the bombs hit, and Jeremy's hurt. He knew about you coming too—weeks ago. You should go to them. Help them."

"I'm here to help you."

A cold, bracing thrill skated through her at the idea of someone like Hugh wanting to help her, but her guardian angel didn't seem particularly enthused with his mission. Then again, she *had* admitted she'd killed him off. She pushed on. "Then go help them after you help me. I'm worried I might still hurt you somehow, and I don't want to do that."

He stopped and turned back toward her, his expression

unnerving her. There was something deep in Hugh's eyes that she didn't want to explore too closely, a strange whisper of a memory she could almost grasp, but didn't dare. What did she know about her angel in her story? Not nearly enough. He could have been a polar bear for all the backstory she'd allotted him.

Then again, he wasn't supposed to be *real*. None of this was supposed to be happening in real life.

"What did you leave behind in this place, Katana Midland?" Hugh murmured. "What are you searching for here? It's not a map. Not here."

Kat stuffed down her swirling hysteria. How did he know these things? "No. It's a thumb drive that contains a story I wrote. It came to me like a vision—it *was* a vision, I guess. I copied it all down, made sketches, illustrations."

She swallowed, then flapped her hand at the shadowy corridor. "I sold it to people who work here. That was a while ago, but I came here this morning and gave the opening of the book to my editor. Then everything went down today almost *completely* like what I saw and—I don't know what's happening anymore."

By the end of her speech, she was barely whispering, but Hugh nodded encouragingly.

"But you do know, right? You wrote the story, so you know what's going to happen."

"I..." She swallowed, trying to regain her bearings. Could this gorgeous creature seriously be her guardian angel? Did angels still do that? "I guess I do. But I wrote it all down and put it on that drive, so anyone could find it, and then they'd know it too."

He gave a low, dangerous-sounding grunt. "That's more of a problem."

"I know. And I need—we need—to get to Sorcerer City.

As fast as we can. We have to follow the story exactly to do it. If we don't follow it exactly, then it might not end the way I saw it. And it has to—like if this is all really happening, if there are evil wizards out there and they're trying to take over the world with magic and kill all the lesser magicians. That's bad, right? That's bad."

"Very bad." Hugh nodded as if he understood her, though of course he couldn't. She wasn't making any sense to herself, let alone to him.

Kat grimaced. In her story, Hugh had been the perfect guardian angel for her heroine. Grim, beautiful, deadly, and here to protect her. In real life, though...there was no Sorcia Steele. There was only Kat Midland. So now what?

An unreasoning fear that had gripped her since that morning reasserted itself. What if Kat needed to be Sorcia to make this all work out? Because she wasn't Sorcia, not even close. Some of the panels she'd drawn involved Sorcia kicking ass...while others...

"What's wrong?" Hugh asked sharply as her cheeks flushed. "I can't read your thoughts."

She gave a strangled cough, resolutely studying the wall. Enough light still seeped in from the front of the lobby that she could barely make it out. "Of course you can't. That would be terrible." Some of those panels had shown Sorcia and Hugh together, wrapped in each other's arms. Holy crap, was that in her future? Surely it couldn't be. Hugh was an *angel*. He had *wings* for chrissakes.

Beside her, Hugh's brows lifted, as perfectly arched as his now-missing appendages had been.

"Where did your wings go?" she asked baldly, because at least that was a safe question—then she flushed again at her rudeness. What was *wrong* with her? You didn't just ask someone about their missing body parts.

"Never mind." She cut off her own question, though Hugh hadn't made any attempt to answer. She needed to refocus. Sorcia hadn't chatted up the angel warrior who'd demanded that she cut short her retirement and save the world. Kat Midland needed to get on with it too. She'd been given the story of *Dead End* for a reason. She'd switched it around and changed it up, but it was still a story downloaded from...well, maybe the angels.

She raked her hand through her hair and ruthlessly retied her ponytail. She pointed to a door marked EXIT. "Those are stairs, I'm pretty sure. That's where we have to go next."

"I know." He sounded entirely too amused with her, and Kat pushed into the stairwell, not surprised that the angel brushed by her and climbed the stairs ahead of her. Her skin tingled at his touch, and she scowled, trying to remember how Sorcia had originally reacted to him.

Had she tingled? Kat seriously doubted it. Sorcia wasn't the tingling type. So what did it mean that Kat was? Maybe there was some allowance for variants to her story. Hugh was here, after all—in a place Kat hadn't imagined him originally.

If variants were allowed, then maybe Kat didn't *have* to run the story exactly as she had originally imagined it. Because the more she thought of that, the less possible it seemed. She would get something wrong—she would do or say something stupid. It was inevitable.

She wasn't a hero. Not even of her own story. Especially not that one.

"There's no movement," Hugh murmured ahead of her, and she quickened her pace to catch up.

"Do you know what happened today?" she asked. "Out there in the world?"

He hesitated. "I do."

"Oh, thank God. Tell me."

When he didn't say anything more, Kat lifted her hand to nudge him, then drew her fingers back, as he kept climbing. Were you allowed to reach out and tap an angel on the shoulder? Was there some protocol she should be following?

"We're at the third floor," he said abruptly and stopped, cutting off her thoughts. "We can talk later."

Together, they stepped out into the eerily silent hallway, and Kat tried not to notice the crumpled bodies on the floor. "Great. That's fine. Third floor. I've only been here once, but my editor's office is at the end of the hall. She had a window."

He peered down at Kat, clearly surprised by the detail. "So? You think she jumped?"

"*No*." Kat made a face. "No. It's just... She was really happy about that window. It meant a lot to her."

He didn't respond. Kat's hysteria mounted as they moved down the corridor, more memories coming back to her.

"This is where it starts," she murmured. "Sorcia wasn't here, but it was this same type of hallway, dark and gloomy. She's walking along, feeling something in the shadows, her eyes narrow and a little angry—nervous, even. She hadn't done the badass-merc thing in a while, you know? She wasn't used to this whole scene anymore. She'd quit."

Hugh the Destroyer didn't respond to that either. Kat suspected he didn't do fear very often. But she wasn't sharing this for his benefit. They walked under a wall sconce, and it flickered.

"Electricity is coming back." She picked up her pace. The crackling wall sconce had been a part of the story, one of the myriad little details that hadn't mattered at all and yet added to the overall ambiance. Sorcia hadn't stopped beneath that light, hadn't spoken. She had moved forward.

Kat could no longer feel Hugh behind her, but that tracked too. Sorcia hadn't needed her angel every second of her journey. She reached the door. It stood open, and Kat was moving across the threshold when Hugh's hand closed around her wrist. She froze.

"There's a woman inside," he whispered. "Behind the desk. Small and dark, with her hair in buns. Some sort of sandals kicked off. She's hurt."

Kat's eyes shot wide. "Is she dead?" It seemed like something Sorcia would say, not her. Or not her before today, anyway.

"No," Hugh said. "But she's not moving."

"Oh, *no*." Surging forward, Kat swiveled her pack around, then yanked her flashlight free and flipped it on—only to feel it knocked away from her hand, winking out as it clattered against the wall.

"No lights," Hugh ordered. "And don't move until I tell you to. They can see us through the window."

Her throat constricted, making her voice little more than a squeak. "They...who's they? More demons?"

He sent her a cool look. "Do you know of anyone else following you?"

"No." She scowled, her feet shifting slightly. She needed to get to Emily. "I mean, I don't think so. But then, I didn't think they were following me either."

"Who else knows you're here?"

"I told you, nobody does. I'm just—I'm an author, okay? I wrote a story and delivered it here this morning and, um, that story is what's been happening. What I think has been happening, anyway. And I need to get it back to make sure nobody else gets a hold of it until I can get through it. Because if I can get through it—"

"Do you see it here?" He cut her off, and she glanced up, startled to see his purple eyes had taken on their own spectral light. Something about his eyes...

"It's on a thumb drive," Kat said, pivoting toward Emily's desk, though it was impossible to see it in the greenish gloom. "Shaped like a little pink cat." Would a guardian angel know who Hello Kitty was? Hell, would he know what a thumb drive was, for that matter?

Hugh scanned the room. "I'll find it. Go to your friend. There's no one outside anymore." He pushed Kat toward Emily as a streetlight flickered in the street below.

"We don't have much time," she muttered, even as she rushed to Emily's side.

"How do you know that?" The question was flat, but Kat ignored Hugh as she reached Emily's crumpled body. Her editor's hair was matted with blood. It tracked beneath her nose and along her arm, and a deep purple bruise extended down her jaw.

"Oh, my God," Kat gasped. "*Emily*."

She dropped to her knees beside the woman, and Emily groaned, sending a surge of relief through Kat. Emily's glassy eyes fluttered open, rolling around in their sockets as she tilted her head. One of her Princess Leia buns had come unraveled, making her look impossibly young. Then she looked toward Kat, and her mouth dropped open. "Katana?" she murmured.

"What happened to you?" Kat whispered fiercely. "Did someone hurt you? Did you get blasted or something by the bombs?"

"Bombs?" Emily frowned at Kat as her eyes slid away. "Why are you—oh, your book. It's on my laptop. It's really good, you shouldn't worry so much, it's—"

"Laptop." Kat looked up, squinted. She didn't see a laptop, but she spied the Hello Kitty thumb drive at the same time Hugh's large hand closed over it. He plucked it out of a pile of SpongeBob, Wonder Woman, and Angry Birds toys. But the desk otherwise remained conspicuously laptop-free. "You downloaded it?"

Emily nodded, then groaned a little as she lifted her hand to her brow and touched her cheek gingerly. "I needed to log it into our server and get it up to the cloud, but I got blocked and didn't want to wait. So I downloaded it to the laptop. Quicker that way."

"The cloud," Kat practically moaned, but Emily made a face.

"Well, I *tried* to get it to the cloud, but I didn't get very far. I downloaded it to the hard drive." She blinked at Kat, then her eyes sharpened, sudden awareness filling them. "My God! That storm that came rolling in—the electricity went haywire, and the sky turned green! And then...then..." She shook her head. "Those were bombs? Somebody dropped *bombs* on New York City?"

Hugh growled a low warning from the windows. "Someone's coming."

"What?" Emily gaped at Hugh, clearly startled at—what? His size? His intensity? His sudden unexplained presence in her life? Kat could relate. He stood silhouetted in the glow from the street, looking down, but unease zipped through Kat at the sight. That wasn't where the danger should be coming from! Everything was happening out of order.

"This is all wrong," she groaned. "We should already be in the hallway—I should be in the hallway when you say that, when you think that, when I had that thought." She was talking too quickly again, not making sense, and Hugh turned to stare at her, clearly thinking she'd lost her mind.

Their eyes met. Kat shivered, her retinas practically seared by the sudden, full force of Hugh's harshly angelic beauty. He was so *incredibly*—

Gunshots fired down the hall.

Beside her, Emily jerked with surprise, then her eyes rolled back in her head and she slumped back to the floor, out cold.

Hugh stepped to the door, locking it. Even Kat knew that wouldn't afford them any sort of protection for long, but he didn't hesitate. He strode back toward Kat and grabbed her arm. "We've got to go."

She yanked it back. In Hugh's original scene in *Dead End*, the one Kat had changed for her agent, the librarian had already been dead. But Emily wasn't.

"We can't leave her here," she blurted—and somehow, he understood. With a growl of annoyance that sent Kat flinching back, he swept by her and picked up the broken, bloody body of the editor. Then he turned to the window.

"Now."

He didn't give Kat time to object. Sorcia was a badass mercenary, Kat was not, so she could only stare as Hugh brought down one shoulder and broke through the thick glass as if he blew through industrial-strength windows as a daily pre-workout warmup. He leapt out, Emily clutched tightly to him. A stream of gunfire erupted behind Kat, blasting through the door and ricocheting in all directions.

Kat's heart was in her throat as she gaped at the broken window. If she stayed, she was dead. If she ran, she was probably also dead, but she had at least a few more panels before that deadicity would happen, right?

She lurched forward, scrambled up on the glass-strewn sill and—

Jumped.

6

*H*ugh watched as Katana flung herself from the third-floor window like a spider hoping to catch the breeze on its way down. Her arms and legs flailing wide, she twisted in the air as if she'd rethought the idea of exiting the building and wanted to return to the sill. It was the exact opposite of how anyone should jump, at least anyone who was a fragile human.

He had accrued six thousand years of experience with fragile humans, though. He dropped the broken one to the sidewalk as gently as he could, then rushed to meet Katana's plummeting body. She crashed into his arms with surprising weight. He swung her around, the heat of her sending a strange wave of awareness through him.

Before he could analyze that too closely, he set Katana on her feet, making sure she was stable before he let her go completely. Lights swept on all around them. The panicked roar of hundreds of starting vehicles crashed through the space. Thirty feet down the street, a man in uniform struggled upright before turning toward them and jerking into a run.

Police, Hugh thought. They'd have their work cut out for them this day.

"Help! Help!" Hugh shouted, shifting his glamour down a few notches for the benefit of the officer, whose panicked face didn't inspire confidence. He pitched his voice high and feeble as he pointed excitedly to the woman on the pavement. "She's hurt."

The policeman was only a few feet away when a blast of gunfire rang out above them. A bloom of blood and gore sprayed from the man's shoulder, spinning him around.

"*Fuck*," Hugh barked as the man collapsed to the sidewalk.

"Oh shit! Emily!" Katana half knelt, half fell to her knees and hovered her hands over the other human, clearly afraid to touch her. "Can you get her to a hospital? You can fly, right? You can get her there?" She twisted around to stare at him. "We have to keep her safe."

Hugh growled with frustration as another spray of gunfire rained over them. He covered the woman on the ground while Katana leapt away, shrinking into the shadows. She made small gasping noises at him as the bullets flowed right through him, then passed out the other side, fully spent, to bounce off the collapsed human's skin. No human could kill a demon.

Still, the problem was complicated. The human Kat had asked him to carry did seem to know something of this Sorcerer City story, whatever she'd been able to see before she'd been attacked. More of that story was on the thumb drive that Hugh now had safely in his pocket. But Kat was the real prize here, whether or not the gunman above them realized it.

"How much does she know?" he snapped.

"Everything—a-all of it!" Katana stammered, but the

additional assertion struck him as off. Once again, the human was lying. "More than she thinks. You have to keep her safe!"

"I have to keep *you* safe—and will you fucking *stop!*" Hugh spit with fury as another round of bullets pelted through him. Just because the bullets couldn't kill him didn't mean they didn't hurt. It also meant the person wielding the weapon wasn't a demon, because the horde didn't have the dexterity to manage mortal guns. Or at least, they hadn't the last time he'd checked.

He twisted around to peer into the windows, but the gunman had edged away—probably figuring he needed to get down to street level if he wanted to bag his prey. Which meant that Hugh needed to get both women off the street, and quickly.

"Keep her safe," Katana yelled, but her voice seemed too far away, too breathless. God's teeth, she was *running*.

"*Katana*," Hugh shouted after her, but the human was gone. With a snarl of frustration, he scooped up the second woman from the sidewalk, spun around, and started running in the opposite direction.

When he caught up with Katana Midland again, there would be hell to pay.

"Now *this* is some good reading."

Finn of the Syx had his legs up, his boots resting on the coffee table in the overdecorated suite of the fancy boutique hotel in Vienna, Austria. Now that the world was back online, the room had been officially secured for the Syx by Death, who apparently now held dominion over their team, at least temporarily.

She didn't look happy about it. Blue stood at the window, surveying the chaos outside. Sirens blared in all directions, lights blazed. The streets were choked with cars, people trying to flee what they didn't understand, fear gripping the city all the way down to the dregs of society. But it was a nameless, baseless fear, Hugh knew—that of the general unknown, not the specific perils the world now held. In fact, the ones who should be afraid were the Connected—and they most likely were smart enough to stay hidden, praying for the smoke to clear. They alone could see the creatures that now roamed through the city, set free from their dark realms.

"How long will it take for the fog to fully lift?" Warrick asked, his mind rolling down the same pathways as Hugh's.

Blue answered that. "It's not going to lift. Not for Connecteds, anyway."

Hugh peered at her, torn between wanting to hear more about the fog and wanting to read what Finn was learning. There'd been multiple files on the thumb drive he'd taken from the Manhattan office. The first contained pages and pages of pictures—comic book panels, as Gregori had tried to explain. The second wasn't really a story, more like the bullet points of a story. The basic outline of an ex-thief who learns she's the only person who can stop a group of elitist magical assholes from taking over the earth. And then there was a third file, what looked like bits and pieces of the original story, but taken out and labeled "archive." Additional files had more pictures, according to Finn, but not as fully rendered. More sketch work than illustration.

Death waved him away. "And Hugh, yes, you should read the story as Katana laid it out. Read it and memorize it."

Hugh scowled—he hadn't asked that question aloud. Another trick of the archangel that Blue had picked up, clearly, and one that would eventually get irritating. But right now, there was too much fucked up in the world to worry about the niceties of their transfer of power.

If the archangel had thrown the Syx to Death to manage, it meant there was still a chance for them to fulfill the mission he'd set. Their path to redemption hadn't been ripped away along with the archangel's wings. Hugh needed to hold on to that belief.

"What does the fog contain?" Raum asked from the corner of the room. "And how dangerous is it? The majority of the people out there still cannot see the pockets of magic that have opened up, correct? These hell blocks that Katana identified... Can humans be harmed by them even if they don't know they exist?"

"Yes and yes," Death confirmed. "But unless they're Connected, they won't know what's lurking in the dark. To them, it'll simply be the same experience they might have walking down the wrong alley at the wrong time. They might think it's not their lucky day, but they won't know they were attacked by ghouls or goblins."

"What about Katana?" Hugh persisted. "Why can't we find her? If Michael encoded the mission into that fucking feather of his, why isn't it working to track her ass down?"

Blue bared her teeth at him. "Maybe because she doesn't need you right now."

"Yo, did you already kiss her?" Finn asked, cackling as he flipped pages. "Because that'd be a good reason to avoid your ass, so far as I'm concerned. Once would be more than enough."

"You were supposed to kiss her?" Warrick asked, and even Raum looked at him curiously.

Hugh recalled the pale-eyed, dark-haired human, practically vibrating with urgency and panic. He curled his lip in what he hoped conveyed dismissal. "I didn't kiss her. I barely had a chance to talk with her before we were getting shot at." He squinted at Finn. "I was supposed to kiss her? When?"

"Guardian angels don't kiss humans," Raum informed them all as Finn fanned back through the pages. "Only the Fallen do."

"Yeah, well, guardian angels do in this human's story," Finn said. "The timeline's all fucked up, so maybe not yet. Still, you weren't supposed to leave her ass, that much is for sure."

"I didn't intend to leave her. She ran away from me."

"Clearly nothing wrong with her sense of self-preservation," Stefan put in. "At least my human wanted me to stick around."

Hugh rolled his eyes. Stefan's path to redemption had been almost as strange as Hugh's was turning out to be—caught in the snare of a human witch. "Your human trapped you in a spell to do her bidding."

"Like I said. She wanted me."

"Did Katana's heroine escape from the first demon attack in the story?" Death asked over them both. "Is that part of what she wrote?"

Finn leaned his chair back, perilously close to toppling it. "Well, in this version, she was in a library, and the librarian bought it, so that's different. Beyond that, we've stashed this Emily chick in a hospital, which could potentially open up all sorts of storylines, you know? So we're off track no matter what."

"Katana did say something about that." Hugh nodded. "The events of this morning were familiar to her—enough of that came true that she understood that her inspiration for the story was something like a vision of the future. But she also said that after the opening attack on the city, nothing was following the exact path of what she'd envisioned. She desperately wanted her friend to be safe, and lied to protect her. She definitely believed the woman knew more than she should. I'm not so sure."

"Well, either way we've got it covered," Stefan said firmly. "We've got two members of the local coven standing guard at the hospital. Nobody's getting in there, and if the Shadow Court sends members of the horde, they'll be dealt with."

Finn made a face. "But the fact remains, we're going rogue from the original story now. So how good is this comic book?"

Hugh rubbed his hand over his brow. "Katana seemed convinced that if she could find her way back into the story, if she synched back into the timeline, she'd be able to take the same path she'd originally mapped out to save the day. She needed to find a place called Sorcerer City. That was where the bad guys had holed up."

"Sorcerer City?" Stefan frowned. "Never heard of it."

"Maybe it's an inside name for these dickheads' magic treehouse. She's got the place in sketches, but nothing more exact than that," Finn said, flipping through yet more pages. "It looks like a collection of old moldering stone houses, more like a city block than a citadel or an actual city."

Finn leaned forward, leaning over the printout to type on his computer. He turned the screen toward them, displaying a series of disjointed illustrations. "These designs aren't in the finished part of the story. They're from the jumble of images she had for the rest of it. How the hell she was ever gonna meet her deadline, I got no clue."

"If the archangel wanted us to follow this human, then chances are her instincts are correct," Gregori commented.

"She needs to rejoin the timeline, then take the path through."

"There's definitely some serious mappage going on in this section," Finn agreed, pointing. "She starts, it looks like, in Central Park. At least as far as the part where she's leaving New York. The actual story began in Chicago."

"That was the second version," Hugh said. "She said she'd received the initial vision all in one piece, but she changed it, updated it. In the original version of the story, the guardian angel died early. But she was pretty clear that she kept trying to kill him even in later versions."

Finn snorted. "Always nice to meet a fan."

"You'll need to recover her and rejoin the timeline quickly." Gregori reached over from another set of printouts to punch in something on *his* laptop. "All power systems are back online. According to multiple news reports, the world shut down as a result of a massive solar flare. Scientists and governments are pushing the same narrative, and no individual faction is taking credit for any resulting deaths so far. Even more curious, no one is mentioning the big gaping hell blocks filled with smoke that were left behind from this little party."

Hugh scowled at Gregori, though there was no reason to dispute his report. He'd become much more adept with computers in recent weeks, which was fine by Hugh. Human technology changed so quickly there was no point in keeping up.

"We still have a problem," Hugh said. "We've got the thumb drive, and we'll get Katana back, but the editor's laptop was missing from her desk. Whoever took it has at least some of the story, and possibly has already figured out how to take the byways Katana mapped out."

"Maybe, maybe not," Finn said, waving his printout.

"Only the first third of the panels are finished with actual copy added. If all the woman got transferred over was this first set of images and this kind of rough outline of the middle chapters, then the bad guys don't have shit. They know how the story begins, that's all. The latter pages are, like, there—but kind of impossible to read, you know? Katana probably knows what's happening in them, but someone else? Total guesswork."

"Regardless, we need her to get us to Sorcerer City." Warrick stabbed his finger at the drawing. "Then we go medieval on the Shadow Court. So find her. She trusts you."

"She trusts Hugh the Destroyer," Finn corrected. "Kind of a catchy name, gotta say. If you're curious how you look to her, it ain't bad. I mean, this guy clearly goes to the gym a hell of a lot more than you do, but you know. A girl's allowed to dream." He flipped to the middle of the stack of pages, then turned the sheet around.

Hugh peered at the artistic rendering. He definitely looked like an angel, or at least the typical human depiction of them—broadly flaring wings, dark hair, purple eyes. "She wasn't surprised to see me," he mused. "This is how I appeared to her, at least to start. Which means she has accepted the idea that what she imagined has come to pass."

A few more pieces dropped into place. Katana's predictions, her derisive comment about her imagination. This human female had written a story that had been pulled off the pages and made real. That made her...what? A channel, passively receiving information about the future that someone pushed toward her? An actual psychic, able to legit see the future?

Or...something else altogether?

"You guys left each other on good terms, right? You didn't freak her out?" Finn pressed.

"I've got another hit on Hugh the Destroyer," Gregori cut in, peering at his screen. "Does the name Jeremy Bollings mean anything to you? He's a miniaturist in Jersey. He blogged on some site a few days ago, teasing the character."

"She mentioned him," Hugh agreed. "She said he knew about me too. But Michael didn't say anything about him."

Warrick grunted. "You think he knows anything?"

"Probably, though he may not realize it," Gregori said thoughtfully. "I suspect he's a low- or mid-level Connected. If he's picking up on your energy, he may have the rest of us coming through as well. He definitely knows Katana. He mentions her in his blog. They had some event this morning, which would have placed them together outside of New York City right around the time of the initial attacks."

"Interesting." Finn cocked a brow at Hugh. "Did this Jeremy guy work with her on the story? Was he the illustrator of her book, maybe? He might know where she lives."

"I don't think so," Gregori said. "This article says he makes...dolls. For collectors."

"You mean we're all going to have action figures?" Stefan asked brightly. "Excellent. I always wanted to be famous."

"Like any of you need more to feed your egos." Death rubbed a hand over her brow.. "Still, this is something we should pay attention to. If both this man and Katana got the same download, other people did too. Finn, you and Warrick need to track this Jeremy Bollings down. Question him. Find out if he's planning to reveal your secret identities or whatever."

"Roger that, General Death." Finn saluted.

She rolled her eyes. "What's the storyline of this *Dead End* anyway?"

"It might-maybe sound a little familiar to you." Finn

said, spreading his hands theatrically. "The one-percenter magicians of the world try to blow up everyone else who's even the tiniest bit magical. A small group of intrepid psychic warriors stops them from taking over completely, but in the process of them taking down the bad guys, the world cracks."

Stefan snorted. "Cracking is never good."

"It isn't, but in chaos there is hope," Finn continued, with appropriate gravitas. "Those who sought to establish control are scrambling as much as the rest of us, trying to understand what the world has become. All sorts of paths to magic have opened up. The ex-mercenary thief that Hugh the Destroyer hooks up with—and not just metaphorically, my man—is a bitch on wheels named Sorcia Steele. Together they take one of those paths to get to Sorcerer City and unlock the place to let the good guys in. Things get pretty fucking hazy after that—she hasn't finished all the art. But you can bet there's a big ol' fight at the end. There's gotta be, right?"

"We don't want anyone to shut down those paths before we take the one we need," Warrick mused. "We need to find her."

Blue scoffed a laugh. "We don't have to find her—the demons will. Then she'll summon her guardian angel again." She slanted her hard, ice-blue eyes at Hugh. "Try not to lose her this time."

"*Think*," Kat moaned. She'd run as fast as her legs could carry her away from Sixth Avenue, then had hidden in the shadows as the entire world came back online. Her phone had started working again about thirty minutes ago, and she'd hoofed it up to the neighborhood near Lincoln Center, where people and businesses were starting to stir. She'd texted with Jeremy—leaving it to him to tell Gable that she owed him a new bike. Jeremy hadn't said anything about Hugh the Destroyer showing up, and she hadn't mentioned the guy either...even though she'd really wanted to.

The fewer people who knew about all the crazy she'd predicted, the better.

She chewed on her lip, huddled over a cup of coffee. Though she had no way of confirming it, she felt certain Hugh had gotten Emily to safety. He also had her thumb drive, so presumably, it was safe. Assuming she could trust him. But why wouldn't she be able to trust him? He was an *angel*.

He certainly looked like one. Kat clasped her fingers

around the coffee cup, willing its heat to seep into her skin as she brought Hugh's face to mind. There was something familiar about him—yet strangely off. Kind of like the coffee she was drinking.

She peered down at her cup. It smelled normal. It tasted normal. But it wasn't warming her up. Maybe she was the abnormal one.

She gave a quick, stealthy glance around the small shop —it seemed pretty ordinary, other than the fact that it was open. Most of the businesses in downtown Manhattan were closed for the rest of the day, but this block still seemed functional. She'd chatted with the baristas about the crazy hazy greenout that had shut everyone down and woke them up as fast—most without realizing anything had happened until they'd confirmed it on their watches that three full hours had elapsed in the meantime.

According to the news, it'd been a solar flare that'd temporarily short-circuited all electricity. And though everyone expected conspiracy theorists to hijack social media for the next few days—blaming aliens, most likely— the two young baristas hadn't been all that fazed. Basically, the whole world had gone offline all at the same time, and that seemed to make it all okay. Nothing had been damaged in the store either. Customers had slumped to the floor the same as the baristas had, and everyone had woken up unhurt. Better yet, their manager had offered to pay them overtime to keep the store open. Win-win.

Kat hunched over more, feeling exposed. She could almost buy that it'd been a solar flare too. Except...except she'd woken up early. And then she'd watched her guardian angel reduce a demon to an black stain on the pavement. And then she'd realized there'd been no computer on Emily's desk.

And now she was here.

Kat took another long sip of her coffee, glancing at the phone charging next to her. Even after a half hour, it only showed thirty percent. The world might have come back online, but that didn't mean every device on the globe wasn't going to be dealing with tech issues for the foreseeable future. "Freaking great," she muttered.

She'd been seeing similar complaints across the internet...though not enough of them, in her opinion. The power grids were up again, sure. But phones were on the fritz, and cellular networks and Wi-Fi hubs were spinning wildly out of control in some of the major cities. Still, even with all the news stories of utilities companies overwhelmed with service calls and people demanding answers, the reaction to the flare had been...weirdly muted, as far as she was concerned. Mostly because no one was talking about the bombs. Power grids dropping, cars shorting out, people fainting—yes, yes, and yes. Deaths because of all those things—yes. No one was disputing any of that.

But green smoke boiling out of nowhere? Bombs falling from the sky? Demons and other creatures stirring down shadowy alleyways, moving in the murk?

Nope, nope, and nope.

The only people who were talking about bombs and smoke-filled streetscapes were fringe YouTubers and people who'd been in the process of tripping out on controlled substances at the time of the sorcerers' attack. Not exactly credible—and those stories were getting buried by all the mainstream coverage of what was already being called the Super Flare—an outta nowhere solar blast that created a unifying threat for the entire world to face. Government officials were calling for global solidarity, but what else could they say? The shouting would die down in a few days, maybe weeks.

But the hell blocks full of green smoke? The demons? What if those were here to stay?

Kat's phone chirped, indicating a new text, and she grabbed for the device as she saw it was from Jeremy.

Where are you? he asked. *Still okay? Please respond.*

Her brows shot up. She'd already texted him, and they weren't that close—though surviving a solar flare had maybe elevated their relationship some. But...was this really Jeremy? And if it wasn't, what if he was in danger? There certainly hadn't been a Nerd-God miniaturist in Kat's version of *Dead End*, but there'd been a lot of variations to the story so far. If Jeremy was being held against his will...

She chewed on her lower lip, then keyed in a question. *What is the alignment of Hugh the Destroyer?*

There was no response at first, then three small dots appeared, indicating that a message would be forthcoming. Depending on what Jeremy answered, she might not know enough to proceed, but it was worth a shot.

It should be lawful good, but I don't think so, came the text. *I don't get that sense for him, Angel of the Lord or no. I don't get evil though. I would have to say chaotic neutral, but that seems to be doing him a disservice. So will opt for chaotic good and give him the benefit of the doubt.*

By the end of this assessment, Katana was giggling. This was definitely Jeremy, and wherever he was, he wasn't under duress. He would doubtless be puzzling over the question for hours now that she'd posed it to him.

You're okay? she texted, not wanting to stop the one connection she had to normalcy quite yet. *Are you hurt? Is Gable?*

We're good. Gable used to be a med tech. Popped my shoulder

back, patched me up, No looting at the store either. G didn't
understand why, but he was glad.

Holy ground? Kat suggested—mostly as a joke, but she
couldn't discount the shiver that slid down her spine.

Even all the way into New Jersey, Jeremy didn't miss the
inference.

I think maybe, yeah. He texted, *Something's happening. Half*
the block's still covered in green smoke, but people are acting like
there's nothing there. Gable and I have stopped saying anything.
It's too weird.

Katana sat back in her chair, toggling her laptop so the
screen displayed again. The illustration from *Dead End*, page
twelve, depicted a young mother and two kids. One of the
kids dangled a limp, stuffed teddy bear from one hand.
They stared at an alley between two tall, forbidding
buildings. Green smoke poured out of the alley, lightning
bolts glittering from deep within the angry clouds. All
around the small group, people bustled along as if there was
nothing to see but their phones and the traffic. They
couldn't see the smoke that was right in front of them. Just
like what Jeremy was reporting.

Be careful, she tapped back.

You too.

A movement outside the coffee shop drew her attention.
A man walked along the other side of the street, but like the
coffee in her hand...he didn't seem quite right. He was too
big for his bones, that was the only way she could describe
it. He slouched along more than walked, as if it took a
second for skin to catch up with his movement.

Despite the rudeness of it, Kat watched the man, unable
to look away. Then the man stopped, turning her way as if
alerted to her attention.

She dropped her gaze, but it was too late. He was now

slouching his way across the street directly toward her, never mind the jaywalking rules in Manhattan.

Shit, shit, shit. Kat slid off the stool and closed her laptop, then yanked her charging cord out of the outlet. She shoved it into her bag, her knuckles scraping against the figurine of Hugh the Destroyer. The figurine didn't give her much reassurance. Where would she go? Where *could* she go? She didn't know what hospital Hugh had taken Emily to, and she was afraid to text her editor in case the bad guys had the woman's phone. She was pretty sure she could sync up with the story near Central Park, but that would require her walking right by Mr. Slouch.

Maybe she'd just...

Kat scanned the room, another chill stealing over her.

Something was wrong with the other patrons in the coffee shop. Their arms and legs—even their hands looked like they'd become slightly longer, their skin looked weirdly plastic, and their eyes seemed to bulge a little.

Even worse, they were all staring at her.

Kat caught a whiff of sulfur and nearly choked. "*Shit,*" she muttered again, this time out loud. She'd flat-out gotten attacked by a demon on Sixth Avenue, but these didn't look like that one. These people looked human.

They are human. Scary as fuck, but human. Kat grimaced at her own spiking hysteria. Slowly and deliberately, she tucked her laptop into her pack and zipped it closed. She looked over at her abandoned coffee on the counter and choked back a whimper of surprise.

A tendril of green steam wafted up from the cup.

Green smoke swirled along the floor too. She could see it out of the corner of her eyes. There was no sound at all in the coffee shop anymore, and nobody moved for another long second—or maybe it only seemed long to Kat.

Sweat trickled between her shoulder blades. How could she fight...whatever these people were? She had no weapon. Even the pens jumbled in the bottom of her pack were felt tip. Sorcia Steele was trained in hand-to-hand combat and had muscles you could bounce quarters off. Kat Midland was about as badass as a Tater Tot.

"*Think*," she muttered again. But she couldn't think of anything except how the smell of sulfur got stronger as a couple of the weird customers stood. The baristas now loomed behind the counter, easily a foot taller. *What in the hell?*

Kat gripped the strap of her backpack, a new fear taking root within her. She was alone here. There was nobody but these weird creatures in this coffee shop. Four patrons and two baristas, all of them looked at her with a slavering hunger.

She glanced at the window, then jolted. Slouch Man now stood pressed up against the glass, peering inside the coffee shop. Kat gaped at him—he was surrounded by thick green smoke. How was that possible? How could she have missed the fact that she was stumbling onto a hell block? And who in the world would put a hell block this close to the *opera*?

"Oh, come *on*, man," she groaned as Slouch Man stepped back from the window, then took one long, exaggerated step and entered the coffee shop straight through the glass. He strode forward three more steps, then came to a stop five feet away from her, a grin stretching his strangely squashed features wide. None of the other patrons so much as blinked.

There were suddenly more patrons too. Like two dozen, crammed into the bench seats, perched on stools.

I'm hallucinating. All this had to be a hallucination, some weird feature of the hell block, but if it was, it was a really good hallucination, and Kat's stomach clenched.

"Hugh?" she tried to whisper, but no sound came out. Could he hear her, wherever he was? Was he still on angel duty? She'd written him into and out of *Dead End* so many times, she'd lost track of his exact appearances, but she sure as hell hadn't illustrated a coffee shop attack in a popup hell block next to an opera house. How would he know where to find her if it wasn't in the book?

Slouch Man took a step forward, arresting Kat's attention. He stretched his jaws wide—but when he spoke, it sounded almost as if a speaker had been switched on in his throat.

"You have a choice, Katana Midland." He spit out the words in a crackling, tinny whine. Kat involuntarily took a step back, but there was nowhere for her to go. Was this a *robot*? Were all these creatures robots? But that didn't explain his ability to enter the coffee shop. It didn't explain how the coffee shop customers had multiplied either.

Slouch Man kept going, his glassy black eyes rolling wildly before they latched onto her. "Come with me or die. You are not the only scribe, you are merely the first."

She squinted at him in confusion, curiosity hijacking fear. "The first?"

Another eyeroll, followed by a dialed-in stare. Slouch Man's mouth sagged open again, and a parade of tiny words fell out. "Serve the Shadow Court or be crushed beneath it."

The other patrons didn't move, but somehow, they seemed to be pressing closer to Kat. Towering over her, trapping her in place.

Fear once more took the wheel. "Oh, well, hey, not that your sales pitch isn't enticing, but I'm afraid you're talking to the wrong girl," she babbled. "I don't know what the Shadow Court is. I don't want to know. You guys can go ahead and do your thing, I'll do mine, and everybody will be happy, okay? Why don't we do that instead?"

Slouch Face paused and tilted his head as if considering her offer. The eyes whirled again, stopped, fixed on her. Then he grinned widely and murmured a soft command.

"Take her."

_____

8

"*H*ugh."

The summons was quiet, but so intensely panicked, it almost dropped Hugh where he stood. He staggered to the side, jerking his head around to search the back of the hotel room, though there was no way the human female had made her way to Vienna.

What's more, the other members of the Syx eyed him like he'd lost his mind.

"*Hugh!*" The cry came again, and this time he gritted his teeth against the queasy shot of fear, need, and pain that blasted through him. He'd been summoned to a human in need of deliverance from demons before—tens of thousands of times—but always through their prayer to the Father. Never in a prayer asking for him specifically. It wasn't a good feeling.

"She's summoning me directly. Can she do that?" He gasped as another scream ripped through him.

"It would seem that—" Blue started to say, but her words were cut off as Hugh launched himself through the wall. He soared out over the mirror-bright streets of the city, then rocketed across the ocean until he descended into a whorl of shadow and smoke that billowed out of a half-block section of Manhattan.

He landed next to Katana. Her pack remained slung over her shoulder, and she held on to its strap with a white-knuckled grip. In her other hand, she held out her cup of coffee like some sort of weapon.

She was surrounded by two dozen completely jacked-up demons—their energy unlike anything Hugh had ever experienced. To Katana, they probably appeared mostly human…though definitely screwed up. With his demon eyes, he could trace the currents of electricity crackling through them like some sort of whacked out force field.

A primary demon stood closest to Kat, its glamour flickering erratically as it rolled its eyes at him. It was barely holding on to its conscious form, the goop of its primordial ooze pulsing beneath the surface of its waxy skin.

"Who controls you?" Hugh barked, and the demon recoiled as if suddenly recognizing him. Its voice chittered and whirred, before emerging in the telltale demonic garble the spawn used to communicate.

"The Sssssssssyx…" it lisped, and Hugh scowled. That wasn't the right answer. Clearly, he wasn't the only one posing questions.

"It told the others to take me," Kat blurted. "It said 'take her,' but I screamed and they stopped and then you showed up and now we're all standing here. Standing is better than taking, but it probably should be switched up into leaving, I'm thinking. How about we leave? Leaving seems good."

"Who sent you?" Hugh tried again to address the primary demon, but the creature jerked as a new surge of electricity blew through it. The other demons began to mewl in pain, their glamour slipping to reveal an elongated arm here, a thick, pitted claw there. Their eyes were rolling too, as a few more of them recognized him for what he was. The farthest ones had started to edge toward the door, despite the current holding them in place.

"Stay behind me," Hugh instructed Katana as he glared at the demons, angrier than he expected to be. The human female had been his charge, and he'd let her escape—catapulting her directly into danger. She had stumbled into this hellhole because of her own stubbornness, but she was still one of God's children. And for the horde to be stalking her this way—to be held to their positions even when faced with one of the Syx...that wasn't right. Someone was definitely controlling them. "And lose the cup. Humans can't kill demons. Not even with bad coffee."

She jerked her gaze toward him, the still-hot brew sloshing. "What?"

The demons attacked.

Hugh leapt in front of Katana, giving himself over to the battle with a relieved roar of pent-up frustration. He needed this battle, craved it. There was too much here that wasn't right—and after six thousand years of fighting demons a particular way, he wasn't thrilled to be making a change. Yanking free a set of knives from his belt, he dove into the horde headfirst, scattering them into arcing waves of black goop.

As he fought, his mind churned. How in the fuck had these demons found Katana so quickly? She wasn't a witch, so she couldn't have summoned them herself, and there was flat-out no *way* the Shadow Court could be this far ahead of the Syx. Especially because there hadn't been a coffee shop in any of the illustrated panels Hugh had seen.

So how had they found her? "This...is pissing...me *off*,"

he growled, punctuating his words with brutal blade strikes. "How are they here?"

"I don't *know*," Katana now cowered against the wall, shaking with real fear. Fear of him?

Oh, *shit*. Hugh burned with sudden, unexpected shame. How much was she seeing of his native glamour, instead of the beautiful angel she'd drawn in her comic book? Too much, clearly.

Continuing to battle the horde, he used the cover of his blurring movement to round out any ragged, scaly spikes that had poked through his disguise, smoothing the skin and restoring color and the illusion of warmth. He fought against the tide of nausea to form the hint of wings as well.

It worked. As he spun around the room in his restored glamour, he caught glimpses of Katana's confused face. Then her pallor receded, causing a second wave of nausea to snake through him. She was deeply, inherently afraid of him, he suspected—repulsed by whatever her more instinctive brain had been able to perceive beneath his glamour. Hugh didn't normally care how he looked to the outside world. He knew how his demon body presented when he wasn't worried about humans freaking out, and generally speaking, he needed his focus to be on kicking demon ass, not looking pretty. But this was Katana, and she was expecting him to play the part of a beautiful angel.

He couldn't afford for her to doubt him. He also couldn't lock in her trust completely while he was dealing with these fucking ankle biters.

Hugh doubled down in his efforts to eradicate the horde. As usual, they seemed to duplicate on the fly. No sooner had he taken one out than three replaced them. With each successive wave, though, they got physically smaller and weaker. Their howls faded from outraged to resigned, and eventually, they didn't even cry out. Another five minutes more, and there was nothing left standing in the coffee shop but the two of them in a sea of black goop.

"Management's not going to be happy," Katana murmured.

Hugh used an apron that had been left behind on a counter to wipe a trail of gore from his hands, then turned to Katana, who stared around the room. Slowly, carefully, she set her coffee cup on the counter in one of the few clean spots left.

"What else did the demon say to you?" he asked her quietly. She didn't respond at first. She was shaking, but he held back from going to her. The trauma of the attack would wear off, and he needed any information he could get from her before her guard went back up. "I need to understand how they found you."

She made a face. "I have no idea how they found me. It's not like I posted on Tinder."

He folded his arms. At least she was talking in complete sentences. That was progress. "Are you a witch?" he asked, though he knew full well she wasn't. "A sorcerer? Spelled in some way?"

"Oh, please. I don't even have a tattoo." She winced as she regarded the large black stain that marked all that was left of the primary demon. "Mr. Slouch—the main guy—he did say more to me, though none of it made sense. I mean, you might know what he was talking about, but I sure didn't. He said I was the first scribe, but not the only one. And he told me I needed to come with him, to join something called the Shadow Court. You know what that is? Because I've never heard of it."

Hugh kept his expression bland. "You didn't write anything like that into your book?"

"I did not. But there's a whole shit ton happening now that I didn't write into my book. I didn't write this scene at all, for example." She waved her hand at the walls painted in demon guts. "This didn't happen. Sorcia was followed and bad guys did try to catch her—the watchers from Sorcerer City—but—"

"Sorcerer City," Hugh interrupted. "Shadow Court."

"SC. Cute." Their eyes met, and Katana nodded slowly. "Yeah. Okay, well, fine. So maybe the Shadow Court is just the real world incarnation of Sorcerer City. But the people who tried to snatch Sorcia off the street were freaking human beings, not demons. And you... Even in the version where you lived longer, you weren't here. You didn't show up until Sorcia got to her apartment on Central Park. And once you both arrived there..."

She broke off and glanced away, her cheeks once more stained with color. Hugh kept his own expression steady. He'd seen the panels set in the apartment that Finn had printed out. He'd followed what he could of the story that Katana had outlined along with those panels. He knew the scene she was thinking of—hot, intense sex between the heroine and her guardian angel. Finn had made sure to bookmark it.

It was his favorite scene in the book.

"What did Sorcia leave in her apartment?" he asked. "Is there anything the Shadow Court could find there?"

"Maybe," Katana muttered. "I honestly don't know. Too much of the story has changed, but if we intersect there, I know we can get back on track. Or, maybe if I go there myself, I can—"

"No," Hugh said, harshly enough that she jumped a little. "You have to stay with me. Until we figure this all out, I have to keep you safe. We can't afford to lose you to another round of demons."

"Yeah, um...about that."

He looked up to see her staring at him, doubt and worry once more looming large. *Oh, yeah. Here it comes.*

"You looked different while you were fighting those guys," she said, her pale eyes fixed on him. "Kind of like them. I didn't draw you that way in *Dead End.*"

Hugh lifted his brows in amused condescension, but this type of deception came easily to him. All he had to do was play into her own doubts about her abilities...as much as he hated to do it. "And because you drew me, you think that's all there is to me? That you know more about my creation than God Himself? Or—even better. You think you're some sort of god now?"

"What? *No.*" She stepped back, but caught herself in time before she planted a foot in the demon goop. She didn't completely abandon her questions, though, or her incessant need to know more. Humans rarely could. "Not at all. It's just... You looked familiar to me, somehow. Like that. That's all. That's all I meant. You made me remember—"

"Remember what, Katana?" Hugh pressed, sensing danger here. She couldn't have seen him in his demon form before now. If she had, she wouldn't have drawn him as some sort of hero in her screwed-up comic book. But what had she seen, specifically? Another of the Syx? Maybe demons harnessed by the Shadow Court? "Think hard. It's important."

"I don't know." She ran shaking hands through her hair, and ruthlessly tightened her ponytail. "It's gone. It's like that sometimes. There's a lot of noise and imagery and ideas, and then it goes away. If it's important, it'll come back."

Hugh bit back his disappointment, but it was probably

for the best. He had to keep the woman focused on getting them to the Shadow Court, and he couldn't afford to get too entangled in her emotions. That way lay danger of an entirely different sort.

"Let's get you out of this place," he said, deliberately gentling his tone. "Take my hand, unless you want to step in all that muck."

He held out his hand to her, and she studied it a long moment before slowly, tentatively placing her fingers into his palm. Hugh gritted his teeth at the dizzying surge of warmth that spun through him, and tried not to yank her to him. "I'll pick you up now. Lift you free."

"I...oh!" Katana broke off in a gasp as Hugh stepped directly into the smear of filth surrounding her and lifted her in his arms. She was a sturdily built woman, but not big, and her weight felt strangely foreign to Hugh—as if he was lifting a precious object from the earth, not merely the fifty-seven-thousandth human he'd plucked out of danger.

"Shh," he murmured as she began shivering again, then they were through the doors and out onto the sidewalk. The green smoke still boiled all around them, and Hugh didn't set Katana down until they reached the street. Even then, he kept his hand on her shoulder—for her benefit, not his. Her skin was so warm to the touch, so vital, that he wondered how he hadn't noticed it in humans before.

"We have to get to the apartment," she muttered, refocusing his attention. "This is all wrong, and I have to get it right again." She stepped out from under his hand and scurried onto the far sidewalk.

"Is it close?" he asked as he stepped up beside her, though he already knew where her heroine's apartment was, a dual tower fortress of golden brick, overlooking the large lake near the north end of New York City's main park.

He'd memorized the panel featuring the apartment complex—and all the ones that followed it. Blue had asked him to do so, after all.

"Central Park West. Probably about a half an hour's walk from here." She pursed her lips. "It's a hike, but we've got to go. I can't keep making things up on the fly."

Hugh shrugged. "Why not? What if you wrote new panels, or drew them, whatever it is you do. What if you built a bridge to wherever we need to go?"

She rubbed a hand over her face, clearly distressed. "Maybe that would work? It seems reasonable it would, but I don't know. I've never done it. I've never done any of this. All I know is that Hugh the Destroyer never killed a bunch of demons in a Carlotti's coffee shop looking like...looking like you did, at least for half a second. It was a great scene, but I didn't write it."

"Well, making things up seems to be working out okay for you."

Kat's chin came up. "But is it? Are you sure? I know what I wrote. There was a path and a map and most of all, an *ending*. Sorcerer City is shut down, at least for the moment. The creatures of *Dead End* are held back from doing their worst. If I start rewriting the story, I don't know how it ends. And maybe it won't end so well."

"Maybe it will end better."

"Or maybe we'll all die and it's the world that ends."

He snorted a laugh. He couldn't help himself. "For you and those like you, it already has, I suspect. But the rest of humanity? Look around you."

He pointed to the veil of green smoke across the busy street—but there were plenty of people navigating through that smoke. Cars moved, people walked. Life went on.

"How are they doing that?" Kat protested. "How can they

just keep walking and not see? Who owns this block? Will they even know their property values have tanked?"

"You still don't get it." Hugh raised a hand, and a jogger running toward them stopped, slapping his hands to his ears as they approached.

"You, what do you see across the street?" Hugh asked. "What's there?"

The runner scowled at him, then glanced across the street. "Carlotti's Coffee. Its window is broken out, and it's closed. There's places like that up and down the street after this morning's solar flare."

"Is it worse here than other places you've seen?" Kat asked him.

"Eh, this is about par for the course." The man shrugged. "Random assholes most likely—not real looters. They didn't do too much damage, didn't steal anything, but you sure can tell where they hit."

Hugh released him, and the runner went on his way, while Katana scowled at the opposite side of the street.

"That's not what I see," she said. "To me, the building is whole and perfect behind all that smoke. Hell, at first, I didn't even see the smoke. How can I protect myself if I can't see where the danger lies?"

"That's a good question," Hugh allowed. "How does it work out in your story?"

"That's my *point*," she ground out. "This wasn't part of my story. My heroine had a map, a plan. I'm running blind and there's no *time*."

Hugh went still. This was new. "Explain that. Why isn't there time, specifically?"

"What?" Katana furrowed her brow at him. "What do you mean?"

"Did you write a time element into *Dead End*?"

"Of course I did. I mean—I think I did." Her frown deepened. "I'm sure. It's part of the story. The magic of *Dead End* is like a living thing, sentient. These hell blocks? They will keep growing and spreading until Sorcerer City is shut down, and only then will people know how much of the world is left and how much is broken. The people who can see any of this, anyway."

Far up the street, beyond the hell block, a pane of glass shattered, a car screeched to a halt, somebody screamed. The shouts of angry drivers clattered along the concrete and metal, vibrating in the heat, but traffic lurched into motion almost as quickly as it had stopped. The city's gears relentlessly turned onward.

Kat pulled out her phone, and Hugh went still. "Give me that."

Mutely, she handed it over.

"You can be tracked with this. I have to destroy it. You understand?"

"But..." She swallowed, then nodded. She looked away as he crushed the device with a quick and punishing squeeze, then dropped the pieces to the sidewalk. "That was my phone," she whispered.

"I know. We'll get you another. It will be okay." Sometime during the last half century, humans had transferred their need for connection to their devices, and Hugh had learned to his peril how dangerous it was to mock them for it. "Where do we go next?"

"The apartment," Kat said, gusting out a sigh. "There will be answers there. It was always a place I knew I could stick stuff for Sorcia to find. Maybe the map is there too."

"I thought the map was in the library."

She flinched at that, seeming genuinely confused and even alarmed. "How do you know that?"

He scowled. Had she mentioned the library when he'd first met her, or had Finn told him about it? Or both? It took him a moment to recall her specific words. Kat was so disoriented, she could easily be led to believe whatever he needed, but he found himself curiously glad that he didn't have to lie this time. "You said so when we first met. You said we should have been at the library, that that was where your heroine had learned what she needed to know."

"That's true—that *was* true," she corrected herself. "But you were already dead in that version of the story. In the second version—and third and fourth versions—we met outside the apartment in Central Park. You didn't go inside. Totally, not at all."

He studied her as the blush rose again in her cheeks. He'd seen every last one of the panels she'd had on that thumb drive. He'd definitely been inside the apartment. Katana needed to get better at lying.

"Well, we're going to have to risk that," he told her. "Because I'm not leaving your side."

9

*K*at pressed her lips tightly together and clenched her hands into fists. She didn't want Hugh to go to her apartment...which, of course, wasn't her apartment. Most likely, it didn't exist at all. But if it did exist, it was where Sorcia and her guardian angel had had toe-curling, mind-blowing sex...right before she'd led him straight to a gang of demons and watched him die protecting her. Another time, the demons had attacked them on their way through Central Park. A third, they'd made it all the way to Sorcerer City, and the magicians there had killed him.

Why had she been so determined to end this guy? What had he ever done to her?

He left me.

The answer was so real, so visceral, Kat stared spellbound at the rushing traffic for a moment, seeing nothing at all.

"We're going to need to figure out how you do what you do."

"What?" Kat jumped as Hugh's voice pulled her back out

of her head. "Well, that's going to be kind of tricky, because I don't even know how I do what I do. And what I do isn't all that...impressive." She broke off, forced to acknowledge the ridiculousness of her protests, given everything that had happened.

"Walk this way," he said.

Mutely, she headed down the street beside her guardian angel. One block, then two. With each step away from the coffee shop, she felt better. Her breathing eased; her shoulders came down. Eventually, they found a small Turkish café, this one conspicuously demon-and-green-smoke-free, and Hugh ushered her inside. It was nearly empty, but the coffee looked and smelled like coffee. They sat with their tiny mugs of the intensely strong brew, and he watched her carefully.

"You need to tell me your process, Katana," he said quietly. "It's the only way I will understand."

"Okay," she sighed, focusing on the curling wisp of steam from her delicate cup. "Well, it's like this. When I was just sitting at home, coming up with ideas to see how they worked out on the page, drawing my pictures and dreaming that maybe someday I could write a story that people would want to read, that I could draw illustrations that would make people feel something, it was no big deal, right? It didn't matter that I didn't understand what I was doing or how I was doing it. It didn't matter until somebody bought the book and made it real. But that's not what's going on anymore is it?"

Hugh shook his head. "It's not. You know it's not."

"Well, I haven't known it for all that long, so give me a break." She glanced toward the bustling street, then back in his general direction, though she still couldn't meet his eyes. "This morning, everything was going great. My life wasn't perfect, sure. Nobody's is. But I'd sold a book to a New York publisher five months ago, with a deal that was going to help me finally get out of my crap apartment and into a slightly less crap apartment. Let's be serious here, the money was good, but it wasn't change-your-life good. However, it *was* change your address good, and that was good enough for me."

Hugh blinked several times as if he was having trouble following her mental processes, but too bad, he needed to keep up. Kat cradled her tiny cup in her hands. "But anyway, we were all at Gable's store and Jeremy was going on about his miniatures. He should go on about them, though. The man has a gift."

Hugh lifted a brow. "A gift for painting tiny dolls?"

She snorted, but she felt easier now, talking to him. More relaxed. It...it was nice. "I'll have you know that painting tiny dolls brings a lot of pleasure to people. Both the guy who's doing it and the people who are lucky enough to get his artwork. Because he not only paints them, he crafts them too. He makes the mold, he casts the metal. I don't even understand how he does it, and it doesn't matter. He does it, and it works. He's a true creator."

She bit her lip, glancing down. Was she afraid to admit she was a creator too? Was that what she was having such a difficult time trying to explain?

Hugh simply nodded at her. "Does he have other miniatures planned?"

"Like you, you mean?" She brought her head up with the sudden rush of memory. "Actually, yes. He said there were six angels in the series—I think he got some sort of vision about it. Why? Is that important? Should you talk to him? I can take you. I'm sure he'd *love* to meet you. He'd probably faint straight out."

He shook his head. "We can do that—but later. He's not my focus right now. I need to understand what *you* do."

"Shouldn't you already know?" she asked weakly. "You're an Angel of God or whatever. Doesn't that make you omniscient—is that the right word? All-knowing?"

He huffed a laugh. "Not exactly. There are some mortals whose minds I can read, generally because they are in distress. Not yours."

Kat laid a hand on her chest. "I'm in distress. I promise you."

He chuckled, almost in spite of himself, it seemed, a quick flash of humor that lit up his entire face. She barely kept from gasping. Her guardian angel was objectively gorgeous—from the dark, swept-back hair to the deep purple eyes to his sinfully suggestive lips. How could an angel get requisitioned a mouth like that? It seemed unfair. His size and the sheer force of him was intimidating too—not in a bad way, though. She didn't feel safe with him, but she did feel protected. It was the first time she'd ever imagined those words being mutually exclusive.

Beneath his sheer beauty, however, something about Hugh tugged at her in a way she didn't expect. He'd seen some terrible things. More than she had, and she hadn't had an easy life.

"Could you maybe tell me a little bit about yourself first?" Her question came out unexpectedly, and he looked at her with surprise.

"That's not what's going to help," he said, his low tone of foreboding making her shiver.

"Well, maybe—but maybe not. You said yourself that it was rude of me to think that I knew you just because I drew a picture of you, and you're right. All I know is that you fought all those demons for me." She leaned forward, warming to the idea. "And even if you're my guardian angel, I bet you do it for other people too, all the time."

Something flickered in his expression, and she grinned. "I'm right, aren't I? I know I'm right."

"It's my job to fight demons," he said oppressively. "That doesn't matter to our conversation here."

"Sure it does." Kat's brain darted back to the image she'd glimpsed of her beautiful angel, scarred and taloned and so hideously, breathtakingly ugly, she'd almost swooned. But he'd been right, he'd been good. And he'd been saving her ass six ways to Sunday. "That's why you turned into one, I'm thinking. You might not even have realized it—it was so fast. But it's why...what? What's wrong?"

He'd gone still as a statue, his dark purple eyes gleaming dangerously. "By all means, continue," he said softly, and she swallowed.

Kat wanted to shut up—she did. But she couldn't. "It's just...maybe that's what happens when angels fight demons. You look like souped-up humans when you interact with us, you know? Whereas in reality, you're puffs of light or whatever?"

His lips twitched. "Something like that."

"So when you fight demons...you take on more of their look, maybe. That's all I'm saying. That would make sense."

"It would." He nodded solemnly, and his expression shifted into...one of almost pride? Could an angel be proud of her? Once again, the idea knocked against something lodged deep within the furthest reaches of Kat's mind, where nothing stirred but dark and oily memories from long, long ago. "Not many humans would be able to understand that."

"Oh..." She tried to quell the blush yet again creeping up her cheeks, hating that her emotions were so transparent.

"Well, I just had to make sense of it. Because I really did feel like I knew you in that other form. When you clearly would never look like that. God would never do that to anyone on purpose..."

Hugh was waiting for her when she glanced back at him, his amused expression telling her he'd followed her brain down this rabbit hole too. "An angel's appearance is somewhat misleading. You can't always believe what you see."

"Yeah, right," she muttered. "Like you're not perfect in every way."

Something dark and pained flitted across Hugh's face, and before he could deflect her, she reached out and touched his hand. He stared down at her fingers, his entire body going rigid. "Tell me," she whispered. "If you're not perfect—tell me how."

"I trust too easily." The words seemed to spill out of Hugh before he could stop them.

"That's a bad thing?" Kat asked as he slowly, carefully lifted her fingers off his skin and set her hand away from him, as if her touching him caused him physical pain.

"It can be. If you let down your guard, humans can be hurt. Angels can become demons really fast that way."

"But how does something so perfect become a demon? How is that a thing?"

"Because angels aren't perfect." He pressed his fingers into the tabletop so hard, she was surprised he didn't gouge the surface, but he kept going. "Most of the spawn are made out of primordial darkness, a living expression of the shadow energy left over from the first creation. They are neither good nor bad, but humans perceive them as evil because demons are different—and not obviously good."

"Oh." Kat frowned, but his explanation made sense, sort

of. "We don't understand them, so we categorize them as evil."

He smirked. "Well, that and they kill humans."

"Right." She huffed out a breath. "You said most of the spawn are made that way. What about the rest? Can humans become demons?"

He met her gaze evenly. "No—but angels can, if they sin. Fortunately, most angels prefer to seek the joy in their creation, not the darkness."

When he said the word joy, he smiled, and Kat found herself arrested by the pure, unrelenting beauty of the expression. This was an angel born to smile—to laugh.

To love?

She shoved the thought away before she betrayed herself with another blush. "I want to know more about that. What makes an angel happy? Unicorns and baby kisses?"

Hugh snorted. "Most unicorns are assholes, and babies are moist."

The comment was so unexpected that Kat barked out a laugh. "I mean, you're not wrong," she said. But he was eyeing her curiously now in a way that made her stomach tighten.

"You don't laugh enough. Why is that?"

She fought the urge to contradict him—though it was the same thought she'd had about him. She much preferred the flow of information to go one way. But there was something about the way he asked the question that made her neither willing nor particularly interested in avoiding it. Being an author and even a graphic designer dedicated to remote work was, well, remote. Isolating. She had friends, she supposed. But...

"Remember, I can't read your mind," he said, almost

chidingly. "If there is something you are thinking you will have to say it out loud. I mean, if you imagined something you wanted to put into your story, it would need to be on the page for it to be real, right?"

She lifted a shoulder, dropped it. "Actually, I would argue that, up until super recently, it wasn't even real when it was on the page. It wasn't real until somebody read it and reacted to it. That's what makes the story real. But now I don't even need that anymore. Because there's stuff happening that never made it to the pages that I sent my editor or agent. There's stuff happening that I drew one day and discarded because it was stupid. But those images... I saw them. They're in my head, and once they're in my head, I can go back to them, live within them, whenever I need..."

She broke off, shaking her head. "What did you ask me? I'm sorry, I get distracted."

Hugh's lips twitched. "What makes you happy, Katana? And do you need to be happy in order to create?"

She snorted. "Yeah, I can tell you the answer to the second question is a big fat no. I've written some of my best work when I was at my lowest point, and sometimes when I'm happy, hopeful about the world or whatever, I can't write for crap. Or if I do write, it comes out sounding like a monkey wrote it. No offense against monkeys. So it's not about emotion when I create. It's more about...letting go, I guess. Letting myself get fully immersed in the story or the work. I'm probably not all that different from an engineer or mathematician. We all have something we're really good at, something we were meant to do."

"And you were meant to write stories?"

"I don't know." She sighed. "If I was really good at it, I'd already be rich, right? So I don't know."

"Can you show me how you do it?" he asked quietly.

Kat fought down the surge of self-consciousness. "It's not really all that mysterious. I can do it with a computer or notepad, but a notepad's probably easier here. You just sort of start, you know?"

Feeling vaguely stupid beneath his curious regard, Kat slid her pack around and drew out a yellow legal pad and a couple of pens.

"If I don't care about the final result, if I'm not trying to create something that's perfect, it doesn't matter what I use. If it needs to be perfect, I'll use the computer drawing tools or pencils with generous erasers. Things are rarely perfect on the first go."

"Things are rarely perfect in the final incarnation," Hugh put in.

"That's true too. But we can always try, right?"

"Is perfection the goal?"

His voice was already fading a little, and she sighed, distracted, images bubbling up in her mind as the chaos stirred.

"Perfection is unattainable, but it's still the goal," she murmured. "If you could just do everything right, maybe..."

She bent to her drawing, transferring the images that flashed into her mind onto the page. She didn't bother with borders. She didn't care about composition or action or structure. She drew the room they sat in, a large angel with furled wings despite the fact that the feathers were hidden, a small woman curled over a notebook, scribbling fiercely. And then she moved to the room around them, and her sketches grew less exact. Doors and windows opening onto worlds she couldn't quite see—cityscapes with long lines of buildings, hints of color, running people...and smoke. So much more of that damned, green, roiling—

"Katana," Hugh said, the word spoken without urgency,

but with enough intensity to break through the spell. She realized with a jolt that he'd reached out to cover her hand with his. His hands were large, beautifully formed. But the nails were ragged, the finger pads calloused. She could sense that the bones beneath had been broken. And that didn't feel right.

"You shouldn't be injured," she murmured, and she lifted her other hand and put it over his, ignoring the swirl of colors and noise that surrounded her. That chaos always surrounded her when she was deep in thought. But all that mattered right now was Hugh's hand. All that mattered was her need to knit his bones back together. "You should be healed."

"*Katana*," Hugh said, more urgently this time. She blinked, pulling away as his hands became unbearably hot—

Then she looked around and gasped.

The world had spun into madness.

10

*D*espite not wanting to hurt Katana with his now-scorched hands, Hugh lunged for her, if only to keep her from bolting. She would have every reason to run. While she'd worked, the energy around her had leapt and hummed at first, reacting to her intensity. That in itself wasn't alarming. Humans rarely understood their effect on the world around them.

When the Father had granted His children dominion over all things, they had chosen to implement that dominion with strife and war, exploitation and destruction more often than not. That was the easiest and clearest dominance to enact. But humans could do far more. They could create art, coax plants to grow and harvest them, and convert the fruits of the land into food for the masses.

Or they could manifest their thoughts into reality. They rarely did, but they could.

And Katana was the most powerful one that Hugh had ever seen. What she'd created...

"What's happening?" she whispered as she stared at the room around them. The simple coffee shop had been transformed into a metaphysical waystation. A room of relative serenity surrounded by chaos. Doors and windows and archways, holes in the tile and even in the ceiling stretched out around them, leaving approximately a twelve-foot square for their table, chairs, and coffee cups.

Through the doors and windows, often right next to each other, were scenes of dramatic differences. In some, thick green smoke obscured the view. In others, the sun shone clearly onto glistening streets. In half the images, people ran, and some were empty and deserted.

"What were you thinking of when you created this?" Hugh brought her focus back to him, but she trembled and flinched away from the flashing images around them.

"This has never happened before, I swear," she managed. "I don't know what's going on." She nudged the pad of paper as if she hadn't been the one who'd drawn on it. The rendering was good, but too amorphous to really show what she'd intended. There were two rough figures sitting at a table, one much larger than the other, with luxuriously tenting wings that thrust up over his shoulders before cascading down in graceful curves. The woman beside him was almost comically small in comparison, and rendered with a few hurried strokes. The doors and windows and archways contained billows of smoke and fire, but only a hint as to the rich tapestry of images that he could see. Katana hadn't needed to even flesh them out for them to take shape in real life.

"What were you thinking about?" he asked again. "Specifically."

"I was thinking about everything that had happened," she finally said, still not looking up at him. Instead, she focused on the opening and closing doors, the gaping holes that vanished as quickly as they were created. "What was now possible, and what would happen to people who were caught in the middle. I didn't...I didn't imagine this."

Hugh nodded. "So when you imagined what was happening to people, did you see them running and fighting? Were you aware of what you were seeing?"

"No. I'd like to say it doesn't work like that, but honestly, this isn't what I normally do." She glanced over his shoulder, frowned. "Are those doors real? Could we walk through them?"

He grinned at her. "Would you like to try?"

"I mean..." She stood up as if in a dream, and Hugh stood with her, reaching for her hand when she hesitated.

"I'm not going to let anything happen to you, Katana," he told her with the ease of the established liar. But in this case, he didn't feel like a liar. Because to the extent that he was able, he would make sure he was telling the truth.

His mission was to find out what this woman knew and what she was capable of, to help preserve humanity from the magic that had just been unleashed upon them. She wasn't going to die on his watch, not if he had anything to say about it. Furthermore, the archangel wouldn't have assigned the task to him without being damned sure Hugh could see it through.

Granted, there were only two demons left who needed to pursue their path of redemption in order to gain their freedom, but this was too important to fuck up. If Hugh hadn't been up to the task, the archangel would have assigned the job to one of the others of the Syx. So he knew he could do it, and what was more, Michael most likely needed Hugh's particular set of skills...if only to carry off the deception of being an angel. That would have been tough for any of the Syx to swallow, even Raum, who certainly had the voice for it, because Raum seemed to have a personal vendetta against angels. Without a doubt, his sin had involved those holier-than-thou bastards. Hugh looked forward to finding out how.

But first he had to nail down his own assignment.

"Which one should we choose?" Katana asked, but though she asked the question aloud, her voice was soft, thoughtful. As if this too was a puzzle she simply had to figure out.

Hugh stayed silent, trying not to think about the fact that she'd wanted his hand to heal from some break that he'd long ago forgotten—and it had healed. The reality of that, the implications...

It boggled the mind. He was a demon—she was a human. Some lines simply should not be blurred.

A second later, she sighed.

"Fuck it, who cares?" she announced abruptly. "The whole goal is just not to die, right?"

With that, she tugged him forward, and almost at random, it seemed, angled to the side, where there was an open door cut into a wall that looked slightly crooked. As they approached, the wall got taller, one end seeming to stretch higher than the other, as if it were drawn deliberately askew.

They broached the door and stepped out into an empty city street fronted by faceless gray buildings. In between those buildings, one after the other, were more of the strangely formed structures that they'd used to enter this place, rectangular buildings that were tall and thin and formed slightly off center, their bricks painted myriad colors —blue, green, gray, violet. Mostly violet.

"Does it mean something to you?" he asked.

"No. Yes. I don't know." Then she scrubbed her free hand through her hair and looked away. "You asked what made me happy. And it made me think of this painting I'd done when I was a kid. I'd been working so hard on it, but I couldn't make the walls line up straight. I wanted to paint it freehand, but no matter what I tried or how long I took adjusting the walls, they weren't even, and the roof was always at a slant. My art teacher told me not to worry about making it even. That if I wanted to see the world on a slant, there was a reason for it and I should just lean in."

She gestured at the little brownstone buildings in their myriad colors. "Slanting windows, slanting doors. Almost right until you look at it, and then you see that it's horribly off-kilter. And around that building, I put other buildings, and every single one of *those* were straight and tall and true. My teacher said I was remarkable that day." Katana smiled a little, shaking her head. "I'll never forget that."

Then she glanced up at him. "Why is it so silent here?"

He lifted his brows. He had no idea. "Maybe because it's a memory, not a real place?"

"We walked into a *memory*? Is that possible?"

He looked down at her with a surge of unexpected emotion, taking in this fragile human who understood so little of what she was capable of and yet created it anyway, hoping—no, knowing—that it would somehow all work out.

"I think with you, anything is possible," he murmured, and though he'd intended it only as a positive affirmation, a tool to gain trust, if he was being cynical, Katana straightened. She gaped at him as if he really was an angel and not a demon most foul.

"You think so?" she asked, her voice trembling slightly.

Hugh reached out and lifted his finger to her chin, tilting it up toward him. She was so pure, so good. She was not for the likes of him.

He hadn't been lying about trusting too easily. Rightly or wrongly, he'd trusted humans to take care of themselves. They hadn't. And while they'd experienced a fleeting death for that mistake, he'd paid the price for six thousand years.

But his truth wasn't important here—Katana's was. What would an angel do in this moment? Not an actual angel. They were assholes. But the angel this woman clearly believed in?

Angels didn't kiss humans. But they did in Katana's world. And it was a world he didn't so much mind living in, at least for this moment.

"I know so," he said. He leaned down to kiss her on the forehead. A benediction, nothing more. Only she shifted at the last minute, once more creating a reality he didn't expect and hadn't planned for.

She lifted her head, tilting it to the side, and her mouth met his.

Hugh had lain with humans before—as a Fallen and as a demon. It had generally been brief, energetic, and wildly entertaining...but in a distant, unemotional way. With Katana's kiss, a hot rush of sensation swept through him, not cool and comforting the way he imagined human affection should be, but desperate, needy. In that moment, he wanted her like he had never wanted anything in his life. Had never realized that he *could* want something so much. To hold her, pull her to him, devour her—

He stepped back abruptly. Katana gasped, lifting her hand to her lips.

"Sorry. I'm so sorry. I wasn't thinking. I'd imagined—forget what I imagined. This is wrong, bad."

"It's not wrong or bad," he assured her a little unsteadily, but for once, he couldn't sell the lie. "I just don't want to hurt you."

"You won't hurt me. You couldn't. You're the most perfect being I've ever met. For God's sake, you're an angel. I believe in you."

He flinched, but didn't try to contradict her. During the kiss, the world had gone back to its usual appearance. They were back in the Turkish coffee shop, all the doors and windows to other possibilities gone.

"No one's come in here looking for us," he said, his voice rougher than he wanted, but that was too damn bad. "We should keep moving."

11

*T*his was going from distracting to devastating, and the guy wasn't even trying.

Hugh had pulled her out to the sidewalk, presumably to restart their walk, but Kat's mind was still spinning out of control. To recapture her sanity for half a second, she shoved away the amazing, spectacular, brain-melting kiss *with an angel*, relegating it to Things to Think About Later™. Difficult to do, but essential, because otherwise, she'd dissolve into a gibbering mess right on the street.

Meanwhile, bits and pieces of *Dead End* were coming back to her, but she needed time to study those pieces thoroughly. And as she'd most certainly made clear in her story, time wasn't a luxury she had enough of.

She needed to get to Sorcia's apartment, and she'd told Hugh as much...except for the fact that the apartment wasn't actually hers. She'd found it months ago on a real estate listing, complete with a dozen professionally shot photos of the interior—and mouthwatering views of Central Park. It was elegant, beautiful, and *not hers*. As she'd done in the coffee shop, she was getting her realities mixed up.

So how could she fix this? If she wanted to sync up the story by returning to a place that served as a proxy apartment—like her hotel—that could work, right? But if there was somebody from this Shadow Court looking for her, surely they'd be watching that hotel, right?

And what if there *was* an apartment on Central Park registered to Sorcia Steele? What would that mean?

"You have an address?" Hugh asked as he stepped off the curb and lifted a hand. There were no cabs on the street, but that didn't seem to bother him.

She made a face, knowing the location he meant. "Sure I have an address. Of course I do. Why *wouldn't* I have the address for an apartment complex with homes that cost millions of dollars?"

She turned toward the street, and something shifted awkwardly at her hip. She brushed her hand over it as a distinctive yellow-bodied vehicle turned onto the street a block up.

She squinted at Hugh as the taxi approached them. "Is finding cabs one of your superpowers?"

"The minds of humans are easily turned."

She shook her head, her thoughts automatically turning to her usual frugal travel mantra as the cab pulled up. She didn't have money for cabs, not yet. Not until the first deposit...

Her frown deepened. Maybe not ever, now. Would Emily even have an office to go back to? Would she want to go back to it? Would she blame Katana for what had happened to her—maybe even send the cops after her?

All these thoughts converged in Kat's brain as Hugh opened the cab door and turned toward her, gesturing her inside. She piled into the car's back seat, wincing again as she felt the bulky bulge over her hip bone. "What in the hell," she muttered.

Then Hugh slid in beside her, and she felt trapped, crowded against the door as his long, heavy frame bent nearly double to get into the car. Once again, she absolutely did not think about their kiss—the touch of his unexpectedly soft lips, the surge of heat—

Nope. Not gonna think about that.

The cabbie—a small man with big eyes that bulged beneath a fringe of grayish-black hair—looked up, and before he could ask where to, Katana rattled off the address of Sorcia's trendy residence. She dropped her hand to her hip as she did so, wincing at another stab of discomfort. Tilting her hips, she tucked her fingers into the pocket of her jeans and pulled out a Hello Kitty keychain. Only this one didn't have a thumb drive attached to it. Instead, two metal keys and a slender strip of coated plastic dangled free.

"What's with the cat?" Hugh rumbled as she studied the foreign objects in her hand.

"I have no freaking idea," she murmured. She didn't dislike Hello Kitty, but her choice of the cartoon feline had started as a joke with her editor. Something she'd learned when her agent had brokered the sale of *Dead End*.

"Those are the keys to your apartment?" Hugh prompted.

"Ah...I guess so?" Kat swallowed. She didn't have an apartment. Sorcia Steele had an apartment. After all, superheroes had awesome apartments, so why not ex-mercenary thieves? Nobody had taken any exception to that element of *Dead End*; not her editor, not her agent. Her agent...

Kat fought down a surge of anxiety as the cabbie navigated through the thickly congested streets of the city.

She hadn't heard from Natasha since she'd dropped off the manuscript this morning, handing it over to Emily like she had been some sort of secret operative reporting to a drop.

But Natasha hadn't called Kat to ask how she was after the bombs. Then again, Katana hadn't called Natasha either. Calling people wasn't something she did, especially since she had no one to call. As a result, nobody ever really knew where she was. She'd always preferred it that way. Had Sorcia preferred it as well?

Kat's cheeks colored. She'd included several panels of Sorcia looking dark and gloomy, maybe remembering a past she didn't like to think about. But that was it. She hadn't fleshed out her heroine's back story. She could have been any woman, every woman. She always looked forward. But nobody came into this earth with no past.

Except for maybe a guardian angel afraid to trust anyone.

Then again, she'd killed said angel in her story like sixteen different ways. So maybe he had a point.

She slid a quick glance his way, but Hugh stared dead ahead, focused on the traffic before him, which, from the pleased huffs and hums of the driver, was proving easier to navigate than expected.

"Are you doing that?" she murmured.

The corner of Hugh's mouth tilted up into a wry grin. "We are only given the right to travel without time passing when the need requires it. The need of one of God's children," he corrected, sounding distracted. "Otherwise, we are constrained by the limits of this world. You find ways of getting around those limits that still fit within the protocol."

"Why not just change the protocol? If I had a superpower, that's what I'd do."

Hugh didn't shift his attention from the traffic ahead. "You'd change the future to suit yourself?"

"Sure I would. Who wouldn't?" A chill skated down her spine, making her shiver. "Theoretically speaking, of course."

"Theoretically speaking, you are changing the future now."

"Sure I am," she agreed. "We all are, every minute of every day."

"You know what I mean. You have changed the story of *Dead End* already, haven't you? You're changing it right now with those keys that weren't in your pocket until a few minutes ago. How long have you had that skill?"

"I don't have that skill," Kat said automatically.

"Clearly." Hugh said drily. "Don't lie to me, Katana Midland. You're no good at it."

"I'm not *lying*." She glowered out the window, feeling mulish. "I don't know if I have a skill or if it's the story demanding to be told. That's why stories exist, right? I change the pieces to suit my mood or the plot all the time, but I don't know if I'm doing it or if I'm getting the story from somewhere else. I legitimately don't know."

"Then how do you know what's true and real?"

She closed her fist around the keys until the plastic edges and the sharp tines of the metal bit into her palms. It was a question various therapists had asked her over the years, at least when she could afford to go. She'd never wanted to think too much about the answer.

The car broke free of the traffic and crossed a wide boulevard to enter the park between two pillars. Katana glanced around, surprised. She knew the cabbie shouldn't have needed to enter the park to get to Sorcia's apartment, but with traffic, it was anyone's guess what the best route was. And of course, she'd never actually been to the apartment building before. Not in person. She'd Google mapped it and even then, only the street directly in front of the building.

"Were you okay this morning, sir?" she asked abruptly, drawing the cabbie's attention. "With all the electrical outages and smoke?"

"Slept through the whole thing." The man chuckled, his slightly protruding eyes seeming remarkably unconcerned. "A lot of people did. Dropped straight down to the floor or the sidewalk, wherever we were, passed out. New York being New York, when we came to, we first wanted to fight, you know? But then we...suddenly didn't. Everyone I spoke to felt...wonderful. Very, very good. I did, for certain. I wasn't on the street. I had worked an all-nighter last night, and I was home in Brooklyn. The wife passed out with the kids in the living room, and when we all woke up, the kids were happy, she was happy. I was happy. It wasn't such a bad thing, no?"

"No," Katana murmured. "I don't think I read about very many deaths."

"No deaths. Well, very few deaths," the cabbie agreed. "It was as if everyone stopped in place, then started up again, a bit better than before."

Better? That was a relief, at least. "Ah, have you noticed anything different about the city since then, anything wrong with the buildings or the streets, any neighborhoods that seem different?"

"Fewer people out at first, though that's been steadily changing as the day goes on. Otherwise, no. The city bounces back, always, yes?"

"Always," Kat murmured as they passed a stretch of park boiling over with smoke. People walked right in front of it without even turning to the side, while lightning crackled within its depths. She could see the danger plain as day, but ordinary people were spared that experience. Was that what Hugh had meant when he'd said the world had ended for her, but not for everyone?

Had to be. Still, what was in that hell block, exactly? Why had it erupted there, as opposed to thirty yards back? And why didn't she know more about what was supposedly her own creation?

Because I didn't create it, I just saw it and reported it.

Was that true, though? Was she really blameless in creating the havoc that now was wrecking all these pockets of New York, and God only knew where else?

Then they were past the hell block, and the trees fell away as the boulevard opened up again. The cabbie pulled to the side, still within the park. "This gets you closer than I normally would coming this way, but to get right up on the building, I'd have to circle the block. You want me to do that?"

"No, this is great." She slid her bag around and nervously eyed the meter.

Hugh leaned forward and gave the man a bill.

"Oh! Um, you have a card? I don't have enough to make change," the guy began, but Hugh stopped him.

"Keep it." Then he pushed out the door, reaching back a heavy hand to pull Kat with him.

The man's thanks was heartfelt as Kat gently closed the door, swaying a little, trying to get her bearings.

"This isn't right," she murmured. The images she'd seen had been mapped when the building was still under construction. A new façade and shops now gleamed from the first floor, while the upper floors were scaffolding-free.

"You don't recognize it?" Hugh asked.

"No. I mean yes, I do, but it's different than I remember." She squinted at it, trying to stamp down her sense of unease.

"Is it within a hell block?"

She grimaced. "No—well, at least not that I can see. Why, do you see something? Is there evil here?"

Hugh's lips twisted. "Evil is everywhere. It always has been. The magic that's erupting in the hell blocks you're seeing, that's new, but the evil within those hell blocks is as old as time itself. That said, no. There's no more evil here than there is anywhere else in the city. You live in this place?"

She held up the keys, grimacing as they caught the sunlight. "I sure hope I do."

12

*H*ugh experienced a growing disquiet as they approached the quietly dignified apartment building that apparently held Katana Midland's fictional heroine's home. It wasn't as showy as most of the residences on the block, but it was older. More sure of itself. As they'd driven closer to the building, he'd felt the pull on his energy coupled with the urgency of flight, the kind of sensation that usually preceded him being yanked from one corner of the earth and thrust into another to save one of God's children in need.

He had resisted it. His job was with Katana.

But now he wondered if it had been an actual call to serve, or simply the emergence of an ability to move Katana to this place instantly. To transfer locations in a heartbeat simply because it was easy to do so, not to save a life. To change the protocol, as Katana had put it.

He'd had a sense, a knowing, that he could make that change. It was a simple thing, really, unremarkable by many standards...yet cataclysmic. Nothing in a demon's life was supposed to be easy.

Being with Katana was easy, though. Hugh scowled as the thought came to him unbidden. Yes, she'd freely admitted her intention to kill the fictional version of him several times over. She also clearly remained worried that the fiction-to-life transition of her story might result in his death whether she wanted it to happen or not. But she'd called him back to her side when she'd needed him anyway. She'd swayed toward him when she should have swayed away. And when she fixed those pale gray eyes on his, with the mercurial fire sparking in their depths, he knew she saw something in him that no other human had.

He would use that connection against her if needed. She was his job, and he wasn't about to forget how dangerous she was—especially given that she'd put a target on his back. He knew he couldn't trust her, and he wouldn't. And yet...this part felt almost absurdly natural to him. Being with her, protecting her. It was...right. It was good.

He carefully kept from eyeing Katana too closely. He got the distinct impression that not much had been easy for her up to this point in her life, yet she had keys to what was undoubtedly a lavish apartment by any human standard. And she seemed at once surprised and strangely accepting of it, as if it shouldn't exist, but it did.

Hugh's experience with truly Connected humans was scant. There was, of course, the Arcana Council, whom he and his kind avoided as much as possible. Still, the Council comprised more than a dozen souls who possessed the strongest psychic abilities in the world. And, generally speaking, they had developed the emotional maturity over centuries to handle those abilities.

Most humans had not. Their brief lifespans precluded great wisdom, and their quest for power and control over their own lives and the lives of others made temptation to do harm an almost irresistible force. The tides of magic had been shifting in recent years, but nothing ever really changed.

Except for the powers that were emerging in this human, who made no sense to him.

There was no doorman at the front of the building, nor any obvious place to insert a key. Instead, there was a code box.

Katana squinted at it, worry crossing her face. "What are the odds?" she muttered. Leaning forward, she keyed in four quick digits. The door clicked open, and if anything, she looked more upset.

She hadn't expected her code to work.

"Play the part," he grunted, then reached for the door and held it wide. Clearly no coward, despite the hysteria likely rising within her, Katana entered the building with her chin high, her shoulders back.

"What is the significance of the numbers?" Hugh asked, genuinely curious. Humans were simple creatures.

"That's the thing," she bit back, giving him a smile that was all teeth and no joy. "My heroine has never put in a code. There's always been a doorman. So it's the first time I've even considered keying in a code. It's your name, by the way. Four-eight-four-four. And I didn't know you even had a name other than Angel until today. So, I guess I made that happen too? Or is that also part of the story?"

Hugh studied her. Katana kept going back and forth between the idea that she could change reality as she embraced it, and the belief that this path she was walking was part of someone else's premade plan. He wondered momentarily if her mind was breaking, but he didn't think so. Which was, if anything, more worrisome.

There was a key slot by the elevator, next to a reader. Kat

waved the slender strip of plastic on her keychain across the panel and punched the button. The elevator engaged, and a moment later, the door slid open. They entered, and Katana peered around. There were mirrors on the walls that caught her attention immediately. She froze, staring at his reflection.

Hugh saw it too. His wings had reappeared. But they had changed. Now, snowy white at the tips of the great arch that rose above his head a good six inches, they fell in waves of sumptuous feathers to the floor, the ombre pattern growing gradually darker until their base brushed the floor with feathers as black as ink.

Katana swiveled toward him, fixing him with curious eyes. "Why do they show up in a reflection, but not on you?"

"For most humans, they aren't apparent at all," he replied. Not really an answer, but she seemed to accept it.

She nodded as the doors slid open, the tension returning to her body as she exited into the hallway. Another large mirror hung over a gilt table adorned with two bowls of flowers. She turned right down the short, windowless hallway and marched up to the only door Hugh could see along this wall. He pivoted back and picked out a matching door down the other hallway, a twin apartment to her own.

When they reached the door, Katana keyed it open with her card. So far, the bit of plastic had been doing all the heavy lifting.

"What's the purpose of the other keys?" Hugh asked.

Katana grunted a soft laugh. "As soon as I figure that out, I'll let you know."

She pushed open the door, holding her breath, and Hugh had to nudge her inside, then push her forward far enough to close the door.

"How is this happening?" she whispered, swaying on her feet.

Hugh glanced around, taking the place in. He had to admit...as created realities went, this one was pretty good.

The apartment was immaculate. Pale wooden flooring extended throughout the space, punctuated with soft white rugs and darker gray furniture on top. The walls were gray as well, the trim white, and the curtains drifted down over the floor-to-ceiling windows in a fall of white gauze. The only color in this space came from the large, colorful paintings—all of them of what Hugh now understood were the illustrated panels of comic books. Five feet square at their largest and no bigger than a foot square at their smallest, they'd been painted with bold, slashing strokes in vivid colors. Reds, yellows, blacks, and blues. And most of the pieces were action shots.

"Your work?" he asked, but Katana ignored him, her feet finally moving her across the room to approach the artwork.

"I've never painted anything this big, and this is actual *paint*. I work on the computer mostly. I haven't done real sketch work since..."

Her voice faded as she stopped again, having spied a corridor that extended along the back wall, presumably leading to the apartment's bedrooms. A series of small framed pencil sketches appeared along that wall, awkwardly rendered, but full of energy.

"Jesus," Katana whispered, lifting a hand, then drawing it back as if afraid to disturb the pencil sketch under glass. "These...I did these. I drew this one when I was a little girl. Holy shit, I haven't even seen these since..."

She waved at Hugh to follow her. "We've gotta see what's back here, then we should probably talk. This is seriously starting to freak me out."

They walked down the hallway, and Hugh took in the sketches as they made their way through the rest of the apartment. The drawings improved in form and confidence as they continued down the hallway, until the last one showed a woman standing tall, her hair swept back, a faint impression of the city behind her. In her hand, she held a long curved sword.

Hugh eyed the sword with particular interest, but Katana's startled exhalation drew his attention sharply ahead.

There were two doors at this point in the hallway, one open, one closed. Katana hesitated in front of the nearer one, which was open, then started in. He expected it to be her bedroom, but this open space had an office with a large desk and drafting board, and floor-to-ceiling windows that let in the late afternoon sunshine. A long couch extended along one wall, with a pillow and blanket haphazardly thrown up against the cushions. But Katana's eyes were fixed on the double-screened computer setup with a gleaming computer station.

"Wow," she sighed. "There is no way I could have afforded this, I don't care what reality I was playing in."

She unslung her bag and pulled out a brick of a laptop. She set it on the table a good six inches from the screens, her hand shaking as she swiped for the connecting cords.

"You've never been here before?" Hugh asked.

"Never—and the apartment is completely different than it looks in *Dead End*. Like, Sorcia Steele doesn't decorate with my childhood art, for example. And when she's here, she's either in her kitchen or living room, or in her bedroom, passed out. This room—this studio overlooking fucking Central Park, for fuck's sake—doesn't exist. It doesn't *exist*."

She swallowed. "I've never been in one of these apartments physically. But I've got keys and it uses your name as a code and there are pictures I drew decades ago framed on the fucking wall." She dropped the keys on the gleaming white surface, the Hello Kitty keychain staring up. Another of the small cats was tucked behind the docking station, dressed like a ninja. "What's going on, Hugh?"

At the very real pain in Katana's voice, Hugh hesitated. He wanted more than anything to tell her it was going to be okay, and of course, he was exceptional at lying. But he couldn't. Not only did he not know the outcome of the strange tide of events this woman was either predicting or creating, but he didn't want to lie to her. Not about this.

Not yet anyway.

"What do you think you'll find on the computer here?" he asked instead.

"A new path," she said without hesitation. "The old path doesn't hold because we changed it."

"You changed it," Hugh said.

Katana shrugged a little helplessly. "I did, yeah. But I changed a lot of things, I'm coming to realize. The apartment didn't survive the first incarnation of the book any better than you did. By the time Kat had fled into the hell block that would take her to Sorcerer City, New York was under attack, and her apartment building was in flames."

"It was? Could that still happen?"

She lifted her brows, fear skating through her dark brown eyes. "It could, yeah. I suppose it could."

"Don't think too much about it," he directed her, and she smiled.

The sight rooted Hugh to the floor.

He had seen human smiles, of course—expressions of

relief, of pain assuaged. He'd attracted leers of an entirely different sort when he'd caught the attention of a human female—males too, for that matter. All the members of the Syx had. But every time he saw Katana smile, it swept through him like sunshine after a hard rain. It made him feel like a new person—not demon, not even angel. He didn't know what this was.

He simply wanted more.

A tremor of fear slithered through him. His growing obsession with Katana was more than dangerous. It was stupid.

He didn't care.

Oblivious to his clenching fists, Katana turned away from him and powered up her laptop, then plugged it into the console on her drafting table. In a few moments, the screens flickered to life, a flood of images filling the monitors with bold, vibrant colors.

"What do you plan to do with these?" he asked.

"Read them," Katana said. "Because, look—you see that?"

She pointed to one of the images, the angel Hugh rocketing up to tackle a demon midair, while a woman in dark clothing trained a gun on other creatures lurking in the green smoke.

He frowned. "You didn't have a gun."

"I didn't have a gun," she agreed. "But more to the point, I—Sorcia, I mean—wasn't attacked by a single demon and saved by the angel in any version of the story I ever wrote. That's new. The gun is window dressing, not a detail that necessarily matters, though something good to keep in mind. But the action of the panel changing completely? A panel that I have no recollection of creating, even though it's totally my style? That's a bigger deal. If we find more of those panels in the future—and if there are panels that lead us all the way to Sor...to this Shadow Court you keep talking about, well then, we've gotta follow whatever path they lay out. Someone is maybe trying to send us a message."

"Or you are sending us the message, in the only way you know how. Through the pictures of this book."

She grimaced, her eyes still trained on the screen. "I guess that's a possibility too."

Hugh watched Katana a moment more as her fingers flew over the keyboard. She narrowed her eyes as she scanned forward through dozens of images, then back—then forward again. She was afraid, he realized. So afraid, she practically shimmered with it.

"What is it, Katana?" he murmured.

"Do you really think I'm the one doing this?" The question was so quiet, it was barely a whisper, and Katana didn't look at him. Her mouth worked, but no more words followed for a second. Then she swallowed and tried again. "Do you think I've always been able to do this? That every shitty thing in my life that happened to me or the people I love was something I did? Is that possible?"

"*Katana*," Hugh said, arresting her attention. "No. That's not possible. All of God's children have their own free will."

"Yeah? Well maybe someone should have told that to Emily before she got blown back against her office wall. Or m-my parents, who got repaid for their kindness in adopting me by dying. They died in a car crash, Hugh! What if I caused that? What if I somehow made that happen?"

"You didn't."

"You don't know that!"

"I *do*." He weighted his response with all the heft of the angelic host and doubled down as Katana's lips twisted. "You would not have reached your twenty-sixth year without realizing this ability. It would have manifested in small ways that gradually became abundantly clear. The death of someone you love is not small. Arguably, it would have been more devastating to you than creating hell blocks full of demons. One is terrible, but a general threat. The other is... your parents. Am I right?"

"I..." She nodded quickly, her eyes shimmering with tears. "Yes. My parents' death feels way worse than what happened to me today—happened to the world. I guess that makes me a bad person."

Hugh's chest hurt, watching her, and he spoke as gently as he could. "It makes you human. Your hearts are made for intense personal connections, first and foremost. You didn't cause the terrible event that killed your parents—nor did you create the harsh conditions of your own life. You likely didn't have the ability to manifest at this level at all until quite recently. Don't you think you would have known?"

"I mean...maybe?"

She sounded so lost that he yearned to reach for her, to pull her close, but he didn't trust himself to let her go again. An urge to protect surged up within him, hot and fierce, but this time, it was accompanied by a need of a far baser kind, a dark, sensuous pull to gather this woman into his arms, inhale her scent of fear, hope, and dawning wonder in her own cataclysmic abilities, and take her right on the floor of the apartment she'd conjured into being.

What the hell was wrong with him? She needed his comfort. His understanding. His—

Fuck all that. She needs me. This human had abilities that no child of God—or angel, for that matter—could handle on their own. She wasn't a threat. She was a miracle.

And she was his.

Even if she might eventually cause his death, it didn't matter. She was *his*.

"Hugh?" Katana searched his face with an expression that, if anything, had grown more frantic, though she couldn't have any possible idea of what he was really thinking. "If I'm making things happen, and I start doing it wrong, will you promise to stop me?" she asked in a rush. "Because it's great that I've created a fancy New York apartment and a kickass Angel of the Lord to help me and hey, maybe even a pathway to stopping the bad guys from doing their thing...but what if I do other stuff that's not so great? What if I break something that shouldn't be broken?"

"You won't do that." And if she did, he would protect her.

"Oh, so now *you're* the psychic one?" Katana's lips twisted into an ugly line. "I want to believe you, I really do, but if I'm wrong and you're wrong, will you promise to take me out?"

Hugh looked into her stormy eyes and saw the suffering there, not only the confusion of the last few days, but a lifetime of doubt and pain. Katana Midland had been telling herself lies for so long, she no longer knew what she was capable of. And she had no idea of the gift the Father and she had cocreated within her fragile form, no idea of its strength and might.

But Hugh was finally beginning to understand it. Understand and want nothing more than to see her alight with all its glory.

His.

"I promise," he lied.

13

---

*K*at exhaled a sigh that held more fear than she wanted it to. Hugh was her guardian angel, and she supposed that counted for something, but it was more important that he made sure she didn't do anything she couldn't take back.

"Good, good," she said, nodding. "I should look first at the story doc by myself, in case it's bad. I can maybe explain it better if I have a second to see it first. You know, to process it, since technically, I sort of created it, even if I didn't create it like a normal person would. Or even a normal me would. You know, normally."

"Of course," Hugh said gravely. She wasn't entirely sure he understood her babbling, but he didn't object as she scanned the gleaming screens of a workstation that she'd neither bought nor ever used. Her setup at home was nowhere near this sweet. What scared her most, however, was that she had never even imagined a setup that *could* look like this, the same as she'd never imagined her graphic panels turned into artwork that would grace a New York apartment wall, or that the drawings she'd hoarded as a child and then set on fire when she'd been rejected from art school could be resurrected and lined up in lockstep down that apartment's hallway.

There was a whole hell of a lot about this that wasn't right. She'd never imagined the best of the best things happening to *her*, yet she was standing in a multimillion dollar apartment with ten thousand dollars' worth of equipment staring her in the face and a straight-up guardian angel close enough to touch. She hadn't imagined the world ending *in real life*, yet she'd just driven through a series of war zones in New York City that were only visible to a handful people...and those people's lives would never be the same.

What if she dreamed that she killed someone? You know, like she'd already imagined Hugh's death? That hadn't come true yet, but would it? Could it? Would she end up betraying him with her overactive imagination, without any way to stop it from coming true?

I have to get control of this.

Hugh's low laugh made her realize she'd said the words aloud. "You only need to control your reaction to it."

"No. You don't understand." She was used to talking out loud to herself, a hazard and privilege of living alone for so many years. She wasn't used to having to defend those random blurts. "I did this—this room. This computer. The shit that's on this computer. I did this and I still have no idea what's going to happen next. That's insane. I can't live like that. No one can."

He didn't say anything to that, and she successfully fought the urge to look into his eyes, his face. She didn't want to see whatever judgment might be there—or worse, pity. She'd had her fill of pity from her school counselors, her adoptive parents, even her—

Her traitorous mind latched on to her errant thoughts like a leech.

Have I killed before? Did I somehow hurt Frank and Jodi? Was their car accident my fault, no matter what Hugh said?

"What is it?" Hugh's question snapped out like a lash, but Kat was already shoving the thoughts away, far away, completely away, like she had when she was little and she had when she was older and like she did whenever her throat closed up and she couldn't breathe. *I'm not thinking about that!* she ordered herself...

And suddenly, she wasn't.

"Katana?"

"Nothing. It was nothing," she said, all her attention on the screen, as if nothing else was more important than that, because that's why they were here—to go to Sorcerer City and stop the bad guys from taking over the world. That's why these things were happening. That's why she had a guardian angel in her studio. The only reason.

She hadn't been making terrible things happen her whole life. Like Hugh said, she didn't have that kind of power. Or she hadn't until now. Everything she was experiencing right now was tied to this one story, this one time. She needed to focus on that.

The laptop finished opening the first set of images. Kat moved to click open the second set, then hesitated, mousing over instead to the file directory folder and clicking it open. The file she'd opened sat at the top of the list, but the last recorded save made her lips tighten with a genuine spurt of fear.

It had saved five minutes ago. Well before she'd fired up her computer.

Who had saved it—and how? This was a secure server, wasn't it?

Sure, if she considered her brain a secure environment.

"*Fuck,*" she muttered, then clicked the file open. It wasn't the design file where she made her images, but the more traditional page layout program where she dropped the low-res versions and moved them around, storyboarding as she went with the notes file open alongside.

She quickly scrolled to the last scene before they reached the apartment building, then shot forward quickly as Hugh drew closer to her, peering over her shoulder. It was a full three pages before she got to where they were at this moment. Two figures stood close together in her sun-drenched studio, a small, ordinary looking woman, and a hulking, gorgeous, heavily winged angel.

"You've drawn two of you?" Hugh asked, pointing to a detail that had completely escaped Kat.

She flinched. There was a third figure in the panel, sitting on the couch with her hands behind her head. She looked a lot like Kat alright, but she wasn't Kat. "Ahh...not exactly. That would be Sorcia Steele."

"Your graphic novel's heroine." Hugh squinted. "She's laughing. Why is she laughing?"

"Why, indeed," Kat muttered. It was bad enough that Sorcia looked beautiful and lithe and strong even as a secondary line drawing—but Hugh was right. She *was* laughing. And Kat had a good idea of what she was laughing at.

Like many authors, Kat had created a character in Sorcia that was everything she wished she could be but wasn't, rounded out by enough flaws to make her interesting. Importantly, Sorcia's flaws were not Kat's. Her fictional stand-in wasn't racked by doubt or terrible dreams or permanent underemployment. Permanent underemployment until now, at least.

Okay, maybe still now. They'd left behind a *lot* of wreckage in Emily's office.

Hugh rocked up on his toes, the same move he'd made before going medieval on the demon horde, but his eyes stayed locked on the screen. "Perhaps she does exist, not only in *Dead End*, but in this plane. Perhaps I'm supposed to connect the two of you."

"Yeah, no." Kat had no doubt that meeting Sorcia in the flesh would be a lot like getting introduced to your ex's new trophy wife. "I think I'll take a pass."

A whirling disc appeared at the top of the page for an instant, then disappeared. Katana's brows tented.

"That's weird." She chuckled as Hugh grunted. "Okay, fair. Weirder. The file saved on its own and, um, there are more pages now. Pages I didn't add."

She scrolled forward again, past the jumble of colors until they changed to a new series of images. Like a completely new set, ones that she'd imagined but hadn't fully created yet. They were fully formed now.

"That's Earth," Hugh said

"Yeah, a seriously fucked-up Earth." She panned through the images, and the view shifted to an image of Earth with several billowing plumes of smoke spinning upward, clearly visible from space. Then the perspective zoomed in again, and as the world got closer, new sparking yellow lines erupted across the terrain, zipping across Europe and Asia, then crossing over the ocean to the United States. The lines exploded out across the States in miniature fireworks, each burst connecting to other cities—other countries, even, stretching throughout North, Central, and South America—then once more, they shot back across the Atlantic to several points in Europe and off to the far eastern horizon.

The scene locked onto Paris next, then arrowed in closer still, until the crypts of Montmartre gleamed up from the screen, glowing with a spectral blue.

"Montmartre," Kat murmured. "Okay, that's still the same. The path still leads to Montmartre."

"The cemetery district of Paris? Why?" Hugh protested. "It is a place of magic, to be sure, but it's far too down-market for the Shadow Court. They are a group fueled by pride. The homes around Montmartre—"

"Shhh..." Another whirling disc appeared at the top of the page. When it disappeared again, she clicked forward to the next page, and it showed Hugh and the nondescript version of her disappearing into Central Park, with lightning shooting overhead. A complete sense of calm washed over her, soothing her anxiety.

The path remained the way she'd first envisioned it all those months ago. Even with Hugh's objections, it remained. Finally, something was going her way.

"Okay, well, like it or not, Montmartre is where we've got to go. Which tracks—we're back in the story, and the story has a happy ending, so long as we keep following it. Everything that should have happened in *Dead End* so far has happened, and we need to move forward from here."

"Everything has happened?" Hugh asked blandly, and Katana's heart jacked into her throat.

Okay, not everything. The second version of *Dead End*—the one she'd given to her editor—had been fairly spicy, for her. Instead of kissing him in some random coffee shop, she had kissed Hugh here—her guardian angel. Well, Sorcia had. And the kiss had gotten out of hand almost immediately, landing them in bed in a flurry of need. Kat hadn't wanted to get too graphic, but her editor had been absolute on the book needing heat. You couldn't have a giant hulk of a guardian angel who was hotter than any human being ever formed and not at least *try* to hook up with the guy, Emily had insisted. It had to happen.

And so it had. Once Kat had gotten started with the scene, the images had crashed into her brain, the intensity of the connection between Sorcia and the angel palpably real. Kat had lived vicariously through the passion they'd shared on the page, but it was the passion of two *made-up characters.*

Like her fancy new equipment had been made up. And this apartment. And the billowing green-smoke-filled hell blocks.

She tightened her jaw. There was no *way* she needed to have sex with Hugh in order to succeed in her quest to shut down Sorcerer City. The Shadow Court. Whatever. That interlude wasn't needed to make everything work. She refused to believe it. *Refused.*

Out of the corner of her eye, Kat saw the spinning circle erupt again.

"What is it?" Hugh asked as she froze. He was so close to her, his body warm and vibrant, the wings she could no longer see still somehow seeming to loom over them with the assurance that everything was going to be okay. She had a guardian angel on her side—and he was smoking hot, real, and fierce. He wouldn't do anything he didn't want to do, and he sure as hell wouldn't hurt her. And she knew in her heart of hearts that she needed to follow the story. So surely that meant it'd be okay if she followed the *whole* story. Like, if she wanted to—and if he wanted to. However that story, you know, happened.

The spinning circle winked out as her resolve weakened. The page count didn't change.

She should listen to her editor, shouldn't she? Or she

should at least try. Besides, it was possible Hugh *hadn't* read all the frames on her thumb drive. It was possible he didn't know the flow of the story. Still, why was he standing so close to her? Why was he leaning in, his glittering eyes intent on hers, his face set, his chiseled jaw...

She swallowed. Her hands had begun to sweat.

"What is it, Katana?" Hugh asked again, his words a soft whisper against her skin. "What is it you want to do?"

"I..." Heat flashed through her, demanding action. She curled her hands into fists, still staring at the screen, the spinning circle—anything but him. "I want to kiss you, Hugh. I wrote it into the book—and more than that. Full-on sex, really, but I don't need—I mean all that's not necessary. But kissing you...I think kissing you is necessary."

His chuckle was low and sensual. "I agree. But first you have to look at me."

"Oh." She turned toward him, awkward but resolute. "You're so beautiful," she whispered. "Through and through."

He didn't say anything for a long moment, just stared at her with his electric-purple eyes. Then he lifted his large hand to cradle her jaw, and his lips came down on hers.

The heat that had been banked into a pile of unruly embers blossomed into a firestorm so full and intense, Kat's entire body practically levitated. Time seemed to rush forward, then hold still, rush then freeze, the perfect representation of panel by panel images spilling out of Kat's mind, a tangle of colors and lines, curves and possibility.

Somebody made a sound, it might have been her, a half groan, half whimper as Hugh deepened the kiss. She brought her own hand over his, her long fingers with their calloused tips and jagged nails gripping his perfectly formed hands. Hugh's skin vibrated beneath hers as twin flames of need and darkness flowed through her—need and darkness, pain and pleasure, life and death. Then the darkness was chased by a light so pure and full, it took her breath away.

She broke away from him, the taste of his lips on hers. She sucked in a gasp of air, then clamped her mouth shut in a futile attempt to hold onto that taste forever. The feel, the reality of him. Because surely this was all a dream. A dream that would fade along with the smoke that still filled New York City, leaving behind a hazy memory she would carry with her to her grave.

"Are you okay?" Hugh murmured. Kat blinked up at him, startled she still held his hand, gripping it absurdly since his dwarfed hers. He stood unmoving, as if anything he did might break the spell. But, Kat knew, the spell was not his to break.

She was doing this. He was letting her, but this was her story to write.

There was power in that realization. Power and more than a little fear.

"No," she admitted shakily. "I'm nowhere near to being okay. But I did learn something—I mean, beyond the fact that I like kissing you."

He nodded, and in his smile she could see a depth of experience and knowing that somehow unnerved her more than anything that had come before.

"We should go to Montmartre," she announced. "Right now. Immediately."

Action was what she needed, never mind the panels she'd seen of her and Hugh together, with their bright flashes of colors and curves. She'd kissed him—twice now —and it had been glorious. Surely that was enough, right? Surely the story didn't need anything more? Right now, everything was perfect. She wanted to keep it that way, perfectly formed, imprinted on her mind forever. "That's where Sorcerer City is—or the path to it. I saw it."

The lazy curve of Hugh's lips once more hinted at a sly confidence she wasn't sure she was ready for. How could a freaking guardian angel have more game than she did?

"We don't have to leave yet," he countered. "The images you showed me of Montmartre were right before dawn. We've got another few hours to wait for that. In the meantime, we'll have to come up with something to keep us busy, I guess."

"...Busy," she echoed, her mind filling with all those images she'd drawn.

"Definitely," Hugh agreed, then gave an exaggerated glance around. "Like for starters—do you think you conjured up any food in this place?"

14

———

"Food." Katana's surprise was palpable—but there was a shimmer of disappointment there too, Hugh knew. Disappointment he shouldn't be stoking, or enjoying quite so much. He knew the danger this woman represented for him, and eventually, he might pull back. He should pull back—for himself, for the Syx. He should.

But not yet.

"Food, yes," he agreed, as breezily as he could without overselling it.

Her blush flared, then faded. "Oh. I didn't, um, plan for there to be any food here, but it's not like there couldn't be, you know? Of course not. Surely if we've seen all this, food shouldn't be a thing, you know?"

She stepped away from him, and he didn't miss her quick glance at the computer. But there was no change to the screen, no whirling disk that seemed to give her such concern.

As they exited the studio, Katana stopped so quickly that he nearly ran into her. He didn't have to ask why. The second door down now stood open, a warm spill of sunlight brightening the corridor. Clearly, that room possessed the same type of enormous windows overlooking the park.

"Well, *hello* to you too..." Katana murmured. She moved forward, pushing into the room. A large four-poster bed dominated the space, which was smaller than Hugh would have expected. The wash of neutrals continued here, with a wood plank floor covered with a thick shaggy white rug. A small white writing desk and chest of drawers were the only other pieces of furniture. It was simple, almost Spartan.

"It's my room," Kat murmured. "Like a million times nicer, but otherwise, it's my room from back in North Carolina."

"It's pretty," he offered, not knowing what else to say. Humans were brittle, and he was getting the impression that Katana was more brittle than most. Walking into this room hadn't helped her. If anything, she seemed more wound up, not less. Not helpful considering there was a whole lot of information he still needed to pry out of her.

Yeah. Like he was mostly interested in information at this point.

Still, he was on a mission here, to get them both to the stronghold of the Shadow Court, and pave the way for the Syx to strike those bastards flat before they had much time to regroup. It'd been less than twelve hours since the Court had launched their attack, and it surely hadn't gone according to plan. But they knew about Katana, and they'd found her already—twice. He couldn't forget that.

"We should make the most of the time we have before we leave for Paris," he said, and color scored Katana's cheeks once more. He had not imagined her reaction to their kiss— either now or the first time. She'd wanted him, and desire was one of the most powerful ways to control a human.

But was her desire real or part of this script she'd made

up in her mind? And what about the surge of need he'd felt when he'd held her in his arms? He was a demon, for fuck's sake, not the angel she believed him to be. She wasn't the first woman he'd ever kissed, and unlike most of the Syx, he'd never tired of pursuing humans for their mutual pleasure. He just didn't trust them. Nor would he ever.

Meeting Katana hadn't changed that. If anything, it just made him double down on the value of lying.

His lips curled. Ask most true believers and they would argue that none of the script of their lives was the design of the human—only the dictates of the Father. But Hugh knew that wasn't true. It had never been true. The Father had not sought to create mirrors of Himself on this earth, nor thoughtless drones to do His bidding. If that had been His goal, He wouldn't have given humans free will, nor would He have allowed—or in some cases, commanded—His angels to fall to the earth to teach His children.

Sometimes, those angels made dire mistakes that consigned them to damnation, because even angels had free will, in the end. Most of them never realized that, of course. Which is why they stayed angels.

"I'm sorry," Katana said abruptly, though she'd done nothing wrong. Another curious habit of humans, the constant flow of apology. "You said you were hungry, and here I am gaping at a random bedroom."

Hugh studied her, another piece of the puzzle falling into place as she hurried past him—careful not to touch him, he noticed—and practically ran out of the room. Katana used her polite bluster as a shield, erecting a wall of words to keep her distance from whatever or whoever she thought she had offended. And she was constantly in motion. Even now, her long, dark hair raked back into a ponytail, her compact, functional body moving quickly and efficiently, she strode down the hallway, this time sparing no attention for what he presumed were replicas of her childhood artwork. Childhood artwork that she had chosen to hang on the walls of her imaginary home.

Hmmm... As he strolled along in Katana's wake, Hugh lifted a hand and skimmed his finger along one of the picture frames. He wasn't surprised to feel the slightly gritty layer of dust. This apartment was real, not a figment of Katana's imagination. This world that they were now navigating was real. Her creation had intersected with the events of the Shadow Court, but if they had not chosen to act, to look for her, would she ever have realized that she owned property on Central Park? Or perhaps better stated, if the Shadow Court had not acted to set her into the motion of this adventure, would *she* have acted on her own?

Most humans didn't.

"How long have you had this place?" Hugh asked casually as they entered the living room again, and she headed to the kitchen.

She gave him an amused look. "I haven't," she said, modulating her words as if talking to a child. "Surely you've figured that out by now. The best I can guess is that this is all some powerful, mind-bending reality that we're walking through in a fugue state until we accomplish the goal I set for myself. I expect it to all disappear at that point."

"No," he said, hiding the smirk at her carefully constructed explanation. She really did need answers to whatever she couldn't explain. He wondered what had happened in her life that now required her to know what would happen around every turn. "You misunderstand my question. How long has it been since the first time that you imagined this apartment as being the domicile of the character in your story? Perhaps not everything inside it, but the first time that you wrote it into a scene or created a picture that included it?"

"Oh..." Kat had scooted around the large gray-and-white granite-topped island, and finally slowed, planting her hands on the cool stone. It seemed to ground her—that and the fact that something solid now stood between them, Hugh suspected. "I don't really... I guess maybe ten or twelve months ago? When I really started writing *Dead End*?"

"When specifically?" he pressed. "It's important."

"Well, I've had the idea of someone *like* Sorcia Steele for a while, like probably five or six years. Not the one who ended up my heroine, but bits of pieces of her in other people. I didn't imagine where she might live, like in a concrete sense, until much more recently. After I started this book, but not long after, so maybe eight months? That's when the idea of *Dead End* came to me, and the real Sorcia Steele took form perfectly in my mind. I thought it'd be cool to set it in New York City. I figured she'd need an apartment and...here we are."

"Eight months," he said. Eight months to plant a seed was not very long by some reckoning, but the Father and all His magic worked in mysterious ways. "And it never once occurred to you to come to see the New York apartment in person? You've never been here before today?"

"Of course not." She shook her head. "Honestly, I started drafting *Dead End*, and it consumed me. I was making enough from my other work to pay the bills, and I lived pretty frugally to make sure those bills didn't get out of hand. The only time I left was for writing and gaming cons, and those were few and far between."

"Cons?"

She shrugged. "You know, like conventions. Fantasy conferences. Places where people meet to discuss stories and magical settings, that sort of thing. There's stuff to buy and workshops on magic and a ton of B-level celebrities out promoting themselves. That's how you get the word out if you're someone like me, especially if you suck at social media."

"Are these people truly magic?" he asked.

She stopped, standing at the refrigerator, but turning back to peer at him. "You're asking that like it's a serious question." She chuckled, then eyed him more intently. "You really do think that's a serious question."

He shrugged, watching her pull items out of the refrigerator that he knew she had not stocked. The human brain's capacity for resilience was astonishing. "Humor me."

She snorted, glancing down at the package of cheese she'd plucked from the shelves. "Fair enough. Okay, no. I would say the majority of them aren't actually magical. A few of them would want you to believe that they are, but frankly, if any of those people had true psychic powers to any degree, they wouldn't be dressing up as superheroes, they'd be using their abilities to get ahead in the world."

"Yet you go to these places."

"I go because these are the people who read my stories. Without them, I'd be nowhere."

"So they *are* magical," he offered, and was rewarded when Katana stopped and laughed.

"Yeah, I suppose you're right. The people who help me tell my stories are magical. Without them, there would be no me."

Hugh nodded, still trying to guide her gently to the truth of who he suspected she really was. "But you don't know anyone you would consider overtly psychic? None of your friends or the people you work with, anything like that? You're completely by yourself?"

"In more ways than one." There was no denying the harshness of her voice, or the shame that followed. "Sorry. I was a kid in the system—I don't remember my biological parents. I really didn't get knocked around too much by life, though. I was adopted when I was ten, grew up the rest of my teen years as a middle-class only child. We didn't have a lot, but we didn't need a lot. My adoptive parents, Frank and Jodi, died in a car accident when I was seventeen."

Hugh wanted to comment, but kept quiet. Katana's energy had shifted in a way his demon senses could perceive, but likely not the senses of ordinary humans. She was winding herself tighter, and in that tension was a growing strength. Manic—fierce. Not healthy, but needful, he thought. But whose needs was she fulfilling?

"I almost held it together," she continued, her hands moving a little more jerkily now, her jaw tensing. Did she even know? He doubted it. "I had a scholarship—or at least I thought I had, but in the end, those cards didn't fall my way. Without a scholarship, there was no way I could afford college, and straight up art programs rejected me. So, that was that. I graduated high school early, faked my ID to get an apartment, then joined the working poor."

He watched her carefully. She believed the story she was telling him, even though it didn't quite ring true. There was something he was missing—possibly something they both were missing. "Your adoptive parents didn't have other family?"

"They didn't. Or at least none that I know of. My parents were first foster parents, and they kept to themselves. We got on well enough, and I'm grateful for them, but then they died, and I had to move on." Her voice had turned another shade harder, angrier. She was still too young to have fully worked through her grief over losing a second set of parents,

Hugh suspected. Had that been when she'd started manifesting psychically? The loss of the scholarship, the drive into isolation that had fueled her creative fire? She'd been afraid that she was causing herself her troubles—endangering those she loved. He'd reassured her, but maybe there had been some truth to her concerns. Not in the way she feared, but in the chaos she drew so easily to herself. She was a manifestor...that was a power not many would handle well.

"I never asked about my birth parents, of course," she continued. "Never needed to. Jodi and Frank had just enough life insurance to get me through high school, not enough to pay for college, but they'd been the biggest fans of my artwork, and we all just kind of assumed it would work out. Things have a way of doing that, you know? Of course, they didn't in my case, but I did okay. I made enough to survive, worked a bunch of shitty jobs, got hired as a gig worker doing graphic design that paid the bills until I got my big break." She smiled a little grimly. "Turns out that's not going so well either, but I'll figure it out."

By now, she had piled enough food on the counter to feed an army, though she still seemed oblivious to it. "You don't know who your biological parents are?" Hugh asked, though she'd already said as much.

She laughed a little sourly. "I don't. Only vague memories that I probably made up. It's not like they tried real hard to find me either, if they're even still alive. So it all works out. Frank and Jodi were the best, though. They really were..."

She looked away, and inspiration struck Hugh. "You didn't bring about their death, Katana."

She jerked her gaze back to him, so filled with fear and pain, he knew she still harbored those fears. "You said that before, but you don't really know that," she snapped. "How could you?"

He hid a smile—not one of malice, but of an emotion he didn't feel comfortable sharing. Not with Katana...not even with himself. Was this compassion? Could demons feel such a thing? Probably not, but angels clearly could, and he could fake it so well it almost seemed real. Either way, he knew what he needed to say to her.

"Katana, think. You have a purpose in this world, and it's not to cause others harm. Your adoptive parents—your biological parents. Your editor. The people on the street you passed today. All those who have come into your life and all those who leave, they have their own path. You can create things in this world, and that is a mighty talent. But you create situations, events. Things." He waved around the room. "Not the death of other living beings. That's not something you can create purely with your mind. With your hands—yes. Your spoken actions, your directives. Yes. But not with your imagination."

By the end of this, she was gaping at him, and he could see her throat working. She was trying so hard to keep it together, but Hugh was finally seeing the truth she had yet to accept.

"You think so—ugh. This is so dumb." She waved her own statement away. "Of course I don't have powers. What am I even saying?"

But Hugh didn't relent. "You do have powers. Greater powers than you ever believed—and I suspect you've always had them. But not those powers. You can create. You cannot destroy."

"You're sure?"

The bald question caught Hugh by surprise, and he

barked a harsh laugh. "I am. And I'm an angel. As I said before, we know things."

"You sure do." Her brows lifted, and she eyed him with renewed curiosity. "You know, this just occurred to me... Was it wrong of me to kiss you? I maybe should've asked you that already."

He chuckled and shook his head. "You'll be glad to know there are no rules specifically encoded about that."

"Well, there probably should be. You can't have people running around kissing angels out of nowhere. It'd be chaos."

She stopped, blinking down at the countertop as if realizing what she was doing for the first time. On the island there were now two glasses of wine alongside platters of fruit, cheese, and some obscure-looking dip next to a heap of vegetables.

Hugh lifted his brows. "No meat?"

She peered at him. "Angels eat meat?"

"This one does."

"Oh. I guess I never thought..." She turned back to the fridge, gasping a little before pulling out a heavily laden charcuterie tray. "Okay, no lie. When this is all over, I at least want this refrigerator."

Hugh watched her as she muscled the platter onto the counter. "When this is all over, I think your life will not be at all the same. Look at me, Katana."

15

*K*at froze in place. She didn't want to look at him, didn't mean to, but she could no more ignore Hugh than she could stop breathing. Finally, she glanced up.

His eyes gleamed with a crackling purple fire. It was the same fire that had burned in the eyes of Hugh the Destroyer as Jeremy had imagined him for his miniature, the strange color not quite squaring with his angelic air. It was too hot, too intense. And he trained that focus squarely on her now, leaving Kat no room to escape.

"Your mind is filled with chaos," he murmured. "How can you focus on anything?"

The question wasn't meant as a rebuke, but of course she took it that way. Hugh wasn't the first person to ask her that question, and she was sure he wouldn't be last. Anyone she'd ever tried to explain her brain to eventually arrived at the same conclusion.

But for some reason, coming from him, the question didn't sting as much as it normally did. He sounded genuinely curious, not judgmental or even pitying, and Kat found herself wanting to answer him. He already knew so much about her—and she wanted to believe him, desperately so.

Could she? Could she simply relax and...go with it? Tell him everything?

"The chaos sort of acts like an insulator." She reached for a glass of wine, but bypassed it for one of the plastic containers of water. Who *had* stocked this kitchen? She certainly hadn't expected to be here, and Sorcia, if she existed in real life, couldn't have imagined she'd be having houseguests. But someone had to have chosen the specific cuts of cheese, the brand of bottled water. Someone had to think about whether Kat would want red or white wine.

Had she done all this?

And if so, had she *really* possessed these skills before now, as Hugh seemed to think, or were they only tied to the *Dead End* project? How much would she be changed after all this was done? She had a flash of her life returning to its same ordinary patterns—working in her apartment, delivering images to clients, drawing her next book in the quiet, nondescript block of her second bedroom. Was that what she would be faced with once Hugh flew away? And could she possibly survive the crushing reality of her ordinary existence when that happened?

Hugh was obviously waiting for more from her, some explanation that showed how she could have become a superhero with the world's most boring life, so she shoved all other thoughts away and refocused on him.

"I used to try to fight through it, the noise. To stay fully present in the outside moment—school, sports, even walking around downtown or through the back streets near where I lived. I was lucky that way. My foster parents and my adoptive ones lived in white-bread suburbia outside of

Philadelphia, and I didn't look like much of anything to catch the eye. I didn't get picked on, didn't have enemies. But I didn't have any friends either. Friends took too much work, you know? And I was happy enough staying inside my own brain."

She grimaced. "That probably doesn't make much sense."

"It does. But describe what you see in this chaos. What you hear. It may be important. Does it ever change?"

"The noise? No, not really. And it's not all that bad. I did some research after I didn't get into college, wondering if maybe there was some sort of hardship thing I could ask for, though that felt like cheating. What I learned was that there were a hell of a lot of people out there who have it way worse than me."

She took in the far windows, bright white squares behind the gorgeously reassuring and comforting neutrals of her living room. Her living room? Well, someone's. It was nicer than anything she owned, nicer than anything she could have imagined, but it was perfect because it was so calm. Her gaze flicked to the brightly colored paintings that should have clashed with all that serenity but somehow didn't, and she sighed.

"It's like picking up a comic book and flipping through the pages really fast, but it's not just one comic book, but four or five at once, all at different angles, filling the screen of your mind," she said. "But the noise, the sound isn't like that ringing in your ears that some people get. It's more like a steady, low, really quick tapping sound. Duh-duh-duh-duh-duh-duh." She broke off, feeling a little silly. "Like that. The tapping accompanies the rush of the pages flipping, images sliding into one another, lines turning to curves that turn into angles that stretch out again to become lines, squaring off images or piercing through them and muddying the colors."

"You're imagining it now," he said, and Kat shivered, realizing he'd come closer to her. When had he done that? Now both of them stood behind the counter, hemmed in by the expensive kitchen appliances, the creamy gray-and-white expanse of the countertop. He didn't reach for the food but simply looked at her, his dark, gleaming eyes intent. "Do you draw images that come out of the chaos, or whatever you originally have set your mind to draw already?"

"I..." She tilted her head, considering the question. "I've done both. Ordinarily, I have a job to do, and I create whatever artwork is required for the job. The chaos doesn't really get involved with that. It's like it doesn't care. But when I'm writing or creating images for myself, for my stories, I'll borrow more from what comes to me, mostly color and the sense of action. Because sometimes the images are all wrong for whatever it is I'm working on."

"Always? Or just recently?"

She shrugged. "Most of the time, honestly, up until this last story. The chaos sort of made more sense for that one because it all came streaming through. And the more I drew from it, the more ordered it became. For the first time, I could see several panels ahead. Never too far, never to the end—or so I thought until I looked up one day and realized I'd gotten there."

"And did the story come to you all in order too?"

The question made her smile. "I've seen that too. Well, heard about it anyway. Read about it. People who can simply imagine stories and scenes and plop them down and then move them around later the way they want. Wouldn't that be interesting? But that's not the way it works with me.

Sure, I've had the occasional sharp image of a scene out of nowhere, like a really great fight or mood shot. But that's always before I start creating. Once that starts, I get the barest sketch of what might happen until I get to that section of the story. So basically, I'm what they call a pantser...only it's even worse than usual, because I don't get the actual words of the story until after the panels are done."

He nodded as if everything she was saying was totally rational, and she wondered at that. Was she making sense? She'd never had to explain her process before, and her process seemed distinctly off the rails. "And you always work on the computer, or do you ever draw anything out by hand?" Hugh pressed.

"Yes, drawing by hand is how I got started, what I thought I originally wanted to do. And a lot of the tech they have now allows you to blend the two so much more easily, especially when you have backgrounds that you can reuse or change slightly. That happened a lot with *Dead End*. Sorcia would move through parts of a city, and then the same city would pop up later in the book but slightly changed. Different enough to throw everything off."

"Like alternate realities?"

"That's a totally reasonable thought, but it's not that, not really. It's more like everyone got the same idea at the same time and built the same city. Only not cities, more like rooms within buildings and then the same buildings within cities. It takes a long time to build a city, right? But to build a room, to repaint or remodel a building so that it looks enough like what it's supposed to that it becomes a sign, symbol, a gateway..."

She winced. "Sometimes I hear myself say these things

out loud and I think I'm going crazy. But it's all for the story, you know? It's make-believe."

Her voice faltered as she refocused on the spread of food before her. This time, she did reach for the wine. "But then I imagined you, and you showed up, and I imagined a library that absolutely wasn't a library, and I imagined this apartment...but not this awesome of an apartment, I'm serious. Not so, I guess, me. That wasn't part of the story. It would have been an amazing part of the story, but it didn't actually exist. I never came here, not like this. This was more a place that the heroine used as a safe house, a bolt-hole where she rested up. She'd come here to sleep or to bleed if she'd been injured, but that's it."

"I understand. Tell me about the gateways you imagined in the nearly identical cities that had changed."

It was a reasonable request. So reasonable, Kat's answer came spilling out. "Well, that's how you know where the corridors between hell blocks are, right? There's a gateway, and it looks the same no matter where you are. You could be in a park, on a city street, or at the bottom of the ocean, and you'll see the same crooked purple two-story brownstone with its silly crooked..."

She stopped short. "Wait. Those weren't in the original story, Hugh," she whispered. "In the story, there was a map that Sorcia had found in *Dead End*, but I didn't—I never..." She swallowed, glancing back to where her computer was, safely in its own sassy studio. "I wonder if those purple buildings are there now."

Hugh nodded. "Do you draw all your own images?"

"What do you mean?" she asked sharply, pulling herself upright. She hadn't realized she'd been swaying toward him. "Of course I draw my own images. What do you think, I'm copying from somebody else?"

"Well, that computer program that you showed me in your studio kept changing on its own," he countered, appearing unruffled by her annoyance. "You said pages were being added. How are they being added if you didn't draw them?"

"It was pulling them in from an archive. The program was populating images I created earlier." The words sounded plausible, but Kat knew they were bullshit. She hadn't drawn the images of Montmartre in Paris—not like they'd been laid out on the screen. She'd never been there. She'd imagined Paris—that much was true, but not specifically those few square blocks. Yet on the screen, it looked absolutely perfect. But where had those images come from? "Okay, let me rephrase. It was pulling those from my mind. That's what the program was doing."

"And is that what it's supposed to do?"

Kat choked out a laugh. "No. Not even Apple is that good. But that's what's happening anyway. I'm—I guess I'm some sort of freak after all."

Huge jerked back, an expression of pain and even anger raking across his face. She winced and turned away, bracing her hands on the counter. Now he was pissed at her because she couldn't explain herself well, and he should be. She was annoying herself.

"Look, I'm sorry," she finally said. "I'm not saying any of this right, and—"

She turned toward him—but she was talking to an empty space. Her guardian angel had left her.

———

16

"*W*hat in the hell are you *doing*?" Hugh demanded, whirling to face Warrick. "I was finally beginning to understand her process, to understand how her mind works, and you pull me out? *Why*?"

"There's been a development," Warrick said, not bothering to turn and look at Hugh. He continued studying the screens in what looked like the same hotel room they'd been before.

Hugh scowled around the room. "Where are the others?"

"Finn is with me. He's out getting provisions right now, but he's the one you're going to want to talk to. He understands the computer shit more."

Warrick turned from the screen and directed Hugh's attention to it. "Any of this look familiar to you?"

"Is it supposed to?" Hugh grumbled. He peered at the rapidly flickering panels. Unlike the comic book pages he had been treated to in Katana's apartment, these images appeared to be real photos from cities across the world.

Budapest, Munich, Tokyo, New Delhi, Johannesburg, Rio de Janeiro, San Francisco, Chicago.

The cities were identified with captions along their bottom edges, but they didn't need to be. Each city featured two images: a quintessential postcard image and a picture of what looked to be the exact same, completely-out-of-place building, all in different neighborhoods. *The same crooked purple two-story brownstone with its silly crooked...*

Hugh let out a low growl. Windows. She'd meant to say crooked windows next. "When did you get these? When did they start coming in?"

"About an hour ago," Warrick said, his amber eyes glowing with interest at Hugh's obvious distress. "Why?"

Hugh lifted his hands to his temples in a vain attempt to keep his brains from falling out. "Katana's doing this. She's bringing these buildings into existence. They're part of the hell blocks that she's created. I personally think they're doorways. Every hell block you enter, you see one of those out-of-sync buildings, and that's where you want to go. Now, where those doorways take you—that's still in question. But we're getting there."

"Seriously? She's manifesting actual buildings and pathways?"

"She's doing way more than that. Food, drink, an apartment in an actual existing building, complete with custom artwork. Tech. Keys. And these aren't illusions, Warrick. Illusions don't work on demons—or at least not on us."

"True." Warrick folded his arms, glaring at the screens. "Ordinary spawn could be fooled, maybe—though who would know? It's not like the horde is known for nuance."

Hugh grunted a laugh as the door to the suite banged open.

"Coming through," Finn announced. The lanky demon jauntily strode in, his arms overladen with bags of chips, a twelve-pack of cheap European beer, and something that glowed DayGlo orange inside a cellophane bag.

"What the fuck is this?" Hugh asked, remembering that he hadn't eaten at Katana's apartment. Would the food taste like food there? Or was it all an illusion? Despite his assurances to Warrick, did he really know the extent of her abilities?

No, he did not.

"Eat like a geek, think like a geek," Finn said, drawing his attention again. "But hey man, welcome back. There's some heavy shit going down, and you're at the drop point. You see any alts cycling out?"

Hugh eyed him in confusion. "Are you actually speaking English, or are you high?"

"Alternate timelines," Warrick interjected. "They flash in and out of possibility, roads not taken. That's the other thing we've been dealing with, and we figured you should know about it before you left the apartment with Katana."

"That—makes a scary sort of sense. So she's not simply imagining one reality, she's playing through a host of other possibilities. No wonder there's so much chaos in her mind." Hugh grimaced, thinking about Katana and her reaction to the images on her computer screen...especially as the computer program seemed to add pages on the fly, then take them away again a second later. He was a demon and not constrained by human sensory capabilities. No matter how fast she'd scrolled, he'd seen the images she'd attempted to rush by with such embarrassment. They'd remained intact even as she bounced back and forth in the document.

He wanted very much for that particular story path to pan out.

"She believes that she's found a pass-through," Hugh continued. "Like I said—that's what those rickety-looking buildings are for. She thinks those are the doorways that lead to corridors linking together all the hell blocks on Earth, in one way or another."

"And what do you think?" Warrick asked quietly.

Hugh narrowed his eyes, taking in the second set of images that appeared on the screens—the same building replicated across the world. "I believe her."

"We've sent Stefan and Gregori to investigate," Warrick said. "They've opened those doors. In most cases, a clear pathway opened up on the other side. Sometimes going to an ocean, sometimes to another street, sometimes to an interior hallway. And sometimes to a brick wall, or a mass of toxic smoke."

"Because, of course. Nothing can be easy." Hugh sighed. "This is why they're alternates. Katana hasn't worked it all out yet. Is anyone else noticing these buildings?"

"Connecteds only, so far," Warrick said. "We're pulling a few in to serve as eyewitnesses—but funny thing, some of them don't see the buildings. Some see the buildings, but not the corridor through, and some see the whole damned thing. Those are the ones who genuinely look like they woke up on the wrong side of death today."

"Yeah, well, I'm thinking they're gonna have to get used to that," Finn said around a mouthful of cheese puffs.

"Montmartre Cemetery, Paris," Hugh announced, glancing at Warrick. "That's where she wants to go. You see one of those fucked-up buildings there?"

"Not yet, but give me a minute," Finn said, tossing the bag aside as he settled into his chair at the table. He wiped his fingers free of orange-yellow dust, then leaned over the laptop. "All I gotta say is this is a really shitty time for most of the Arcana Council to go MIA. I could use a little tech support here."

Hugh made a face. They'd lost most of the Council in the cataclysm that morning. Not even Blue seemed to know how many of the Council were left, and those that were wouldn't be able to offer much hope or help, not anytime soon.

"Any news on the archangel?" he asked.

"We have Raum on that," Warrick said. "He's still got the tightest connection to the horde, along with you. He can hear the bastards better than any of us, anymore. But he hasn't been able to find anything so far, at least not anything good. We're hoping to have information from him within the next few hours. Michael isn't in Hell, and nobody seems to think he's all the way dead. But he's somewhere between the two, probably not having too good a time of it."

"What about Blue?" Hugh asked.

"Oh, you mean our scary motherfucker of a new boss?" Finn put in. "She of the icy stare of, well, Death? The bedside manner of a serial killer? The charm of a lanternfish?"

Warrick stifled Finn with a glare. "She's gone. Presumably looking for Michael as well."

"You think?" Hugh asked. "She's not out, I don't know, gathering souls to toss over the edge of the earth?"

"She holds herself accountable for the archangel's capture by the horde. She believes the Syx will be able to help her with the search, but only after we've completed our path."

Hugh frowned. "But with the archangel no longer with us, how does that work?"

"Total chicken-egg situation. You nailed it," Finn said,

clearly not willing to remain stifled for long. "But we've got bigger problems, my man. Human problems."

"Worse than the ones I already know about?"

"Sadly, yes. So we've got the Shadow Court's attempt to subjugate the remaining ninety-nine percent of Connecteds, right? That backfired, hooray for our team, but now there are people asking questions."

Hugh winced. "They're not buying the solar flare theory?"

"Most of them are, sure." Finn nodded. "But a few prefer the theory that space junk caught fire and zapped the world, and an even smaller minority think that maybe there's some magical shenanigans going on. That crew hasn't been stupid enough to start talking so far." He tapped the computer. "But it's starting. Private text chats, secure message boards, and it's all over the arcane web—but that's not really the group we're worried about."

"Well, *I'm* worried about them," Hugh countered.

"No, no, you see? They're supposed to know shit's going down. Hell, a lot of them probably were supplying the Shadow Court with whatever they used to make up their weapons. But I'm interested in the ones who don't even know that the arcane web exists. *Those* are the people starting to come out of the woodwork. Most of them are glomming onto 'we've been attacked by aliens' message boards, but a few are more sophisticated." He waggled his brows. "We've got some power spikes going on, Connecteds who're becoming aware they've got skills—skills like our Katana Midland, maybe, only they've got no idea what to do about them."

Hugh took that in. "What about the Shadow Court?"

"Silent," Warrick said. "Clearly, they didn't expect the

Arcana Council to push back so hard. Their grand plan to shut down the psychics of Earth didn't succeed."

"They still did some damage," Hugh countered. "And we've got a major demon problem—some of them are under Shadow Court control via remote control, looks like."

Finn snorted. "Yeah, like that's gonna work long-term."

"Doesn't have to work long-term, just long enough to get a specific task done. I could see how that would be helpful," Warrick mused. "They still want Katana, which means she's still useful to them. Hugh, you need to keep pushing her to get to the Shadow Court."

"Sorcerer City, man. Keep up with the cool kids," Finn said, turning back to his computer.

Hugh nodded. "She thinks there's a time issue. The longer it takes her to neutralize the Shadow Court, the more hell blocks get established. The more hell blocks—"

"The more magic." Warrick pursed his lips. "Humans are already overloaded, and between their advancing access to shit they don't understand and the outpouring of the horde, we'll be overrun. We have to stop them."

Hugh gritted his teeth. "We can't break a human."

"We can't," Warrick agreed. "But we can't allow them to break us either."

The words cut Hugh more deeply than he thought Warrick intended, but Finn piled on too.

"Something for you to keep in mind, my brother," the irrepressible demon finger-gunned him. "You cozy up to Katana, and you're going to experience crazy on a whole new level."

Hugh regarded him coolly. "I've been with a human before."

"Not one that calls to you specifically. You think falling for Dana was a walk in the park for me—or that Warrick here had an easy time of it with his Maria? She's a better shot than he is."

"Careful, Finn," Warrick said quietly. Too quietly. "Say the wrong word and you're a black stain on the carpet."

Hugh glanced between the two demons. Other than Stefan, whose mission had entangled him with a witch the Syx desperately needed in their day-to-day battles against the horde, none of them wanted their humans involved in their work. It had surprised Hugh, when he'd even spared it a thought—Warrick's mission had forced him to partner up with a cop, while Finn had wrangled with a security expert who had more than her share of interesting parentage. Gregori's human, Angela, was in deep with the US government...all of them positioned in very useful places, if only the members of the Syx would let them do what they could.

But demons were territorial and stubborn, and the Syx had both traits in spades—with a healthy dose of protectiveness the horde didn't. And now that Hugh had met Katana...

He scratched his chin. "Nah, I'm still not seeing it. The shit Katana can do is unreal, man. I can't not let her be her. But don't worry. I won't let her get to me."

To his surprise, Warrick snorted. "Spoken like a demon who hasn't had his rotten, charred-over heart healed by a human's love."

Finn laughed out loud at Hugh's expression, fortunately not picking up on his underlying whisper of panic. "I'm telling you, man. It's not gonna feel right, but it's gonna feel good. You'll know what I mean when it happens."

"Right." Hugh kept it casual, but he understood the warning both Finn and Warrick were trying to give him. Katana was powerful—maybe even deadly. What was important was that she was at least trying to do the right thing, though. How many humans with her burgeoning abilities would do the same? Not nearly enough, as he knew from personal experience. "What about the non-Connecteds? Are ordinary people buying the solar flare bullshit?"

"What choice do they have if they want to keep order?" Warrick waved off the question. "The entire world went dark, from the most sophisticated first world behemoths to the tiniest hamlet in the middle of nowhere. Give it a few days, and we'll have the religious nutjobs declaring the Rapture—"

"Already there," Finn piped up, but Warrick kept going.

"—and after that, magic will get weaponized as a matter of public policy. That's a whole lot of churn that humanity has in store, well beyond the real issue of the Shadow Court."

"Fair enough." Hugh sighed. Every generation, it seemed that humans got better at fucking themselves over. "You're wrong about the Shadow Court standing still, though. They've got Katana's story on some laptop, and they're tracking her with demons. What do you have on the editor?"

Warrick fielded that one. "She's still being watched. She's awake and alert and can't remember a thing other than that she fainted when the lights went out."

"Uh-huh. You have a hand in that?"

Warrick nodded. "Stefan and his witches did. Said seeing Katana and a guardian angel out of the book Katana wrote would break her mind, and unless we were willing to risk that..."

"We're not."

"So there you go." He grinned. "Bottom line, she's safe. She can't help us right now, but she can't hurt us either.

Katana is our only connection. And you say she's targeted Paris?"

"Montmartre," Hugh corrected. "As if the Shadow Court would have a base there."

"I don't know, there's some really old shit that went down in that area," Finn said, rocking back on his chair. "I bet if we did some digging, we'd figure out there's all sorts of magical crazy buried in the old homes surrounding that place. Humans love nothing more than burying their dead, then fucking with them."

"Katana isn't focused on the cemetery—it's the gateway, nothing more. But she's identified the district as the location of Sorcerer City, so that's where we're heading." He paused, then ran a hand through his already spiked hair. "There's another problem. Katana didn't make too big of a deal about it, but you should know. The demon dickhead who cornered her in the coffee shop wasn't trying to kill her, but kidnap her. Same goes for the one on Sixth Avenue."

"Well, hell, everything she dreams up becomes real," Finn said reasonably. "I'd like her to come to my birthday party too."

"It's deeper than that. This second one tossed off the comment that she wasn't the only scribe, merely the first."

At that, Finn rocked his chair forward, the wooden legs thunking to the floorboards. "No way," he groaned. "We've got too much shit going on to play find-a-psychic, if that's what you're saying."

"They could be lying," Warrick said.

"They could," Hugh conceded. "But it gets worse—or better, depending on your perspective. That miniaturist, Jeremy? Death's guess was right about him revealing our secret identities. He's apparently got doll ideas for all six of the Syx. Katana says he's reported receiving visions."

"Ooo..." Finn leaned forward, his blue eyes sharp with interest. "Now we really need to talk to that guy. I'm totally ready for my close-up."

"Either way, if he's dialing in to us, others will be too. Better for us to move on the Shadow Court as quickly as possible, which means we're going in tonight. I'll hit the city again, scout the area, and make sure there aren't any other demons lurking around, then I'll hole up in the apartment until we make the jump."

"Good," Warrick said. He smiled, all teeth. "Blue ceded control over the Syx's movements to me. Turns out the archangel could have allowed us to travel at my direction the whole time."

"Which makes him an asshole," Finn put in, and Hugh chuckled. He had to admit, he missed the asshole. He suspected they all did. Wherever Michael was, it probably wasn't a party.

"We'll get him back," he said, fixing them both with renewed intensity. "Please tell me that with this kind of mobility, you'll be with me in Paris as backup for whatever shit the Shadow Court has planned? Like I said, we can't kill the bastards. That puts a crimp on things."

Finn grinned. "We're working on that, my man," he promised, and Warrick nodded.

"There's more than one way to stop humans from slaughtering each other, despite their best efforts," he said, nodding at Hugh. "You two flush the rats out, and we'll make them dance."

17

*K*at jolted awake, immediately registering the half-empty bottle of wine, the partially demolished snacks, and the laptop on the kitchen counter. She'd resisted going to get it for a long time, freaked out about going anywhere near the studio with its couch and its screens and the whirling updater-of-doom on the *Dead End* file. But after Hugh hadn't returned and the hours kept passing, she'd finally screwed up her nerve, slunk down the hallway, crab-walked across to floor of her studio, and snaked her laptop off the table, then raced back out and plastered herself against the smooth, creamy expanse of wall in the hallway.

As she'd waited for her heart to stop slamming against her rib cage, she'd let her gaze play over the framed sketches on the wall. They definitely were all her own work. The last one being the sword-wielding modern warrior she'd drawn when she was a high school junior. She'd been so full of certainty about her future—without a clue of the disaster about to land on her head. Clearly, she hadn't been some sort of great psychic manifester of goodness then. Even if she hadn't caused their deaths outright, she sure as hell hadn't been psychic enough to predict the traffic pile-up that had taken Frank's and Jodi's lives.

Kat had pursed her lips, pushing away the yawning ache that opened up whenever she thought of her adoptive parents. None of this had been their fault. Leaving her hadn't been the plan. She knew that, and yet...

Would it ever stop hurting so much?

Tears had burned in her eyes as she'd tuned out the roar in her ears, focusing again on the frames marching down the hallway wall. The figure in the last sketch had been an early precursor of Sorcia Steele, though it'd be years before Kat would officially create her. From the start, she'd imagined Sorcia as a skilled swordswoman, and though the blue-black linework of the city beyond her was indistinguishable, it...

She'd stepped closer. The image was a close-up of Sorcia with a church in the background, some vaguely cathedral-y looking thing rising high above the city street. Nowhere she'd ever been, but it almost...

She'd fled to the kitchen and yanked open her laptop. A few Google searches later, she'd identified the church. Not that she should have been surprised.

Sacre Coeur. The basilica that soared above the summit of Montmartre Cemetery in Paris.

This realization hadn't made her feel any better. She vaguely remembered the drawing she'd made as a teenager —had she really set it in Paris? Had she intentionally set it anywhere, versus simply cobbling together images from the internet as inspiration? Or, had she drawn something totally different, but since she needed Montmartre now, it was the background that had appeared in the made-up picture in the made-up hallway of her made-up apartment?

She'd nervously returned to the corridor, forcing herself to study each of the pictures in turn for any other clue. The remaining images on the wall hadn't provided additional help...but the last one, the one from her very first attempts at drawing, pulled viscerally at Katana. It was a picture of a...dog, maybe? Something running across a flat green line that could only be grass. She had smiled at first at the awkward rendering, but then real tears had trickled down her face, feelings of loss and abandonment, of not being enough...and she could come up with no good goddamned reason why. It was a *dog*.

At five years old or whenever she'd drawn this, she'd been in foster care. Had there been dogs? She couldn't remember any. Had she somehow wanted a dog and been denied? Had some dog run away from her, rejecting her?

She had no clue. She'd stared at the sketch for what felt like hours before finally trudging back to the kitchen counter.

After that, she couldn't remember anything she'd done at all.

Now she scowled at the mess surrounding her. A notepad lay open beside her, several crumpled pieces of paper alongside it—none of which she remembered drawing on. She did this sometimes, getting so wrapped up in the story playing through her mind that she stepped out of time for a while. A quick glance at the clock matched up with the fading light filtering through the windows. It was nearing dusk. It would be nighttime in Paris, the fog rolling through the tombs of Montmartre.

Kat shuddered, but not in fear, exactly. More...almost relief? All she knew for sure was that she *had* to be the one to go to Sorcerer City. It was her turn. Her time. Art school had shut its doors to her. She'd never broken out of gig work as an artist until the sale of *Dead End*—and now that had gone up in green smoke. She'd been waiting so long for her chance to be worthy, and this was it.

So maybe...maybe she shouldn't wait any longer for Hugh, but go ahead and leave now? She still had Jeremy's figurine of him, stuffed into her bag. Maybe that would be enough protection?

She tapped the space bar on her laptop to wake it up, and bit her lip as the image filled the screen. She'd drawn the building she described to Hugh. Tall, thin, and made of violet-colored stone, like a ridiculously hued brownstone wedged between two industrial-looking office towers. She'd never seen those towers before, she was pretty sure, yet the street seemed so familiar. Had she merely drawn that building into a background scene in *Dead End*? Was it the gateway she was so convinced it was, or simply an aberration of her wine-soaked imagination?

She scowled down at the crumpled pages, picking up one, then another, before unfurling them. It was the same building, worked out in multiple hues of colored pencil. Pink, violet, red, violet again, orange, blue, violet, violet, violet. All her colored pencils lay scattered by the laptop, with one conspicuously missing.

She found the broken remains of the violet pencil in the trash. She didn't remember throwing it away. She didn't remember any of this bizarre, fugue-state drawing sprint.

"Freaking weirdo," she muttered, grabbing another bottle of water and downing it before reaching for the wine with a shaky hand. If she'd slept, it hadn't been for very long, not based on the number of drawings she'd rendered. She closed the laptop with a click and leaned back.

She remained alone in the apartment. Her guardian angel had either given up on her or was taking a prolonged smoke break. She didn't blame him for either, but she was getting antsy. Maybe she *should* go. It's wasn't as if Hugh couldn't find her whenever he wanted.

"Right." Like she should plan on *that* happening.

She scanned the counter for her phone before remembering she didn't have it anymore. But how could she be without a phone? It was impossible to imagine. She'd watched enough police procedurals to know that phones were a risk, but for fuck's sake—she needed a map, if nothing else. And she wasn't going to scrawl one on a piece of notebook paper. After all, what was to say that people didn't already know where she was?

She looked around the sumptuous apartment. It was beautiful, perfect. Real.

And super well-stocked.

"No way," she whispered. But she got up off the stool anyway, moving jerkily to the side of the kitchen where a row of drawers extended.

She found a burner smart phone in the third one. It fired up at a touch.

"Fuck." It took several seconds before the room stopped spinning, and she gripped the phone tightly, trying to make some...any sense of this. The wine tasted like wine. The countertop felt cool beneath her fingers. The phone looked like it worked. Had she imagined all this into being, or had she imagined it and someone *else* had brought it into being? Was all this some kind of setup?

And if so, why? And if so...what the *hell* was Hugh the Destroyer's part in this? What could his angle be? Was he really a guardian angel, or was he something more? Something less? Was he the answer to all her prayers or some threat from which she needed to be delivered?

Gritting her teeth, Kat opened up the laptop again,

relieved to see the page count of the updated *Dead End* hadn't changed. She scrolled to where Hugh had left, and then scanned through several panels of her feeling sorry for herself in the kitchen with her glass of wine.

"Yeah, well. Get over yourself," she muttered. Then she flashed to the next image and stiffened.

In the panel, Hugh stood in the middle of her living room, wings flared, staring out the far window. Katana had always been proud of her ability to render the human form, but this particular image of her angel was definitely divinely inspired. He turned in the next panel to look straight out of the screen, and his eyes practically smoldered with deep-purple intensity. It was almost enough to distract her from his beautifully sculptured face, his powerful shoulders, broad chest, narrow waist, and long, muscular legs. His wings cascaded around him in a fluffy white symphony of feathers, the detail so perfect, this panel should have been one of the paintings on the wall.

"You drew me here, in this place? Before you knew I truly existed?"

The question was so quiet that it took Katana a moment to realize it was spoken aloud and not merely in her head. She jerked back, nearly falling off the back of her stool, then swiveled to see Hugh the Destroyer once more in her kitchen. He'd changed into a new tight black T-shirt and sleek dark jeans, but his wings were definitely missing. So were his shoes.

Kat blinked at the sight of Hugh's bare feet, which seemed intensely intimate to her, there on her kitchen's tile floor. Like everything else about the man—angel—whatever he was, they were also improbably gorgeous.

A sudden thought—memory?—of a deeply damaged Hugh somehow abandoning her shot into her mind, and was gone just as quickly. How was that possible? She'd never met her guardian angel before today...and before, whenever she'd imagined him for *Dead End*, he'd appeared absolutely perfect. Even though he thought he wasn't, even though something clearly haunted him, weighing him down whenever he looked at her, she knew better.

Though there *was* the small problem that she kept killing him off.

Kat scowled at him. "Why are you here?" she blurted before she could stop herself.

Hugh lifted his thick, dark brows. "You summoned me."

"No, I mean why are you *really* here? In my head, on this page. Why are you doing any of this with me?"

"Why do you think? Like it or not, you created a story of the future that has a beginning, middle, and an end in which everything works out. You believe completely in that end. I appeared in the middle of that story, and now we are aligning that middle to match up with the images that you had in your head. How am I doing so far?"

"Pretty good," she grumbled. "But it's one thing for me to imagine a building into being, or a picture, or a bottle of wine. But like you've pointed out—you're a real person. You have thoughts and needs, wishes and desires. I can't just order you around."

"Where I come from, orders were made to be followed. And as long as you trust the one doing the ordering..."

He stepped toward her, and her breath caught. He was assured, intense—and from the way his eyes glittered, he had something important on his mind. Something that felt...shockingly personal. *Her*, she realized. He wanted her.

There was a touch of another emotion she was picking up, almost on the edge of her awareness...fear? Could he be afraid of her, somehow?

Not likely. She should be the one to be afraid. The *literal* love scene of her dreams was potentially coming to life right in front of her, and though she'd had plenty of experience with ordinary humans...Hugh was not that. Would never be that.

"You know what I drew on those panels," she said in a rush. "You know what I imagined when I imagined...you."

He tilted his head, watching her closely. "I know what you imagined when we first came to this apartment, yes. And everything you thought would happen after."

"Right. Of course you do. But even if I drew it, I mean— you're not obligated, you know. You do know that, right?"

Can I please shut up now? Kat lifted her hands to her temples, trying to quiet the chaos in her mind. But this time, it wasn't the tumble of images and lines, curves and colors that was distracting her, but a very real, desperate need that was building inside her, demanding to be satisfied.

"I'm not obligated. I understand." Something seemed to shift within Hugh, a decision made—but what? She didn't have time to parse it out as he stepped even closer, pinning her in place without even touching her. His words, when they came, held a shiver of promise. "Katana, I don't pretend to understand what you're going through. I don't begin to understand the brilliance of your mind, the power that you have to create an idea, draw a picture—and have it come into being. But I trust you."

The words practically vibrated between them, taking on a life of their own, dangerous and dark. "Don't," she whispered. "Please. I don't trust myself."

"Then we'll figure it out together." He took another step. It seemed to cover more ground than that one stride should allow. He held out a hand, and she stared at it, almost as if she were standing outside her body and watching herself lift her own fingers and settle them into his.

Hugh took her hand and pressed it against his cheek, the warmth of his skin thrilling her. Her heart beat harder, her nerve endings practically twanging to attention. She was fully and completely present with him, in the moment...and she was terrified. "I don't understand this."

The fire in Hugh's eyes glinted brighter. "You don't have to understand it. You only have to want it. If you want it and you like it, then why shouldn't you bring it into being?"

She huffed a small sigh. "Well, I like this."

"Good." He turned and pressed a kiss into her palm, setting off a chaos of sensations that rocketed through her. Her toes curled on the cool tile, while everything else in her body fluttered and rolled. "Then I'd say you're doing pretty well so far. What about this?"

She watched uneasily as he lifted his other hand and drew it along her cheek. A new set of sensations went spinning through her body in another direction, making her dizzy.

"Yes," she whispered.

"Even better." He tucked a finger beneath her chin and lifted it. She could feel her lips part, and her eyes met his, seeking out the dark glittering purple flames flickering in their depths. He leaned down and brushed his lips against hers, and for the first time in longer than she could remember, the sound in her mind quieted and the chaos eased.

"Yes," she gasped, though he hadn't asked a question. "Oh, yes."

He pulled back, and it was everything Kat could do not to lunge for him. Her gaze dropped to his lips, feeling the heat flare through her, tugging at something deep and needful.

"Then what do you want to do next?" he asked. "If you could have anything in the world you wanted, anything in the world you could imagine—and it looks like you can—what would it be right now?"

She looked up at him, his beautiful face fierce and vulnerable at once.

"You," she said, without hesitation. She told herself it was because she wanted the story to end correctly but really, at this particular moment, she couldn't give a good goddamn about the story. If the world was about to go down in flames, she at least would have this. "You. I want you."

He studied her for a long moment, and then curled his hand around the back of her head and pulled her to him.

---

18

*H*ugh didn't know what he was feeling, mostly because he had never felt it before. Again, this wasn't the first time he'd hooked up with a human woman since becoming a demon, particularly since he'd generally maintained a very human appearance to God's children.

Even as a Fallen, he'd been no saint, and he'd relied on the fact that he would never intentionally harm a child of God, only give them pleasure. It was what he was best at. But the thing that he was second best at was lying, and deceptions came easily to him, none more so than declarations of reassurance for those weak creatures who believed him too quickly and too well.

He hadn't known the ramifications of his lies until it was too late. But if he had to go back and do it all over again, he wasn't sure he would fare any better. He was made the way he was made, and that was all there was to it.

But pressing his lips to Katana's soft, supple mouth, he experienced a disquiet that he couldn't cover over with lies and deception. She pulled at him, triggering sensations deep within that no human ever had. Other than the members of the Arcana Council and the occasional witch, Hugh had never encountered any truly psychically powerful humans, but Katana was different. She could create reality out of her mere imagination. She could draw the future into life.

He also knew she might betray him. As he'd been betrayed by humans before, so many millennia ago. Right now, he didn't care.

"Hugh..." she murmured against his lips.

Hugh heard the need in her voice, the question. "Yes," he whispered. "Anything. Everything."

With a soft, shaky laugh, Katana snaked her hands around his back, pulling free the shirt from his trousers and pressing her palms against the skin of his lower back. He growled low in his throat. The touch of her hand burned. Also something different, but he didn't flee from the pain of it, almost welcomed it for what it meant. This was yet another way in which Katana was a human unlike the others—not so weak or easily broken. Neither in body nor mind, no matter how much chaos reigned through her.

She curved her fingers and lightly scored his back with her nails. Strips of agony unexpectedly arced through Hugh, causing him to gasp and stiffen. Katana's eyes flew open as she stumbled back, instantly aware of the pain she had caused.

"I'm hurting you," she hissed. "How can I be hurting you?"

"I'm fine," Hugh said, struggling to keep his voice light, easy—but he wasn't fine. Not even close. The fading pain was replaced by yet a new sensation, dark, demanding, possessive.

Before this moment, no human had ever made him feel

anything. He engaged with them to give pleasure, nothing more. It wasn't so much that he refused to take pleasure in return, but it simply never happened. What satisfaction he gained was simply in the knowledge of dominion and control—the one area he could have control, outside of killing demons.

But this was different. Hugh wanted this woman, wanted her touch, even craved the very pain she'd caused him unwittingly. He would have her too. Humans were not built to remain strong when it came to slaking their own pleasures and desires. It was perhaps one of the cruelest cuts the Father could have dealt them—forging for them a path of the righteous and pure, yet creating their bodies as a tuning fork for every possible pleasure and pain. It was no wonder their lives were so filled with chaos.

He could take away Katan's chaos for the moment, but in exchange, he would be thrusting himself directly into that same fire.

And he didn't give a damn.

He stepped back and held his arms out wide. "What did you imagine we would do in those tumbled panels where you worked out this scene?" he asked her. "What did you see?"

"It's not like that," she whispered. His pulse jacked as he took in her tousled hair, her flushed cheeks. She darted out her tongue to moisten her lips, and he nearly lunged for her. "When I imagined, when I made those scenes, I didn't expect you to be here in the *flesh*. Um, oh, hi." She barely murmured this last, her entire body quivering as he unbuckled his trousers and let them fall to the ground, then slid his shirt off over his head.

Hugh was well aware of how he appeared—an angel dropped down from the heavens, complete with fluffy white wings. His lips curved wickedly. He shouldn't be leveraging his cover story as much as he was, but that was too damned bad.

"You're beautiful," she sighed, lifting up a hand as if she could touch him from five feet away. "I've never seen anybody like you." She blinked hard, several times, confusion clouding her face. "You weren't made specifically for me, though, were you?" she asked weakly. "Did I create you like some kind of magical doll?"

He laughed low in his throat. "You didn't create me. I existed before you were born, and I will exist long after you die. I'm immortal."

She jolted in clear surprise. "You can't be killed?"

"Not by a human, no," he acknowledged, recalling vaguely that he'd told her this before. It was not usually information he gave out, but he didn't want to do anything to break the spell weaving around them. Katana was trying to focus on his words, but her body was telling a far different story. She swayed again toward him, taking an awkward step. He reached for her hand, drawing her over to the side of the room where the deeply upholstered couch stood, waiting for them to sink down over it. He tugged, but she held firm.

"But you're only here because I willed it to be, right?" she moaned, her mind clearly having exhausted all other obstacles and been forced to come back to this one. "If we have sex—if that happens, and it doesn't have to happen, but if it does, is it only because of my stupid story? Why did I put that in my stupid story?"

"Maybe you knew I would want it. Need it," he suggested, and her eyes flared, the pupils dilating with desire. She was so close, so close to giving in to the fire he was stoking. And even though he had been forged in fire as punishment and pain, he wanted to drown himself in that heat. He pulled her closer to him, and he could feel her rabbiting pulse beneath his fingers. He itched to taste her, take her—and to feel her beneath him, pliant and free.

"But I'm just using you." Katana's voice was raspy now, her defenses falling like dominos.

"Then let me use you too." He reached out and slid a finger along the collar of her shirt. "Can I take this off?"

"Oh. I can—" She stepped back sharply, as if she suddenly realized that only one of them was nude, and before Hugh could stop her, she'd pulled her shirt over her head, yanking her hair halfway out of her ponytail. She balled up her shirt, then glanced down at it as if surprised it was there.

Hugh reached out and pulled it from her fingers, lingering on the sight of her breasts rising and falling beneath her cheap cotton bra. In the harsh kitchen light, he picked out the bruises and scrapes that formed a patchwork map of Katana's day so far, each one a testament to her resilience, her fire. "You're hurt," he murmured.

"I am?" She looked down, the movement serving to take her focus off him for the split second he needed to move closer to her, tossing the shirt to the floor. She jumped a little as he eased the straps of her bra from her shoulders, his fingers fizzing with sharp, staccato whorls of fiery heat as he skimmed the bra down her arms. This version clasped in the front, and before she could get tripped up telling him how to remove the thing, he reached forward and unhooked the clasp.

"I..." she began. This time, he could see that her flushes started at her belly and suffused the entire upper half of her in the space of three seconds. "I've been with a guy before, seriously. But I'm not used to anyone...quite like you. It's throwing me a little."

He smiled. "I'm glad."

He didn't care if it wasn't fair, he continued using every ounce of his demonic ability to manipulate and control a human to hold her gaze with his, reveling in the soft, shuddery breaths she managed as he dropped his hands to her jeans. He peeled the sturdy denim away from her waist, then curled his fingers around the cotton waistband of her panties.

"Yes?" he asked quietly, easing his control on her just enough to ensure she had at least some shot at stopping him, but she nodded quickly, and he didn't give her a chance to change her mind.

Dropping to a quick crouch, he pulled both garments down her legs, not stopping until they pooled at her ankles. His cheek skimmed her outer thigh, and she half groaned, half gasped a garbled "*Yes.*"

Pleasure and need roared through Hugh as he urged her feet out of the jeans, relishing the touch of her hand as she braced it over him for support. Energy zipped from her palm deep into his shoulder, and when he turned toward her to nip the outside of her knee, her skin burned like fire.

An answering flame roared deep within him. He didn't know how Katana was stoking his need so expertly, but she was playing a very dangerous game.

He stood, the tension going taut between them.

"Better?" she managed.

"Much," Hugh agreed. "Your turn."

"I don't want to hurt you." Another blush warmed her breasts, her neck, and finally her cheeks, and he felt his own body jack into full and urgent need.

"You can't," he assured her, though he grunted when she

lifted her hands and dropped her fingertips gently to his chest, his muscles jumping beneath the soft silk of her touch. Her gaze flew to his, and he held it, nodding slowly.

"It doesn't hurt," he lied, as jabs of fire spilled out in all directions from her fingertips, lighting up his nerve endings. She flattened her palms over his chest, and he covered her hands with his, pressing the flaming brands of her hands more firmly against him. After a flare of blistering heat, the sensation was replaced with cooling ice, and he almost laughed out loud from the sheer shock of it.

He pulled her down to sprawl over him. Now every time her skin came into contact with his, it was as if a mountain stream flowed over him, cooling the fires that had burned since before the time of recorded history. He could feel the change sweep through him, but he was powerless against it. Powerless and triumphant at once.

His body was not supposed to work this way. God had not created his angels *or* his devils to experience such a sensory delight. That was a purely human capacity. Regardless, Hugh reveled in it, drinking deep, and all she was doing was touching him.

"Oh..." she moaned, and drew her body up his, slowly and carefully, until his shaft pressed into the most intimate part of her. She convulsed, shuddering with the mere contact, and when he opened his eyes, she stared back at him, a sheen of sweat on her face and shoulders.

She rocked against him with a gasp, and Hugh jolted with sudden awareness. The air around her had started to supercharge, tiny bursts of light exploding like electric pixie pinwheels. Katana didn't seem to notice as her lips parted, her breath quick and tremulous. "Hugh—"

"Yes." Hugh gritted out, wishing his response didn't sound so desperate, but barely holding onto his own sanity as a new wave of sensation swamped him, dizzying and dire. "Anything. Everything. Always."

"I—yes," she agreed abruptly, as if answering some question only she could hear. She said nothing further, but in one smooth motion lifted herself up and over him, then plunged down, the sudden connection of their bodies so electric, he damned near passed out.

19

*K*at gripped Hugh's shoulders, the war between her body and mind shut down for one blessed, shining moment. And in that moment, all she had to do, all she wanted to do, was savor the sensations cascading through her.

And those sensations *rocked*.

The skin beneath her fingers was warm and smooth—but seemed pulled almost too tight over sinewy muscles that bulged, flowed, and dipped as if Hugh had spent the last twenty years of his life in a gym. She knew better, of course, understood that his body had been made perfect from the start, custom designed for her—or at least, for this moment. A whirl of distracting thoughts tried to converge upon her brain, but she shoved them away, sinking more heavily down on top of him, reveling in the feel of him hot, vibrant, alive.

Too late, she remembered what she should have asked at the outset. "Condom?" she managed. She had no idea if she had anything stocked—a consideration slightly more important than another bottle of wine, and yet she somehow suspected that of everything in this magical mystery apartment, protection hadn't been top of mind.

Hugh merely chuckled. "Angels can't impregnate humans," he said. "I'm pretty sure they cum glitter and fairy dust."

She choked out a laugh that was abruptly cut off as his hands shifted to glide down the sides of her waist and over her hips, anchoring her to him. She closed her eyes tight as she groaned, swamped with the heat and the liquid energy pooling in her belly.

Mostly the heat.

"This...feels amazing," she moaned, rocking forward, meeting him thrust for thrust as he arched up slightly from the couch. She couldn't waste a second of this. Her eyes fluttered open, only to see him staring at her, his face set, his lips parted.

"What are you doing to me?" he murmured, the words raspy with need. Fire lit the pool of what she now understood was straight up nitroglycerin inside her. Flames roared hot and healing through her, galvanizing her senses and her sense of inner power. *She* was doing this. Hugh was letting her, but she was doing it. She was taking her moment, reveling in the possibilities of everything she was, everything she could be. He was her punishment and her reward for every moment that had led up to this one, and the salve against all the broken crazy that would come after.

With that, the chaos threatened again, pressing close, seeking any opening, and she gasped against the pressure in her mind, struggling to hold on to the sensations beneath her fingers, everywhere their skin touched.

"*No*," she moaned, the word almost a prayer. She bent forward, capturing Hugh's mouth once more with hers. The growl he emitted was one of anger and possession, and his hands drifted up, clamping down on her skin as he trailed hot, heavy kisses to her ear.

Curling up in one smooth movement, he pushed her back until she was sitting upright. He shifted further, wrapping his arms around her and switching their positions until she was the one beneath and he loomed over her for the barest second. Then he leaned close again, his mouth capturing hers, his kiss hard, demanding, insistent.

Shifting roughly, he seared a line of kisses along her jaw, down the curve of her neck, his teeth sinking lightly into her skin at her collarbone, her shoulder. She licked her lips, tasting his heat, the smell of burning embers catching in her mind, worrying it, a detail that didn't fit with all the others.

Then he lowered his lips to one breast, and all thoughts fled again as his hand curled around the other and she arched up from the couch, gasping at the unexpected assault. She'd been touched before, but not like this. Never like this. Though they were no longer joined, it seemed as if every touch, every kiss he rained upon her was more intimate than sex could ever hope to be. He drove her to greater heights as he licked and sucked, teased and pulled, raking his teeth along her sensitized skin, his tongue shifting and swirling, tasting her with such thoroughness that she knew by the time it was done, her body would have no more secrets to hold from him. And her mind was dangerously ready to unburden all its truths as well.

She drew in a broken breath as he dropped his focus, skimming down the curve of her belly, the flare of her hip, and kissing the insides of her legs as her knees angled open.

A whimper deep in Kat's throat struggled to break free. "Ohh..." she began, but her thoughts splintered in a dozen different directions as Hugh brought his lips to the vee between her legs, kissing and sampling her with the same passion and need he'd poured into every other touch. A groan rose up from his throat, and he gripped her legs hard enough to make her cry out as he yanked her down the length of the couch, and in a swift, almost brutal movement filled her with one long curse, speaking a language she had never heard him speak before.

"What sorcery is this?" he gasped. But if he meant for her to answer, he didn't give her a chance as once more, he fell upon her, his body long and lean pressing her into the couch, offering her the strangest blend of security and danger. He rocked into her with a smooth, sensual motion as his hands roamed and his mouth pressed against her, murmuring benedictions and curses alike. He hovered at her ear, and she felt the cool stomach-flipping slide of his tongue along the sensitive skin there and his voice was low and husky. "*Mine*," he growled.

The solitary word burst barriers Kat hadn't realized she'd been desperately holding closed. She arched with a cry beneath him, convulsing as once more the chaos was drowned in a need far more primal, more basic, and more powerful than anything she'd ever felt before.

Now it was Kat's turn to curse as the orgasm built, built, then swept through her, harsh and stuttering. Hugh let out a stunned gasp as his body jerked with a fierce shudder as well, his eyes intent enough to drill her nearly through the couch and into the wall as their bodies seemed to break apart and rush back into place again. The pinnacle moment was sharp and true and gone again, leaving utter destruction in its wake.

She sagged back into the cushions as he collapsed on top of her, a boneless sprawl that surprised her most of all, she lifted a hand almost tentatively, then with more confidence to press her fingers along his sweat-slickened skin.

"I didn't know angels perspired," she murmured, and he chuckled low and deep.

"I don't think they do." Then, almost as an afterthought, he added. "Not usually. They're missing out."

He spoke almost dreamily, and she reveled in the feel of him wrapped around her, cradling her. Distantly, she wondered if the pages of *Dead End* had shifted again. They should have, at least a little. She could never have drawn what just had happened between them so simply, so cleanly. The curves and angles, the flashes of colors would have looked like an explosion had rocked the fancy New York apartment, not the intense yet infinitely focused connection of two vastly different souls desperately seeking sanctuary and solace—and maybe something more.

As if hearing her thoughts, Hugh braced himself on one hand and lifted from her, grinning down. "How did we compare to the story?"

"I'll be making updates. My editor may never recover."

His grin deepened. He leaned down and playfully nipped at her lips, the movement making her blink with surprise. She definitely hadn't drawn that, though she could see the panel now, the gorgeous superhero figure of Hugh the Destroyer rolling away as Sorcia Steele blinked, eyes wide, lips parted, concern, confusion, and sudden awareness writ large across her face. An awareness of what, Katana knew all too well. This wasn't real or permanent, after all. Because Hugh couldn't be what he said he was, couldn't be *this* right, this flawless—

Her resigned sigh drew him back around, his beautiful arched brows lifting.

"What is it?" he asked as she struggled upright. "Or was I right about the fairy dust?"

Kat's entire body flushed as she glanced down, half expecting to see glitter exploded against her skin, and vaguely disappointed when she didn't. "Apparently, we need to try again."

Hugh curled his lips in invitation, his expression sly and full of promise as he stretched, muscles rippling. She'd heard about muscles doing that, but like everything else with Hugh, reality vastly superseded her imagination.

"I can do that," he informed her, banked heat still burning in the depths of his eyes. "Anytime, anywhere."

Something shifted hard and absolute in Katana's mind, like a door blowing open. The chaos roared forth once more, rushing into all the quiet places. As she studied Hugh's flawless face, she felt that odd tug, the memory that she had met this angel before—when he wasn't so heart-skitteringly perfect. That she knew him.

That he'd abandoned her.

She sighed a little sadly, but she couldn't stop the question anymore. She had to know.

"Who are you, really, Hugh?"

20

———

 ugh supposed that there were certain creatures wrought by God who, when faced with a direct question from someone who had managed to affect them so profoundly, would be absolutely constrained to be honest. He was not that guy.

"Again, I'm what you summoned," he replied, leaning against the counter and crossing his feet at the ankles. He didn't miss how Katana's gaze slipped from his face to roam the planes and contours of his body. He could present himself as the most loathsome amalgam of hideousness that would haunt her worst nightmares—and she'd seen him that way, though only for a moment.

Alternately, he could appear like he was right now. Perfect, whole. Winged. Both were true in their own way, and both were lies. He was comfortable that those lies coexisted within him, but it did him no service to present one when the other was so much more useful. There was a time and a place to scare the hell out of people, and this wasn't it.

Katana pursed her lips, clearly aware that he was

skirting the question, but not willing to give up. He could practically see the rush and flurry of her thoughts behind her eyes. She'd referred to it as chaos, and there was real truth to that characterization. Most human minds were filled with extra noise—their own terrible judgments of themselves, their worries, their fears. With Katana, it was different. Her chaos had form and function, a magician's cauldron of possibility that had been pushed into true creation.

She was dangerous. She was powerful.

She was *his*.

The reminder struck Hugh with the force of a battering ram to his solar plexus. He had known this human female less than one day. He was immortal—she wasn't. She would die in the barest instant, all her bright, chaotic energy surging up in a flare of heat and ecstasy and then winking out as she fled this plane to return to home, becoming one with All That Is. Neither angels nor demons were smart to fall in love with a human. It was like loving a shooting star.

None of that mattered. This broken, frail woman, studying him with the tumult of the ages in her eyes and desperately trying to bury the power that practically exploded from within her...was his to love. His to protect. His to explore, inch by trembling inch.

She might not know it yet—no. She *absolutely* didn't. Her face was fierce with concentration on the questions she was constructing like spiked walls to keep him at arm's length, and her manner was as brisk and no-nonsense as she could ever try to be. She was drawing a box around him, the same as she did her illustrations. She had to, he understood. It was how she was wired.

But it wasn't going to work with him. Heat and wonder flowed through him like an elixir, more diabolically intoxicating than any poison. The fire in his deepest core stirred to life with eagerness—no longer yearning for mayhem and death, but the mayhem and life of this one woman.

He would champion her until she proved herself *to* herself. He would be the angel she believed he was.

And he would never let her go.

"No, I'm serious," Katana said, oblivious to the transformation taking place in front of her, as humans so often were. "I get that I summoned you and that you're here now...doing things. That we're doing things together," she amended quickly, embarrassment flooding her cheeks despite everything they'd just shared. Hugh felt a curious sensation in his own chest, laughter bubbling up within him, not so strongly as to break free, but enough to fizz and pop in his bloodstream, warming him through and through. It was not a sensation he was used to.

He recalled Finn's words, and the strange, almost spellbound gleam in his eye. *"I'm telling you, man. It's not gonna feel right, exactly, but it's gonna feel good. You'll know what I mean when it happens."*

Oh, yes. He did.

Fortunately, Katana couldn't track his thoughts. "But who and what are you, specifically?" she continued. "What are you allowed to do—and what aren't you?"

He lifted one shoulder, dropped it. He didn't feel like making this too easy on her. Every word she shared, every question, was a window into the spinning constellation of her mind.

"You were the one who originally drew those panels. Clearly you had some idea of what I could be, and what was possible between us."

She flapped a hand at him. "Possible, maybe. But

probable? Not hardly. That's the whole point of fiction. You create things that probably *wouldn't* be possible in the real world, but would be super interesting if they were."

He lifted a brow. "So you think I'm interesting."

"I think you're many things. Interesting doesn't even begin to cover it." She studied him. "Tell me something about you that I don't know. Like, what's the worst thing you've ever done?"

Hugh's heart stopped in his chest, the direct question arrowing through him straight into his rotten core. His Sin. She wanted to know his Sin. She didn't realize what she was asking—couldn't, since she thought he was some beautiful, perfect angel—but she would remember asking this, and she would remember what he said.

He could lie—should lie, really. But why, when the truth was a whisper away?

"I lied to a group of humans, and some of them died because they believed me," he said flatly. "I didn't kill them outright, but they ended up dead all the same."

Katana blinked. "You're not kidding."

"No." *Might as well go all in.* Despite the warnings sounding in his mind, Hugh found himself wanting to confide in Katana. Needing to, even. "I was tired of humans —their endless anxiety. Their questions. I wanted them to be more than what they were ready to be. So I told them to go forth and know they could protect themselves as if they were angels on this earth, blessed by the Father, destined for glory. Some took that advice too literally, and attacked their enemies without their guards beside them. They were slaughtered. When their families cried out against me, the Father listened, and I was punished."

Katana stared at him. "But that wasn't your fault. Humans have free will, right?"

Hugh grimaced. "Yes. But I did not treat them with the care they deserved."

"You treated them with something better," she grumbled. "Respect. I'm sorry, Hugh, but God got this one wrong."

She turned away without waiting for his response, then efficiently began collecting her clothes, clearly thinking that she needed to give him time to recover. She didn't need to, of course—he'd had six thousand years to go over the events of that long ago day. But he enjoyed watching her all the same.

As she slid her shirt over her head, Hugh turned to the counter, surveying the half-eaten food, and the crumpled balls of paper. "You've been busy."

"Not busy enough." Katana's focus latched on to her drawings again, and her energy shifted. It was for the best. It would get them closer to their mission, but it was all Hugh could do not to lift a hand to smooth her hair from her brow, to lean in and brush his lips over her cheek. Focus had never been a challenge for him before, but now...

She hurried on. "I've been working on how all this fits together, trying to remember why I did things the way I did. Why the story has to be the way I wrote it, you know? Like, I get that it does, but why am I so certain about that?"

Refocusing on her words with great effort, Hugh leaned forward and tapped her computer. He didn't go so far as to drop his fingertip on the identifying scanner, but he could have. Human's attempts to protect their privacy were laudable, but they were nothing against the work of a demon.

Still, he'd jostled the computer enough that the screen flared up. Katana moved beside him, brushing his hand aside as she reached for the device. A shiver of awareness skated along his skin, the touch of her hand enough to send his mind rocketing down dark and sensual paths as she logged into her computer and slid forward a few pages.

"Sorcia's holding the map here—it's a maze of connecting points, or that's how I thought of it," she said. "You can move from place to place, but there's no time difference in between, no time passing."

"You've mapped the In Between," Hugh said, nodding. "Of course. That makes sense."

She twisted around to peer up at him. "It does? I did? What's the In Between? That sounds...vaguely familiar, but—"

"The In Between is a network between places on this earth, jumping off and landing points. Various...entities have used it since the making of the world, but it's dangerous and unpredictable. There are inconsistencies in your map, though." He tapped New York, then Paris. "You don't have a line between these two, but I know they connect."

"They should connect," she said, nodding. "But I was drawing for speed, not precision. Besides, to get to Paris, you're either going over water or under water. So maybe I couldn't really map that so clearly. I just knew that I wanted a quicker way to get around—a magic way—and...um, you said this existed already, in the real world? Like, it's a thing?"

"It's a thing," Hugh confirmed, leaning over her and trying not to show his excitement. "But now, I suspect it's your thing. You've reshaped it to your needs, which no one could have expected or prepared for."

"Well, I wouldn't go that far—"

Hugh cut her off. "What happens if you want to go from, say, Budapest to Tanzania? Can you forge a direct path, or do you have to follow the intersections of the map? A direct connection would be better."

"It would," she agreed. "And I think it's possible but...but there's a problem with these pathways." She broke off, shaking her head and glancing over at him. "Okay, this is going to sound crazy."

He laughed at the visible kick to Katana's energy that locked in as she formed a new possibility in her mind. She was a wonder. There was no other way to explain it. He wanted to take her into his arms again, but resisted the urge. Barely.

"As if nothing that has come before has sounded that way," he teased.

"Well, yeah, but hear me out. I think right now, the corridors are open for those who can see them—anyone who can see them can use them. But I feel like, maybe the sorcerers in Sorcerer City don't want people to be able to get around so easily. If so, they'll try to shut that access down. Like, if they're not the only ones able to take these paths, they'd rather give them up entirely."

Hugh nodded. It's what Warrick expected the Shadow Court would do as well. "Humans rarely give up their gains easily, but...perhaps. That's how you imagined it?"

She laughed a little wryly. "Well, no, but I *could* imagine it that way. And it does feel right to me."

"So this is the outcome of stopping the Shadow Court?" he pressed. "You're able to keep the paths open for all?"

"Yes—I think so." She made a face. "Honestly I didn't spell out the ending of *Dead End* completely. I wanted to leave my options open. But I definitely know that my job is to get to Sorcerer City and make sure the good guys get in, and it just feels right that the pathways will stay open after that."

He studied her, drinking in her earnest expression, her

skin glowing a soft blue in the reflected light of the laptop. "Are you sure you're not the good guys all on your own?"

She snorted. "I don't think so. Hell, I still don't know if I imagined all this, or if it was delivered to me. If it's the latter, then there's definitely a pile of good guys out there, waiting for me to get my ass in gear. And check this out too." She scrolled to another image, this one of an oddly shaped building that shifted slightly to the side, the windows almost lining up, but not quite. She had painted it violet.

"I've seen those," he said. "They're popping up in the cities wherever there's green smoke. Sometimes almost as soon as you enter the hell block, sometimes deeper within. They look like they've been there a long time, simply an odd feature of the landscape, but they can't be."

"No, they haven't been there long. I suspect they've only appeared in the last twelve hours. But once you know where to look for them...they're easy to spot. And they're almost always the same color."

She popped open a series of illustrations, and he leaned close. Sure enough, he could see a stroke of purple deep down along a line of silver skyscrapers—buried in a landscape of trees—hidden among a cluster of homes.

"So those doorways lead to...where?" he asked. "All to Sorcerer City?" The question was, in part, a test. How much did Katana truly know about her creation?

She shrugged. "Maybe? For now? Or maybe they're like a ghost town façade where it's just the wall and there's nothing behind it. I don't seem to have a lot of illustrations devoted to what's behind the purple buildings. And by 'not a lot,' I mean none."

He nodded. As he knew from Warrick's research, some of the doorways *had* been dead ends. Some had led to beaches and towns on the other side of the world from

Montmartre. But none of the Syx had allowed any of the humans to enter those strange passages, and they weren't going to go in themselves. Only Katana could lead them.

"Where is there one here in the city?" he asked gruffly, no longer happy with their plan. What if she went in and didn't come back out?

She waved a hand. "No idea. I ended up in that demonic coffee shop totally by accident, and I *guarantee* you there were no purple brownstones in the area. I have no idea where to find the closest one, other than..."

He narrowed his eyes. "Other than where?"

She glanced at the now-darkened windows that looked out over the park, then back to him. "There was always supposed to be one in Central Park, right? Sorcia's apartment is right here. You can see the reservoir, and it makes sense that if something was going to be hiding, it'd be hiding in the park. But a tall, skinny, purple building with off-centered windows and a sloping tilt? Someone would figure that out pretty quick, wouldn't they? They'd almost have to. There are so many people going through that park every day."

"If they're Connected, and they could see it. And if they knew what to look for."

"Fair..." She studied the images, worrying her bottom lip. "I have to be the one to do this," she muttered. "No matter what. I have to. I'm not going to be left behind again."

Hugh slid his gaze from the laptop to her pensive face. Something about all this didn't feel right, and he experienced a deep, disquieting sense that went beyond Warrick's warning to not let the human break him. There was profound Connected ability in this woman, far beyond anything he had seen or imagined, but she was also relentlessly seeking...something. When she found it, what would happen? Would she be at peace, or would she explode like a dying star?

"What are you looking for, Katana, when all is said and done?" he murmured, drawing her attention. "What will you do when you reach Sorcerer City and defeat the Shadow Court?"

"I don't know." She shrugged, waving off the question. "Maybe I'll save the world?"

Save the world. Yes. That tracked. But would she save herself?

He didn't know. He only knew he'd move hell and earth to keep her safe.

"Okay, then," he said, reaching for the bottle of wine. He drained it in one gulp, and gestured to their remaining provisions. "Eat what you can. Take what you need. It's time we went hunting for hell blocks."

21

*E*xiting the building, they struck out immediately for Central Park, Kat still shouldering her own pack, while Hugh carried a similar one that was nearly empty.

The new pack had been lying next to hers when she had returned to the studio, an anomaly that shouldn't exist, but did. She hadn't known she'd even want him to have a pack of his own as she'd walked back down the short hallway under the watchful eye of her childhood drawings. But as she'd entered the now-darkened studio and seen it, the fact of it had seemed exactly right.

She was getting more adept at accepting the strange appearances of needful things for what they were. Bread crumbs she was imagining into place—or, much more worrisome, breadcrumbs someone was leaving for her. She didn't want to think too much about that.

"It's kind of dark in here, don't you think?" she asked as they walked along a footpath in the park. Lights technically flooded the area, and there were still plenty of walkers, and cyclists even, rolling through the paved streets and along the paths, but everything seemed dimmer than it should.

Hugh nodded. He held the folded-up map Kat had drawn of the city around Central Park. It appeared that there was a hell block deep in the park itself, near its biggest pond. He'd agreed with her that the location wasn't ideal, since it would be a little more difficult to construct a purple-fronted unevenly angled building next to a freestanding structure. But it was the closest possibility and, as Hugh'd explained clearly enough, they shouldn't stay in the open in New York for long.

Not with the horde still roaming through the city.

Kat swallowed. At least Hugh's recon of the blocks surrounding the apartment had yielded gratifying results. As far as he could tell, the demons were staying hidden, not so stupid that they would confront him directly. But despite that positive turn, the idea that demons had two brain cells to rub together seemed to have bothered him.

Were the horde being controlled by the sorcerers of Sorcerer City, this group he called the Shadow Court? How far did that control go? Hugh had had no problem dispatching the assholes who'd trapped her in the coffee shop, but he'd explained that in doing so, he'd also betrayed his presence and interest in her. If the demons watching them were being controlled, their handlers would be more careful now. More strategic. That wasn't good.

Maybe she was worrying unnecessarily. In all truth, not much time had passed, and maybe they didn't have access to her story—she prayed they didn't, honestly. Had they realized that there were multiple paths leading to the Shadow Court's hidden fortress? Or were those paths even available to anyone but Kat?

And more to the point, why didn't she know more about her own story?

"It's getting foggy," she muttered. "I know that happens sometimes when it rains in the park. But I don't think it's rained." Her hand twitched toward her bag, and Hugh's voice cut through the mist.

"No phone. Not yet. At least, not until we know it's safe."

She gritted her teeth. "I know, I know. But a flashlight wouldn't suck."

He glanced ahead. "I can see easily."

"So you've mentioned. One of the gifts with purchase of being an angel?"

"Something like that." He ignored her sarcasm and nodded ahead. "We're coming up to a brick building that could potentially be our target. It's off the path, but not too far."

"It's a gatehouse," she confirmed. "It's possibly what we're looking for. It's a single building. I mean, there's nothing else there, but at least it's a building."

In another few steps, the thick fog overwhelmed them. Katana sidled closer to Hugh without saying anything, more grateful than she could express that he reached for her. She slipped her hand into his grasp, instantly feeling safer. He really was her guardian angel, she told herself. She should use that to her advantage.

"Remember, I can see," he reminded her, and she forced herself not to grip his hand more tightly. "What am I looking for?"

"This is all too weird," she muttered, not answering his question as she scanned the path, taking in the other joggers. "There are other people in here with us, only they don't seem to be bothered by the fog here. They're not even noticing it."

He didn't comment. He didn't have to. Besides the runners, there were walkers, couples old and young. Were there others in the mist too, watching them?

Hugh seemed to read her mind. "There will be demons here." He chuckled softly as she drew closer to him, and Kat's thoughts rabbited back to everything that had happened in the apartment—the feel of him surrounding her, the smell of sulfur and...

She frowned. Sulfur?

At that moment, they came around the corner and saw the entryway off the path to the small gatehouse. They immediately turned in that direction, but they hadn't taken more than a few steps when Hugh checked his stride.

"That's it?" he asked. Set back from the main path and accessible over a small bridge, the gatehouse was squat, square, and made of whitish-gray stone...lit up with floodlights that streamed down through the greenish smoke.

However, there was an additional feature that Kat didn't suppose was ordinarily viewable by the tourist gawkers: the southwest corner of the gatehouse had been replaced with an oddly leaning tower of vibrant purple, a single skinny door at its base. They could barely see it through the trees and foliage snugged up against the gatehouse, but it was there.

"That's...oh, *crap*." She gripped Hugh's hand, but though he didn't say anything, he knew what she'd seen. He had to have.

Between them and the gatehouse, a man leaned casually against the railing of the bridge, still as a statue except for his hyperfocus on his gleaming phone. Was that really a phone, Kat wondered wildly, or was he carrying some kind of Shadow Court psychic laser gun? How would she know?

He wore black clothes—a dark, long-sleeve shirt, dark pants. Dark shoes. A heavy-duty mask hung around his neck, but given the fact that flu season might never end again, that didn't make him either more or less scary. Just a New Yorker.

But she knew he wasn't any ordinary New Yorker. She'd drawn him. He was taller in her illustration, but the clothes were the same, and the phone. In the panels of *Dead End*, he'd hulked over the small device like a football player at a kindergarten table. This guy was more normally proportioned, but he still creeped her out. "We can't use this doorway," she whispered.

"But it's right there," Hugh said reasonably.

"Well, so is he."

Hugh paused, turning her toward him as if they were two ordinary walkers out enjoying an evening stroll. "He's not looking at us. He's looking at his phone. Only at his phone, though he clearly knows we're here. Also, he's human, which is interesting."

"I don't care if he's a flying squirrel. If he sees us going in, the sorcerers will know where we are. He's probably texting them right now. 'Dinner on the way. Bring beer.'"

"They already know where we are without his help," Hugh countered. "We need to figure out where they are— and *who* they are. Including this guy. He's got skills, training. He knows we're here, but he isn't moving or giving any indication that he's anything other than some rando with a phone. Which means they told him to wait and watch. They don't know what we're going to do and would rather track us than take us. We should do the jump now and not give the Shadow Court time to assemble the troops or come up with a better plan. And don't worry. We'll jump together."

She glanced up at him quickly, and he gave her his

widest smile. He seemed to be enjoying this way too much. "Together," he insisted. "But we should get a move on."

His confidence didn't make her feel much better. "You think he'll follow us?"

Hugh shrugged. "I'm counting on it, one way or another. Either he comes in after us, or somebody's going to be waiting for us on the inside. Assuming any of this works, of course." He made a show of peering through the fog toward the lit-up violet column. "That's kind of a skinny door."

"It'll work," Kat muttered. "I drew this. It's in the file. The reservoir, the corner tower, even the asshole on the bridge. I knew this would all be here, but it doesn't feel right or safe. If I had more time, I could fill in the details, make the path clear."

"We don't need the details," Hugh said. "We just go in... ah, through the door?"

"I have no idea," she hissed back, her focus shifting from the gatehouse to the watcher on the bench. "It's not like the doors are real, or the windows or the wall, for that matter. We could walk straight into the brick side of the gatehouse and end up with nothing more than a bloody nose."

"Well then, you go first." Hugh said helpfully. "I'll keep an eye on sentry boy."

He squeezed her hand, then nudged her to his other side so he was between the sentry and her. They walked on, Katana gripping his hand so hard, she suspected she'd leave marks. She kept her gaze fixed ahead. It suddenly didn't seem smart to focus on anything but getting through that ridiculously tiny hell block entryway.

"Most of them are bigger than this," she muttered, but Hugh squeezed her hand back, the two of them falling silent as they passed the sentry. Definitely a human, Kat decided, though she didn't have much experience with demons to base her assessment on. It was a testament to New York that no one else so much as gave the guy a second look. Then they were past him and moving up the path, and she didn't need to turn her head to know he wasn't following them. Nevertheless, she remained massively creeped out.

"Okay, so we go up and walk through," she told Hugh unnecessarily. "If it looks like it's a real door when we get up on it, we can try opening it. It'll open inward. Always inward."

"You're doing great," he said, obviously trying to reassure her.

It wasn't working. "Yeah, I'm doing great."

Kat didn't pause at the base of the gatehouse stairs, but trotted up them, angling to the left. She knew she couldn't check her stride. She had to speed up, not slow down. But she really didn't want a bloody nose for her trouble. Squeezing her eyes almost shut, narrowing her vision to the pinprick of space that contained the violet splash of color, she lifted her arm, bent forward, and picked up her pace. The doorway wasn't a real doorway. She could tell that at once. It had been painted on the stone, still leaning drunkenly to the side, but it wasn't a doorway. It wasn't a thing!

She kept going anyway.

At the last second, she felt Hugh's presence behind her, his arms coming around to lift her as if she weighed nothing. Disoriented, she couldn't slow, even if she wanted to now. His momentum carried them forward. And then they reached the stone wall—and jumped.

Straight through the doorway.

She fell through the wall and face-planted on the other side in utter darkness.

"Get up, get up! There's no oxygen here." The

words jangled in her ears, but they were actual words. Startled, Katana drew in a short breath, only to have her throat spasm awkwardly.

Hugh was right. There was no oxygen. But how was that possible? How could she hear him if there was no oxygen for speech?

"Which way?" he demanded, shaking her a little. She realized he'd pulled her upright, both hands on her arms like she might pass out at any second. And she might. She pulled an arm free and gestured vaguely, having zero clue which way to go. Then her eyes rolled back in her head, and she felt herself sliding out of consciousness.

"*Fuck!*"

Hugh's voice thundered in her ears as she felt herself lifted again and flung forward. This time, her feet hit pavement. She stumbled, but a burst of air filled her lungs, so sweet and pure, she almost choked on it. Then she was sprawling forward, her hands scraping on rough brick, her hair plastered to her face as rain pelted down.

A second later, Hugh was beside her once more, scooping her up and half shoving, half hurtling her out of the way as a whoosh of wind blew over them. Then another set of footsteps sounded, and he was up again, turning back.

The man from the park bridge had burst through a tall, skinny mausoleum shaped like the violet brownstone facade they'd seen in Central Park, but even smaller—little more than a door. The man's mask was now over his face— and it was a lot more impressive of a mask than she'd realized. As she watched in horror, he lifted a gun and shot at Hugh.

Kat didn't have the time to get out her scream before the bullets struck Hugh chest-high. He convulsed, then the thin bullets shot through the other side and banged against the large stone monument she was slumped up beside. She mewled a little as she scrambled out of the way, but the guy didn't fire again.

Hugh didn't give him a chance.

Her guardian angel leapt so fast, he practically flew, knocking their assailant flat before dropping on him. Kat winced, wanting to look away, but Hugh only laid his hand on the man's face, ripping his mask away and fixing him with his gaze until the man wailed in terror and passed out, boneless on the wet street.

Hugh turned, twirling the mask in his hand as he came back to her. The wind gusted, and the rain abruptly stopped, leaving the ground around them glistening beneath the fingers of green smoke.

"Well, that was satisfying." He grinned and reached for her hand. "Let's see what other trouble you can get us into."

---

22

*H*ugh knew it was wrong of him to derive pleasure from incapacitating the human, but he *had* only incapacitated him. He hadn't killed him outright. And plus, that human was going to hurt his human, the one he had been specifically charged to take care of. Surely there were rules about that?

Even as the thought crossed his mind, he realized the flaw in his thinking. If Death were to be believed, and there was no reason why she would lie, this was the same setup that had led to the archangel's predicament. Michael had stepped in to save Death, a rarified human who had served in her role of ushering the dead safely to the other side for centuries, even millennia. She alone had probably saved countless lives through the generations, and provided aid and support to thousands, maybe even hundreds of thousands. She was an objectively worthy human.

And here the chosen Angel of God, the right hand of the Almighty, had stepped in to protect that worthy human, and he'd been destroyed for his efforts.

Had Michael known the risk he was taking? Had he known, in fact, that it was his path to take that risk? It was possible. The archangel had seemed eerily prescient on a number of occasions, in a way that was not totally unlike Katana, minus all the pretty pictures. But Michael had thousands of years' more experience than Katana. He would have known the possible outcomes. He would probably have known that he was being tested. And yet when the time came, he still took a human's life. Why? How could he have worked so tirelessly to shepherd the Syx toward their redemption and then turn his back on his beliefs so abruptly?

Who was the archangel, really?

A problem for tomorrow—or maybe the day after. Now, they had sorcerers to hunt.

He and Katana had landed in what seemed to be the farthest back corner of Montmartre, and sure enough, one of the cemetery's mausoleums had become a hell block doorway. It was mostly doorway, in fact, with only the thinnest frames of violet and the hint of a lean-to echo the portal back in New York, but there was no mistaking it. Hugh tried to recall the passage from New York to Paris, but with Katana unable to breathe, he'd not taken the time to do a thorough recon.

Hopefully they'd have plenty of time to explore later. The idea of traveling the pathways Katana had opened— with her at his side—appealed to him far more than it should, but too damned bad. She wasn't getting rid of him now. Not if he could help it, anyway.

The cemetery hell block itself extended about twenty graves by ten, the thick veil of green smoke clearing within seconds of them getting on the move. Hugh didn't know how long the man would stay unconscious, but based on what Hugh had seen of his mind, the guy wasn't an idiot. Hugh expected he'd stay appropriately passed out for at least thirty minutes.

Katana had been silent for too long, however, leading him toward the entrance of the cemetery of Montmartre with quick but cautious steps. She took no turns, but headed straight down the main path toward Avenue Rachel, not looking around her at the ornate cemetery markers or outright mausoleums. Montmartre might have been the portal location for Sorcerer City, but it seemed as if the cemetery itself would remain holy ground.

Hugh spared the cemetery markers a few glances, though, appreciating the artwork if not the sentiment. Humans and their need for immortality...how little they knew. It was why the Father had originally allowed his angels to become Fallen, emissaries of information and wisdom to help assuage a population so caught up in fear that they were missing the point of creation. Things hadn't worked out the way the Father intended, Hugh suspected.

But then again, how would he know? Maybe God did work in mysterious ways. The Father had created demons, after all. And He'd given certain humans access to magic. Both decisions weren't all that bright, as far as Hugh was concerned. Then again, God hadn't asked Hugh his opinion.

He wondered if Finn and Warrick had made any headway on identifying the players currently working with the Shadow Court. He doubted it. They would have contacted him—especially since Warrick could now drag him back into his presence on a moment's notice. So that left Hugh with the job of figuring out what the Shadow Court's game was with Katana.

There was no question that Shadow Court wanted her for her mad skills, but he suspected it went deeper than that.

They needed her. There was no other reason why the demons hadn't torn her limb from limb. They'd also referred to her as a scribe—and had indicated there were other scribes as well, if Katana had correctly understood the demon who'd addressed her. Truth—or more lies?

Either way, Hugh and the Syx couldn't underestimate the Shadow Court. The minds behind the assault on the Connected were some of the most psychically powerful humans outside the Arcana Council. It had taken an act of ultimate sacrifice for the Council to have done as much as they had. Even though it seemed like a rout—what with hell blocks filled with green smoke now dotting the globe, demons running rampant, and magic boiling out of every crack and crevice it could find—the alternative would have been far worse.

They were close, he thought. Close to where the Shadow Court had holed up, even if the cemetery itself wasn't the location of their hidden citadel. The Council's sacrifice would not be in vain.

"There isn't another doorway, is there? Leading somewhere else?" he asked Katana, just to be sure.

She shook her head. "The colors are right for this place. The background tones, the blues, the darkness, the lights picked out in the distance. I can't show you how, exactly, because it's on my laptop, but Sorcerer City is close—it's in this arrondissement."

She shot him a startled look. "I think that means neighborhood."

He gave her an encouraging wink. "I'm aware."

"Yeah, but I'm not. That's the problem. Sorcia Steele

spoke French, but I never had to write it accurately when she used it in *Dead End*. My agent said they'd find someone to translate at the publishing house, and I did my best with a dictionary, but who knows how close I got." She grimaced. "Jeez, my agent. I wonder if she's trying to get ahold of me. I wonder if anyone is."

The words struck Hugh as unexpectedly forlorn. One thing he had learned about humans over the past thousands of years that he had served in their shadows, delivering them from the worst of his kind, was that they always performed better in groups. They lived longer, seemed happier. Those humans he encountered who were truly alone were rarely the ones who called for help when demons struck. They had a more fatalistic attitude about their lives and even their worth. They accepted the attack of the spawn as one more in an entire string of events that was up to them to solve. How long had Katana looked at her life this way?

Since she was seventeen and her adoptive parents had died, certainly, but perhaps even younger? He suspected so.

"Did your parents speak French?" he asked suddenly, and she snorted.

"Good thought, but no. They'd both taken Spanish in high school. Practically everybody does. I only got out of language because I took an introduction to coding class instead, and my school was cool enough to count that. Why?"

He shrugged, peering around at the tombstones and crypts. "It seems an odd choice for your character, the French language, if you didn't already know it or had any associations with it. She could have easily spoken Cantonese, right? I just was wondering if there was some connection between the fact that she spoke French and the fact that we're here now."

"Oh." Katana looked around with greater interest. "You know, I never thought about that, but that makes sense. Why *did* I decide that Sorcia and her angel had to come here? All those cities, all those intersections. But I knew this was it." She sighed. "Once again, am I making this up, or am I following something that already existed? And how will I ever know?"

"You'll know if we get to the end of the cemetery and there's something waiting for us. Something or someone. I have a feeling they won't leave you in the dark for very long once you find them."

"Yeah, well." She made a face. "What did you find out from the guy following us, or did you knock him out before he could say anything?"

Hugh hesitated. Human minds were a jumbled mess, even ones that were more ordered than Katana's. And they were frequently inaccurate in their assessment of situations, except for those who had had formal military or scientific training. He suspected the man who'd been trailing them had neither. But Hugh had sensed his Connected ability. He'd needed it to get into the passageway behind them, to enter the thin sliver of color that had made up the portal in Central Park.

The sentry had also had two other images in his mind, fixed and certain. A grand mansion that sat behind a white stone wall, the wall's wrought iron topper overhung with tree branches, and his bank account. An improbably large number had gleamed in light blue numbers against a white background.

"He was a low-level operative, hired for a specific job, and paid very well," Hugh finally said. "Just Connected enough to be able to pull off the transfer between stations—and ballsy enough to do it even not knowing what the In Between might have in store for him—but he didn't know any of the players."

"Did he have any communications tech?" Katana pressed. "Like, some sort of phone or headset or anything like that?"

Hugh held up the mask. "This comes equipped with the mouthpiece, or it did before I smashed it. The headpiece and tracking unit, I left on him. We want people to know that he succeeded in tracking us this far."

"But doesn't that mean that we're going to be bringing down a raft of bad guys on our head?"

He smiled. "The reality is, that's the fastest way to figuring out what's happening here. You weren't shot at by those gunmen who attacked your editor, and she was left alive long enough for you to reach her. They need you—probably because they understand at least a little bit of who and what you are. That's why you're still alive."

"Well, but by your reasoning, they don't need you alive. Not to put too fine a point on it, but that's a bad thing."

"No human can kill a demon," Hugh reminded her automatically, then added just as smoothly, "Or an angel. Or any of their relatives."

"Well, I suppose that's comforting. But what happens if this Shadow Court has demons on their payroll? Can a demon kill another demon...or an angel?"

There was enough hesitation before she said the final words that Hugh knew her agile mind was moving too quickly.

"Theoretically speaking, a demon can kill another demon, but not an angel. They can make their lives miserable, but they can't kill them." He thought again of

Michael, held by the horde. "But I don't think that the people we're going to be dealing with will have demons too high up the food chain. They're a bitch to keep control of, even with witch handlers."

"Um...with what?"

Then Hugh heard it. The soft footfall of a cautious step in the empty Montmartre, a graveyard that was closed to the public overnight. No one should be here—*they* shouldn't be here. Instead, they were being followed. Everything in him itched to go and collar their newest tail, but he couldn't leave Katana alone. Unlike him, she *could* be killed by a human or a demon, and even if the Shadow Court wanted her alive, mistakes happened. He couldn't risk leaving her alone.

"There could be a battle, if you want," she murmured, and he shot her a sharp look.

"What do you mean?"

"Would that help us? Would we learn something if we drew the sorcerers out in a fight? Or should we walk through their front door and ask them outright?"

Hugh grimaced. "The only reason a fight would be useful is if there was information I needed from it. Is there?"

She looked at him, annoyed. "You're asking me?"

"You're the one writing the story."

"I'm the one *following* the story. There's a difference."

"Is there? If you *were* writing this story, what would you do next? What would be the most natural thing to happen?"

She pressed her lips together. "Honestly, if I were writing this as a story, I think I *would* have a battle to show the hero and heroine working together. Especially if my heroine was Sorcia, a badass femme fatale And that would also display how dangerous their opponents are. But we already know how dangerous these people are. And we don't have time for a fight. And, oh, yeah. I'm not Sorcia Steele."

Hugh's mouth kicked up at one corner. "I don't know, you're doing pretty well for yourself as Katana Midland, and I'm always up to fight some demon ass. Better yet, so is my—"

His next words were cut off as demons fell from the sky.

---

23

*T*he fear that consumed Kat was so real and absolute it was like her body had been invaded by an alien being. All around her, creatures either fell from the clouds or seemed to erupt out of the crypts themselves, a trick of the shadows, perhaps, but effective all the same. Some were small, some were large, but they were all long-gaited, hideously clawed and scaly-skinned beasts, spewing black liquid that flew from their leathery skin and spattered the ground around them with sizzling fury.

Their eyes bulged, their jaws gaped, and as Hugh rush to meet their attack, she drew back, momentarily horrified as he shifted from the beautiful avenging angel that she knew into a creature of pure fire and destruction, his limbs stretching, his neck and shoulders bulging, his long, beautiful fingers turning into claws. The effect lasted only a moment, but it didn't need to last longer. The demons screamed in absolute terror at the disguise.

Hugh roared, then switched back to angelic form, the transition so abrupt that chaos poured into Katana, filling her ears, flooding her mind, a lifetime's worth of pain rushing over her, exploding in fiery retribution. Something screamed at her from the distant past—a thought, a memory, a secret she'd once known and let slip away...

What have I forgotten? Who left me behind?

There was no more time to think. The demons reached her.

With no other weapon, Kat yanked her pack off her shoulders. Grabbing its straps, she swung it at the beast. As she did, the pack changed its form midair, elongating and curving, the straps solidifying into a smooth wooden cylinder, and the rest arcing through the night sky with an unmistakable hiss of metal. She jolted with the impact of her long katana sword slicing into the demon's body, her arms practically vibrating out of their sockets as black blood spurted. The creature reared back and howled as if relishing the pain. A concert of chittering cries filled the cemetery in response.

Hugh would have wanted her to call him for help, she knew. But Hugh was keeping secrets from her too. She didn't know how, but there was something about him as he'd rushed into battle that had struck her on a deeply visceral level. Something that had taken her all the way back to her earliest days—when she'd first known she was a failure, unworthy.

He had to know what had happened to her all those years ago, surely. He was her guardian angel.

He'd told her the harrowing story of the dying humans, but he hadn't told her a damned thing about herself. *Why*? How was that a *thing*?

As her mind churned, Kat chopped off another demon's arm, then flinched back as a gout of black blood arced toward her, landing at her feet and causing the ground to sizzle. What memory had Hugh triggered that had upset her so? Why did she feel so much outrage and shame buried deep within her? Had he somehow lied to her? Had he betrayed her?

No! No, he couldn't have lied to her. Not with the way he'd held her in his arms and kept her safe. Then again, maybe Hugh was her imagination working overtime, that's all. Not an angel of the Lord, but a creation of her own mind.

But if that were true...could she trust anything he said?

Chaos surged and rolled in her mind as she tried to parse everything she'd learned about Hugh, everything she believed to be true. It wasn't like she'd had a hell of a lot of time to process. Was he real? Was he simply an extension of her own twisted mind? Was he an angel at all, or some kind of illusion?

No human could kill a demon—or an angel. That was something else he'd said, something else she didn't fully believe. Was that what had upset her?

As she wheeled around, her sword somehow flashing expertly through the air although she knew *not one thing* about sword fighting, Kat caught sight of Hugh. A mini horde of slavering creatures attacked him all at once, but he didn't back down. He was beautiful and strong, powerful and true. Her guardian angel, in the flesh.

A hair-raising demon scream cut through the night, and as she turned in panic, a flash of violet light caught her eye, winking between the sepulchers. A harder look on a second turn confirmed that a haze of green smoke whispered through the cemetery markers, indicating either a second hell block or an extension of the one at the back of the cemetery. Was it a path through, a path out? She hadn't drawn any of this, but she suddenly knew with absolute certainty that if she followed that winking light, she could escape.

Perhaps it was time for her to strike out on her own and open Sorcerer City for the unseen warriors she knew were waiting in the wings...somewhere.

She couldn't leave Hugh alone to fight, though, could she? He was clearly proving to be a one-angel wrecking crew, but demons were erupting out of the ground like Carrie after the prom. Surely someone was out there who could help him a hell of a lot more than she ever could. There had to be!

"Please—please God, or Archangel Michael, or anyone who's out there listening. Please save Hugh from the horde," she prayed, though she felt distinctly awkward doing so. Prayer had never helped her before...and yet, she'd written an entire story with a guardian angel main character, so clearly she believed. Would it be enough? Was this something Sorcia would have done? Was this right and true? Could this possibly—

A new howl roared through the cemetery, this one of absolute murderous joy.

Three sets of boots crunched into the earth beside her, worn by three tall, dark, and brutal-looking warriors bristling with muscle and attitude. Kat's eyes practically popped out of her head. *Angels.* They had to be more guardian angels—the same warriors Jeremy had seen in his vision.

Well, he was going to make a million dollars if he planned on merchandising these guys.

One of the warrior angels was half again larger than the others, his eyes glowing an eerie green. A second, lean and loose as he turned a full circle, laughed in delight at the demonic chaos, his blue eyes flashing and his grin positively gleeful. The third angel—big, brutal, and somehow steadier-feeling, whipped his head her way and pinned her with his golden-amber eyes.

He stepped toward her as the others raced into the battle.

"We don't have much time," he barked. His voice pounded through her, the same way Hugh's had done when she'd first met him, the effect nearly lifting her off her feet. These guys really needed to make it into more religious art. Church attendance would totally soar.

The big angel flinched back, then grinned, almost as if he could read her mind. Though of course, there was no—

"The rules of this place are changing," he continued. "You're changing them—you need to know that. You're changing the present and the future with every breath."

Who was this guy, and how did he know her? Kat shook her head. "I guarantee you, I'm not changing anything. You work with Hugh, right? Of course you do. That's why you're here."

The angel started to speak, then paused, slanting a glance to where his partners now joined Hugh. The three enormous warriors moved in almost perfect unison, as if they'd fought like this many times before.

"Real live warrior angels," Kat murmured, staring at them. "Jeremy's going to stroke out."

Her words seemed to galvanize the angel. He glared at her with his golden eyes. "What we were and what we are doesn't matter. This is what you must know. You're running out of time. The copy of your manuscript that Hugh gave us is losing pages now, not gaining them. If you had the time to look at your own copy, you would find the same. The ending that you originally wrote no longer exists."

A new wave of chaos screamed in Kat's mind—outrage

and fear too, but mostly chaos. "I *know*," she shouted above the demonic howls of the battle around her. "I know, but I can get back to it."

"No," the angel warrior insisted. "It's gone. That path is no longer open to you. Something you've done has changed the course—forever. It's just happened, for what it's worth. Any ideas?"

"B-but that can't be possible," Katana stammered. "The story has to sync up again. It has to!"

He gestured around the cemetery, a decisive swipe of his hand. "Montmartre was part of the original story. But the panels leading up to it are gone. How did you get here originally? Think. What did you do—or your guardian angel?"

"But..." Kat swallowed. This was a part of the story she'd had to cut to get her agent on board, but she hadn't replaced her original ideas yet with anything more than a few transition panels. "He was never here," she finally said. "In the first version of *Dead End*, Hugh died before Sorcia ever left New York. In the second, a sorcerer killed him at the gates. And in the third, fourth, and fifth versions, he died in various demon attacks—but also before he got to the cemetery. He was never here."

The angel grinned. "You don't like him very much, do you?"

"I do, though! I just..." She flapped her hand at him. "Look, he doesn't die in some versions of the story until the end. In some, I added him back into the story after the cemetery—seriously. He's with me in the mansion."

"Not anymore." The angel shook his head. "Something happened. Whether you did it or he did it, those pages are gone. If you want to get him out of this, you'll have to come up with something new."

All the blood drained out of her brain, chaos howling in her ears. "But how?"

The angel glanced at his fellow warriors, who were barely holding their own against an unending tide of demons. "I'm thinking you'll come up with something. Just...don't take too long."

Kat followed his sightline, and real fear surged within her. Four angels—four. Only four. Against how many of the horde? Fifty? A hundred? They'd never succeed in holding them back. They'd never take them all out—and they had to.

They had to.

Hugh couldn't die

"Why can't humans kill demons?" she blurted. "That seems like a really stupid rule."

The angel blinked at her in surprise. "We didn't write that story. We merely live with it."

"Oh! So I can rewrite it."

"*No.*" The giant held up his hands, his amber eyes glowing fiercely. "That is not the way. Some stories shouldn't be changed."

"You're saying that to the wrong girl. Here." She pulled around her pack and rummaged through it, just as another unholy scream erupted and a fresh snarl of demons surged up out of the cemetery's dark, loamy soil. She flinched and dug more deeply. "Oh my *god*, where are these things coming from?" she moaned.

"A little help here," shouted the blue-eyed angel, who had gotten separated from the others and was single-handedly pressing back at least twenty of the horde on his own.

The angel turned. "I've got to go."

"Wait! I can help you," Katana insisted, rifling through

her pack more earnestly. And she knew she could, because she'd written it that way. In those panels that she'd destroyed, she'd gained power over a demon lord, after Hugh had died protecting her. But fuck a bunch of demon lords. She could come up with something better than that.

The amber-eyed angel only looked pained. "You can help by creating a new path through."

She jerked her head up, searching for the violet light that had danced in the shadows. She saw it again, this time winking at the opening of the cemetery. But how? Surely the hell block didn't extend out into the village of Montmartre.

"We can distract them for long enough for you to get to whatever you see. And then Hugh will find you, if he survives."

"He'll survive," she snapped, her fingers finally closing around two stubby cylinders. She yanked them out and tossed them to the angel. "Take these canisters and use them."

He caught them easily, then scowled down at them. "What's in them?"

"How the hell should I know? Scum spray. But it'll kill demons. Bet on it."

The angel stiffened and jerked back, holding the cans out like they might burn him. He eyed her suspiciously. "Where the hell did you get that backpack?"

"Um..." Kat glanced down at the bag. "Online, somewhere—some college guy in Boston, I think. Why?"

"Never mind," the angel growled. He spun around and leapt toward the others, and Kat ran the other way. She made it to the edge of the cemetery, mere steps before plunging into the brightly lit streets of the village beyond, then a surge of fear ripped through her. She wheeled around again at the last second, searching the cemetery wildly, unwilling to leave Hugh.

She choked back a scream.

There was no longer one battle in front of her. There were two. Two sets of the horde layered over each other, two quartets of angelic warriors fighting them.

In one battle, they pressed the horde back, laughing happily, almost feral in their intensity. Doing what they were born to do, or what they had been made to do.

In the other battle, though, Hugh turned as if suddenly aware that Kat was no longer part of their group. At that moment, an enormous lumbering demon erupted out of the ground, clawed fist first, directly beneath him. Surprise turned to horror as Hugh staggered back, blood pouring out of him. His eyes widened, his mouth grew slack, and Katana couldn't take it anymore.

She was killing Hugh by staying here! This was the ending she'd feared. But if she didn't stay here, he wouldn't die. If she couldn't imagine it, it couldn't happen.

She fixed her mind on the first version of the battle, turned, and fled into the city.

24

"You did *what*?" Hugh demanded, unwilling to believe his ears when Warrick finally reached him in the midst of the horde, the two of them falling into easy battling cadence. "How could you tell her to go? Are you fucking insane?"

"Had to be done, my man," Finn yelled over his shoulder. "The story went absolutely ape shit after you guys left the apartment. It's gone completely off the rails, and your girl with it."

"Give us a minute, Finn," Warrick yelled. The demon enforcer grinned, then spread his arms wide, shearing off to the right while Gregori headed left, giving Warrick and Hugh space as they squared off.

"So it's gone off the rails," Hugh fumed. "How does that translate into you sending her out on her own? I'm supposed to protect her. I can't protect her if I'm not *with* her."

"What do you know about her demon-killing weapon?" Warrick asked.

Hugh stiffened. "What the fuck are you talking about? What weapon?"

Warrick showed him the two canisters. "She pulled these from her pack and threw them at me, said they were filled with scum spray. Do you know what they are?"

"Not one clue. They kill demons?" Hugh took one of the canisters from Warrick's hand. "Son of a bitch. She decided to change the rules."

Warrick nodded. "I think so too. Can she do that? You've connected with her."

Hugh shrugged. "If she gave these to you, she thinks they'll work—though that means they'll kill us too, if we're not careful. But I haven't really connected with her mentally. Her mind is filled with chaos. More than most humans."

In the midst of the demons, Gregori roared in frustration as another wave of spawn belched out of a moldering crypt.

"Did she foresee us coming to help you?" Warrick asked.

"No." Hugh grinned at him. "Which means she hasn't foreseen your deaths, either."

"Comforting."

Hugh laughed as he shoved the canister into his pocket. "We need to get closer."

They battled back to Gregori's and Finn's sides. Slicing, shredding, exploding the spawn back to the depths of hell or wherever they originated. Hugh looked closely into the eyes of each creature as he blasted it back to perdition. They remained insensible, crazed. He knew that humans had been co-opting some of the demons to do their bidding. But that was not these creatures. These had merely been summoned and set upon him and Katana. He didn't know if that made it worse or better.

When they took up their positions next to Finn and Gregori, the fighting reached a fever pitch. The demons howled. The Syx roared. The time-honored dance of evil turned and evil remaining recommenced, until the four of them were in a tight knot, almost back to back.

"This isn't going to be pretty," Hugh shouted, pulling out his canister and waving it at Finn. Warrick held up his as well. "We get any of this on us, we're dead. Like dead, dead."

"Let's avoid that then." A new roar sounded as another crypt burst open, and a swarm of spawn emerged. Finn let out a curse. "Are you *kidding* me with these guys?"

"Do it now," Gregori advised. "Awareness is starting to seep outside the hell block. The humans will start reacting with panic and anger shortly, not knowing what's going on."

"Got it." Hugh locked eyes with Warrick, and together, they uncorked their canisters and threw them at the same time into the crowd of demons while simultaneously pressing back against each other, a tiny pinpoint in a sea of madness.

The canisters exploded on contact with the horde. But while Hugh had half formed an idea of what would happen next, he gaped as the first demon struck cratered into nothing—and then the second and the third. It wasn't the wrath of fire and brimstone that spread among the horde, it was the straight-up breath of God. A weapon he had heard of, but never seen.

A weapon only angels were allowed to wield to kill a rage of demons.

Until today, anyway.

"Holy shit. Don't move," he said tightly as the wheel of destruction spun around them, ever widening, never contracting. The few demons that still stood close to them within the center of that circle had frozen as well, self-preservation rendering them immobile for a full ten seconds as the breath of God spun its deadly poison in broader and broader arcs. Then a few of the demons at the perimeter of their island of safety lost their nerve and bolted into the empty space. They immediately disappeared as well.

The mighty enforcers of the Syx moved not one muscle.

"*Shiiittt,*" Finn spoke first, clearly impressed. "How'd Katana get a hold of a couple of cans of Demon Whoopass? She's now the one human who can kill us?"

"I don't know," Hugh muttered, still trying to process the destruction Katana had wrought without even trying all that hard.

"You do know," Warrick said quietly.

They stood in silence for another few moments, though nothing else stirred in the cemetery. Hugh sucked in a long breath. "What else should I know, Warrick? What am I missing?"

"We found other pages—deleted, but not fully destroyed," Warrick said. "As you know, the book she gave her editor, the one we have as well, wasn't the first edition. But she cut out other pieces along the way. Pieces beyond your multiple untimely deaths. They include Sorcia Steele getting talked over to the side of the sorcerers in Sorcerer City. Betraying you."

"No *way,*" Hugh said, ignoring the stab of outrage that knifed through his gut. "Why would she do that to her heroine? Everyone would hate her."

Warrick shrugged. "Apparently, she realized that as well, but that doesn't change the fact that those panels still existed at one time in Katana's mind. So she could, theoretically, access them again. That wouldn't be ideal."

"She won't turn on us," Hugh said. "It's not possible."

"I'm not saying she would, but it *is* a possibility."

Hugh set his jaw. "No, I've given this some thought. The

chaos in her mind? It's choice. It's a hundred thousand threads of futures she could pull. She maps them out without even realizing it, I think, racing forty-seven steps ahead, and then retracing her steps and starting over when something she doesn't expect happens. But the artifacts of those old paths don't ever really go away. They remain for her to see. Seeing is not taking, though."

"Something she doesn't expect," Warrick mused. "I think it's safe to say that giving a group of demons the breath of God to use as a weapon could be classified as that."

"She doesn't know we're demons," Hugh pointed out.

"And it's a good thing we're hella nimble demons, or we'd be ghosts now," Finn put in.

"The energy is changing. Look." Gregori waved a meaty hand to encompass the cemetery. "The birds are returning, the animals. The horde has left this place, and so has the breath of God."

Hugh slanted a glance to the enormous enforcer. Of all of them, Gregori was the most sensitive. "You think it's safe for us to move?"

The big demon shrugged. "I think it's worth a try, unless you want to stand in the middle of this graveyard for the rest of our unnatural lives."

They didn't have a chance to test out the theory.

A summons, sharp and irrefutable, cracked through their minds, and a second later, they were yanked back to their unofficial headquarters in Vienna, an unamused Death glaring at them with her arms crossed.

"What the *fuck* just happened?" she demanded. "Half the population of spawn in France has vanished. Not just Paris, but into the countryside of France. What did you discover? Who did this? And how?"

Hugh rubbed his hand through his hair. "Katana gave us

containers of the breath of God and we used them. They were...effective."

Death's eyes narrowed. "And you weren't damaged?"

Finn grinned. "We were very, very careful."

"Humans can't kill demons," she reminded them all.

Warrick shook his head. "They still can't. Not directly. But Katana found a way to make it happen anyway by making a tool and placing it into the correct hands. And if she did it, she's not going to be the only one to figure this out."

"Fair enough," said Death. "But is she making this path that she's racing down so swiftly, or is she following it?"

Hugh spread his hands. "That, it would seem, is the question of the hour."

"It's not the only one," Blue said. "This woman doesn't know what she is, but she also doesn't know *who* she is. The Shadow Court does. We've figured out who her parents were."

"Here we go," Finn crowed, and Blue nodded.

"The Arcana Council is in shambles, but the computer network survives. And a few of the Fool's assistants know how to get into it and run an arcane DNA query."

Hugh started. "DNA? But how—"

"We hit her apartment," Warrick said. "It was harder to find than it should be. She has a very small footprint."

"But when did you have time?"

Blue smiled grimly. "Let's just say we made it a priority. Plus, we had some help on that front from her friends from the gaming store. And, of course, our DNA database is highly, highly specialized. What we found isn't all that reassuring. The last known location of Katana's parents was the small city of Bruges, twenty years ago. Ironically enough, I ushered them into the afterworld myself. They'd already sold their four-year-old daughter to the Shadow Court before their car ran off the road—that's a whole different issue right there, but not relevant for this. Regardless, the human trafficking transaction didn't go through. She and about a half dozen other psychic children were intercepted, sent to a safe house, and eventually fostered out to families that were identified as Connected-friendly. She was kept in the system until she was ten years old and the powers that be judged her safe, then permanently adopted."

"She has such chaos in her mind..." Hugh said, rubbing his face absently. "She believes that she was chosen for great things, but failed to deliver. You think that could be a holdover from being told she was, what...going to the Shadow Court? Like that was some sort of prize? She was only a little girl."

Blue lifted one shoulder, dropped it. "She was four. Old enough to have some understanding, maybe—and a few memories, for sure. Her parents were either desperate or shit bags to enter into a sale of their only kid. Probably both. Either way, she's beyond powerful, and once the Shadow Court figures that out, they'll know they've found the key that has kept Pandora's box shut fast. At that point, all they'll need to do is turn it."

"You think they already know?" Hugh asked, his throat constricting.

"Honestly? No. They know she's a high-level Connected, but I don't think they understand what's on its way to them. I don't think we understand it either. Until we do, we need to protect her, in a way that neither antagonizes her nor frightens her."

Warrick looked at Hugh. "Looks like you're up again."

"Looks like." Hugh gave a brief nod. He didn't want Katana to see the full truth of him, but nothing was worth her getting hurt. "If the going gets bad, she's not getting an angel. It's too hard to keep up that glamour and fight. She's going to have to deal with the demon."

"Excellent," Finn said, clapping his hands together. "Hugh the Destroyer is kind of a wuss. Hugh of the Syx is a way better time."

---

25

*K*at slipped through the shadows of Montmartre's cobblestoned streets, but she no longer felt the fear that had dogged her for the last few days, and far longer if she was honest with herself. She knew where she was going. And she knew, once she got there, that she would figure out what she needed to do. Everything had been leading to this.

She swallowed, trying to push out the visions of Hugh and his heroic group of friends standing in the middle of the demon-killing explosion.

She'd wanted to help, and she probably *had* helped, but that didn't mean she hadn't screwed herself in the process.

If the canisters she'd handed the big angel had exploded as she'd envisioned they would, taking out everyone in their midst, Hugh would know that she was the equivalent of a weapon of mass destruction—dangerous no matter whose side she was on. If he was a true angel, would he let her live? Could he let her live? She wouldn't if she were in his place.

Worse, maybe, if the canisters didn't explode at all, and that was a sincere possibility since she hadn't heard a peep from Hugh in the past half hour, he would know that she was a charlatan, a fraud. Just one more person trying to figure out what she was good at in life and failing.

Better for him to know that upfront, than to keep protecting her as she tried to unravel the mess she had caused.

Either way, she sincerely doubted she would see him again. And though she'd only known him for less than one full day, that knowledge lay like a stone in her stomach, dull and lifeless.

When she'd been with Hugh, she'd thought she was something special, different. Not just another cog in somebody else's wheel. "Don't overshoot your station," her adoptive mother would say, "Stay in your lane," her father would chime in, and she'd tried to do that. But what had that course gotten her? She was twenty-six years old with no college degree, working gig jobs to support a writing career that was as ephemeral as the psychic bombs that had rained down on New York City. Supposedly causing no damage, yet completely destroying everything she'd worked for.

What would she do now? Would Emily even want to work with her, given what she'd endured over Kat's manuscript? She doubted it. There were five thousand other people angling for the chance she'd gotten, waiting to take her place, and none of them were freaks.

These thoughts carried her all the way up Rue Caulaincourt until she reached a tiny coffee shop—still closed, of course. Then she simply went where her feet took her, eventually turning onto a tree-draped street where the homes were covered in ivy, and massive estates loomed behind elegantly austere stone walls. And about halfway down the long street was the same winking flash of violet she'd thought she'd seen from more than a mile away. Not a crumbling brownstone at all, but the whimsy of a homeowner who had installed a flickering LED lamp.

Kat looked around, frowning. There was no one out walking the neighborhood but her, and she didn't know what time it was, other than very, very early in the morning. The gloom of the shrouding fog pressing in on her could have been the sign of a hell block, or it could have simply been a wet Paris night.

She exhaled slowly. It was going to happen now. She knew it. She just had to hold on to her plan. And that plan was...what, exactly?

She didn't have time to think any more about it. The door opened next to the flickering violet flame, and the wrought iron gate disengaged, clicking open.

The inference was clear. She was being welcomed inside.

Kat had fled the cemetery in a rush. Her katana had turned back into a laptop pack, she was fresh out of scum spray, and she didn't have a guardian angel anymore. She didn't even know how the story she'd written was supposed to end. All she could do was step forward.

It was her adventure to take.

One step, another, and Kat felt better moving, at least. As soon as she cleared the gate, it snicked shut behind her, the lock hissing into place. Tightening her hold on her backpack, she strode up the short lane, past the trees overladen with heavy branches that looked just on the verge of budding, and marched up the stairs. The door stood wide, but no one loomed beyond it, and she glimpsed an expanse of white marble tile and white walls.

Once again, she wondered what the hell she was doing, and once again, the answer was clear: whatever she could to take this chance that had finally been given her. Whatever she could to succeed.

She walked through the entryway. The moment she did, the bright lights of the foyer dimmed, and movement to the left drew her attention as an attendant she hadn't seen shut the door behind him.

"Bienvenue, Katana Midland." It was a woman who spoke, tall and elegant with carefully brushed gray hair swept back from her face, angular features, and an aquiline nose. "My name is Charlotte DuBois. We've been waiting for you."

She held out a hand to Katana, and Katana grasped it automatically.

"Oh!" she gasped, yanking it back quickly as something jabbed her skin. She glanced down, expecting to see blood coursing across her palm, but the skin remained dry, untroubled. Kat grimaced, imagining all sorts of dire things that had just been poked into her. Someone else was trying to overwrite her story! But she was better at this game than they were.

Schooling her features into guileless chagrin, she shook her head. "Ah, sorry. It felt like something sharp was in—it's nothing."

"Good, good," Charlotte DuBois said warmly. She clasped her hands in front of her, not making a move toward Katana. But her eyes sparked with approval as she tilted her head.

"You must have a great many questions. We certainly do for you. But we also owe you some explanation. What you learned, what you channeled, is nothing short of extraordinary. The work we did was on a very high psychic level. The plans we made were deeply secured. And yet you knew them, internalized them, and created a pop culture fable about them."

Kat tried to summon a blush, but couldn't. Where were her blood vessels when she needed them? "I didn't realize it was real," she offered, as humbly as she could.

"Well, in that, we are even," Charlotte said. "We didn't realize you were real, or even possible. If we had, we would have recruited you long ago. There's so much we want to learn about you. So much we can do together to help the world recover."

Kat blinked, but she didn't have to fake her confusion this time. "What do you mean, recover? You did this. You did *all* of this, didn't you? That's why I'm here. I'm following the path that you gave me."

"Not exactly," the woman said, giving her a sympathetic smile. "You're following the escape route we created, fearing the worst would come raining down upon us. And it did. The plans that you tapped into psychically are not all of our creation, just the pathway through to survive the aftermath of the attack of the Arcana Council."

The Arcana Council? "Wait." Katana's bullshit meter was back to pinging wildly. "You mean the Shadow Court didn't attack the world?"

"Mere de Dieu, non." Charlotte's eyes flew wide. "Is that what you thought you were walking into? No wonder you look so resolute. Honestly, we were surprised that you could make it here as quickly as you did—and that you did it without being captured is nothing short of extraordinary. The Arcana Council has set its agents against us, and they employ demons to do their will. We have lost so many to the horde already, it beggars the mind."

"Ah...Demons. Employed by the Arcana Council."

"You were chased from the beginning, of course you would have seen some of them." Charlotte nodded sympathetically. "But who am I to keep you waiting like this? Come, come, there are so many people who want to meet you, to welcome you home. We learned of your story through our mystics and channeled its path...but there is so much we still do not know."

"Ah, right," Kat began, but she honestly had nothing more to say after that, so she moved into the room, following Charlotte down a long corridor. There were no guards bristling beside her, no apparent weaponry of any sort. The house, though, was undeniably beautiful, the paintings lining the walls looking expensive. "If this is a rogue operation, I'd say you're all doing pretty well for yourself."

"Yes, well, we knew that in order to be successful when the final challenge came, we would have to put all our resources into fighting for our freedom. We suspected a war like this would come hundreds of years ago. So we've had a little bit of time to get ready. But in the end, you're never actually ready, are you?"

She stepped into a doorway and held out an arm.

With the most amiable grin she could manage, Katana stepped in beside her. She didn't know what she'd expected, except maybe a fancy drawing room, people standing around with glasses of champagne. It was an elite Parisian manor after all, and in her book, in her mind, and in real life, it was all lining up. This old stone mansion really did resemble the house she'd drawn in *Dead End*.

She'd made it to Sorcerer City.

Kat's mind churned as she scanned the room, not happy that it was so...unexpected. She sure as hell hadn't imagined the room that she stepped into now, a war room with a long, central table and chairs all around, computer stations bristling at the walls, and large screens, all of them currently blank. The door opened at the far end, and men and women filed through, their faces all possessing the same indefinable element the woman did. Not attractive, necessarily. There were old and young, tall and short, fat and thin, craggy and soft, but there was something familiar and consistent about those faces that nagged at her. Had she seen people like this before, with their speculative, calculating expressions, sizing her up like a side of beef? But where—how?

She received murmurs of greeting and even a few nods of deference as Charlotte waited for them to all file in and be seated. "We are honored to finally have the opportunity to welcome Katana to our home. She followed the pathways that now exist between cities, linking us together to protect what is rightfully ours and to usher the world into a new beginning. Welcome, Katana."

A chorus of greetings sounded around the room, and Katana smiled gamely, her mind racing for suitable words to keep the conversation going. Eventually, the battalion of angels would show up, right? They had to show up.

They'd better show up.

"Look I don't know how much you guys are aware of me," she began. "But I just...I just want to help. To undo anything that I did wrong. I don't know anything about the Arcana Council or their demons."

"That's where you're wrong," Charlotte said, her face soft with understanding. "You had no idea the danger you were in, and we couldn't help you. We couldn't do anything but try to intercept you, and even that proved a failure. We staged the fake attack on Emily Green's office with her willing participation. She's one of ours, you know."

Kat deliberately widened her eyes as much as possible,

reminding herself that this was all bullshit. Really *great* bullshit, but bullshit. "One of yours? Seriously? But she..."

The chaos got louder in her mind as the first trickle of doubt leeched into her resolve. Kat hadn't known Emily had existed until her agent had introduced them six months ago. She'd only delivered her finished manuscript yesterday. And Emily had been frightened, legitimately frightened, when Kat and Hugh had found her. Hadn't she?

"She was scared," Kat said out loud. "How could she have been a part of this plan and be so scared?"

"Well, you can excuse her. Not everybody can handle being so close to a demon as you. And Hugh of the Syx is one of the worst."

"I'm sorry?" Kat protested, but more feebly, as the screens that lined the war room flickered on, then were filled with startlingly horrible images. The slavering horde of demons in Montmartre were replicated in cities around the globe. Kat didn't know all the cities, she hadn't traveled that much, but image after image of demon-like creatures attacking terrified humans filled the screens.

And in one, the unmistakable form of Hugh the Destroyer ran snarling past a cluster of cemetery markers. Kat jolted. In his wake ran the three other warriors that she recognized from the cemetery. They had battled together like a unit—like they'd been doing it for years. Like they were brothers.

"What are you saying?" she asked flatly. *Really great bullshit*, she reminded herself. *Really...great.*

"Only what you have already suspected, but were wise enough not to betray to save your own life, and to save countless others," the woman said. "The world is overrun with demons, and these Syx... They are mankind's deadliest enemies."

26

"Whaddya got for me, Finn?" Hugh asked. They were huddled in a small coffee shop that had just opened for the morning, the petite barista behind the bar staring at six hulking men and a spiky-haired female who more than held her own. Finn was working on some sort of souped-up smartphone that should have been able to track Katana—but wasn't.

"A whole lot of deeply unhappy bullshit," Finn said. "We lost her as soon as she cleared the borders of Montmartre, the lingering effects of the breath of God knocking out any trace of her. She didn't turn a phone on, so that's no good, and the homing device you slipped onto her laptop is being jammed. So that's good and bad. The good news is, she definitely made it to where she needed to go. She's in the belly of the beast. The bad news is, we don't know where the beast is."

"I can find her without your tech," Hugh growled.

"Yeah, well, that's great, but if she's being held against her will, it might not be a great idea for us to go in guns blazing," Finn countered. "And remember, we've got a bigger mission here. Not that Katana isn't central to that mission, but we need to understand what the Shadow Court is planning, who they're going to hit next, and, ideally, how they're using the demons. Not to mention how they plan to use Katana and other Connecteds like her. People who didn't even know of their skills before all this shit went down are now running around like firecrackers waiting to be lit."

Raum cocked a brow at Finn. He and Stefan had been yanked back to the Syx for this next campaign as well. Clearly, Death wasn't taking any chances. "I don't think you're using that metaphor correctly," he murmured.

"Whatever," Finn said, flapping his hand. "We've got a whole lot of crazy happening right now, and we don't know jack. Our number one goal is to get intel and…"

"Give it to who?" Gregori asked quietly. "The archangel is gone. The Arcana Council is broken. Humanity has more access to magic, wild though it may be, than it ever had before. There will be chaos and death no matter what we do. And who are we to set ourselves up as arbiters in this war? If the humans want to kill themselves, why shouldn't we let them?"

"Ooh, harsh," Finn said, "but there's a slight flaw with your reasoning there, O Giant Grumpy One."

"I welcome it," Gregori shot back.

"One, the AC may be busted up, but they still make up what's left of the most powerful sorcerers on earth. And they have an avowed interest in keeping the balance of magic intact, fucked-up though that balance may be."

"We also have groups not affiliated with the Council, the houses of magic, the witches, and, like it or not, the arcane black market," Warrick put in. "Those who are not the toadies of the Shadow Court, but who are making their living doing the best they can. All are children of God. And all are our charge. So even if they are determined to kill each other, we are officially opposed."

"But we *officially* don't have much say in the matter. We're not humans," Gregori rumbled. "They have free will. If it's their choice to kill each other, they can. The magic that's flooding the earth is a gift of the Father. When angels were first called down as Fallen, they failed in teaching His children how to use that magic. Perhaps now we'll have a second chance at it."

"You really think we're going to be any more successful?" Stefan protested. He stood closest to the door to the coffeehouse, keeping watch. "The spawn are flooding the earth. The bad guys look damn close to the good guys, and the Arcana Council is MIA. We've got doll makers channeling us into children's toys and comic book writers changing the world. Who's to say what our right path is?"

"The archangel already did," Hugh said, irritation spiking. "He led us to Katana. She's important to it all, and I will not just *sit* here while you—"

"Hold on to your hats," Finn interrupted, not looking up from his screen. "We've got movement."

"What kind of movement?" Hugh snapped.

"Full on psychic what-the-fuckery, that's what. Astral projection shit like nobody's business, augmented with some kickass tech. Concentrated right up the street from us, Rue de l'Abreuvoir. I bet you dollars to doughnuts they've got our girl."

"Astral projection?" Hugh asked. "I wouldn't include that among Katana's abilities."

Finn shrugged. "I'm not saying it's her. I'm saying there's a whole lot of tech happening right now linked up with Connected ability. It's tipping the scales high enough that my money's on astral projection, but it's a whole lot of something, that's for sure."

That seemed reasonable to Hugh—and to be honest, he didn't know the limits of Katana's powers. None of them did. "Okay, so where is she?"

"Like I said, close. We've got a problem, though. She's not asking for your help. And we ain't got an archangel to send you anywhere he damn well pleases. We're pretty awesome, but we don't do transpo." He eyed Warrick. "Can you get us in there?"

Warrick hesitated. "I can, but I'm not sure if I'd be delivering us into a trap."

"Fine," Hugh said. "Then we get there on foot and bang on the front door."

"Oh, for fuck's sake," Blue said. "I can get you inside any of those mansions. We'll have to go In Between, but as long as none of you are going to be delicate about that, it's the fastest way. Montmartre is deeply tied to the In Between, especially the homes on that particular street. I can get you in."

A few minutes later, they stood at the edge of a dimly lit tunnel, which had been dank, but not wet. Blue had come through on her promise, but none of the demons looked too happy about it. Nevertheless, they now stood at the doorway into the cellar of the largest mansion on Rue de l'Abreuvoir, with Finn's psychometer pinging deep into the red zone.

"That was clean, at least," Hugh offered. "No rats."

"I'll send your regards to the housekeepers," Death said drily. She fixed him with narrowed eyes. "I am not the archangel, Hugh. I don't know your path, I only know that it's unfinished. But if I have to come back to usher your soul somewhere, I'm going to be pissed."

Hugh gave a mirthless laugh. "Well, in that case, you

have no worries, daughter of the Celts. I have no soul to ferry anywhere. That's not how any of this works."

"Yours is a curious creator," she muttered, and he laughed.

"So is yours, priestess. So is yours."

27

*K*at forced herself to keep watching the screens despite the fact that they were filled with violence, if only to keep her expression neutral. So Hugh was a demon after all—at least according to Charlotte, who'd dropped that bomb to scare Kat to pieces.

But was she scared? Did she even care? It was possible Charlotte was lying, but Kat had seen too many videos now, and Hugh simply looked too...right.

And the chaos in her mind had dropped to a low ebb.

Hugh was a demon.

And the crazy thing was...Kat wasn't even surprised. She didn't know why—or how—but everything suddenly felt right in her world. Ordered. The chaos peeling away to reveal something else beneath that she still couldn't quite see.

She was aware that Charlotte was watching her closely, however, so she couldn't focus only on Hugh. She shifted her attention to the older woman. "I assume you're showing this to me for a reason?"

"Does any of it look familiar to you?"

Kat lifted her brows. Was this some kind of test? "You know it doesn't. If you're working with Emily, you have a copy of the book I submitted, and you know what I thought was going to happen. Some of it has, but some of it hasn't— and now everything around it has changed. So I'm not sure how much I can help you."

"Oh, but you can," Charlotte said. "You have a remarkable skill. You can cast forward in time the likely outcomes of any particular course of action. The images appear to you like a map forward. Such a map would be very helpful in any case, but particularly when we're experiencing such a rapidly changing turn of events. None of this is anything we planned for. All of it is sheer possibility. Any path, any turn, flows forward from you like dominoes that fall in succession to an eventual end. We need your help to know which path to take."

Kat made a face. "I already had a map planned out where there was peace. The dark forces seeking to subjugate humanity were knocked back, and magic flowed to all. I just need to sync back up with that timeline and it technically could happen again."

As she thought about it, those images were pulled back into her mind. She nodded, seeing the colors shift, the images warp and weave, imagining how it could come together. This was her story, dammit. She could write it.

"It wouldn't be that difficult," she continued, sliding her pack around. "I just need—"

"Actually, we have a different plan in mind," Charlotte interrupted her. "What you saw, the future you foretold, may have worked for your fictional story. But played out in real life, it's not as useful. The power that's currently accessible is too much for most people to handle. Only a select few can really manage it without causing grave destruction. You are one of those few, which is why you could imagine it in the first place. And eventually, with time and preparation, the utopia that you foresaw is possible. But not right away. For the initial rollout of this magic to work for the greater good, only the top, most capable psychics can have access to it, so they can bend it to their will for the good of all."

"I get what you're saying, but I don't think it's that complicated," Kat hedged. "The magical cores are intense at the heart of each hell block, but I bet the farther away you get from the center, the more it would resonate harmlessly with a psychic of even moderate ability. And of course, individuals who don't have any psychic ability wouldn't be affected at all. Though honestly, if they knew how, everyone in the world could open themselves up to this power. And once it gets accessed, it diminishes, you see? So spread it around to enough people, and everybody benefits, while it doesn't overwhelm anyone. It wouldn't even take that much time."

"No, Katana," Charlotte countered, almost sadly. "The resource of this new release of magic can't be squandered across thousands of undeserving minds,. Some they will simply burn out. And others—"

"But it won't burn anyone out," Kat protested, still trying to keep the game going. "I guess that's possible, but that's not how I envisioned it. And if I don't envision people's heads exploding, then there's at least a fighting chance it won't happen, right?"

The woman flattened her lips into a disapproving scowl. "I appreciate your confidence in your own abilities, but we have a responsibility to ensure the safety of those connected who are not as mentally equipped to handle an influx of magic. Their minds—"

"That's what I'm trying to *tell* you," Kat said, a deep sense of certainty welling up within her. She might have started this tale by spinning bullshit to stall for time, but she was right. She knew she was right. "If a psychic's mind can't handle this new influx of magic, it'll roll over them like, I don't know, like a breeze—not like a wave that will drown them, but literally a breeze that'll barely ruffle their hair. But if they *can* handle it, or if they can expand their minds to handle it, maybe with a little training or something like that..."

"Again, what you're suggesting is certainly a utopia that we all aspire to," Charlotte said, now sounding a little strained. "But perhaps the best way to go about this is to follow two potential paths. How does that sound? One where the world has no checks or balances against the spread of and access to this new magic, and another in which our organization serves as stewards to ensure the safe rollout of such access. Would you be willing to consider that as a possibility? We have scribes in place right now who are able to take down your ideas, illustrators who can expand on your vision and begin bringing it into life. Better than either of those, we have the technology to parse through any potential path and identify how we can be most successful. We'll start with the stewardship scenario and then roll straight into the rapid expansion unchecked."

"But..." Kat understood that she was treading on thin ice here, but she needed to process what she was learning. There was a *system* to her imagination process, dammit. You couldn't take two potential paths at once. You had to follow one until you chose differently.

Or did she have to do that? Had she ever really had to do that?

"All right," she said slowly. "We can start the process, keeping the outcome vague. If the end result is magical access for all, then I see your point about an intermediate step of stewardship. I'll just build that into the equation. And then there won't be any backtracking necessary once we identify the safety parameters we need to put in place. I can see that. Yes, that'll work."

She looked around, still feeling strangely alone. The expressions of the men and women seated at the conference table were no longer quite so welcoming, and Charlotte looked strangely sad. Disapproving and sad.

"We'd hoped to do this with your full charismatic powers to bear, but I think you don't understand that we will do this one way or another," Charlotte said, her voice gradually growing louder and sharper. "We have computers to add in the equations, as you call it. What we need from you is your mind—fully and unreservedly."

"I mean..."

But the woman talked over her. "We've employed some of the most effective scientists in the field of neural stimulation and are quite adept at securing the results that we need after a little trial and error, Katana. Sometimes that trial and error can become uncomfortable, but I'm afraid you're leaving us no choice."

She gestured, and two new individuals entered the room, neither one looking particularly menacing, except for the slim black case the taller of the two men held in his hands.

Well, this wasn't part of any story I wrote, dammit. This part was starting to distinctly suck.

"Hello, Katana," the tall man said.

Without much choice, Kat turned her attention to him as two more men entered the room, and a third beside them, standing farther back in the shadows. The one who'd spoken to her looked like a skinnier version of Gable

Sizemore, only not as likable. He adjusted his square glasses and peered at her.

"Your mother told us all about you. Did you know you heard the noise that so plagues you at a very early age? Practically since birth? Do you recall trying to speak with that noise at the age of two—and then at three, and four? That was when she finally contacted us."

"Um...no?" And after a beat, her eyes flew open. "You knew my mother? My actual *mother*?"

Chaos stirred, and Kat's breath seemed to dwindle in her lungs. She dropped the thread of the story she was trying to write, wanting so desperately to reach for a different thread. A far older thread. "How did you know my mother?"

The man eyed her almost sadly. "She knew you would be best served by being cared for by us. Alas, it was not to be. But now, that noise is what we are looking to help you with. By helping you express your thoughts and images more clearly, we will help you tame that noise."

"Well, I don't really want it tamed..." Kat began.

"Enough," Charlotte interrupted, her voice clipped. "Secure her."

"Hey now." That was enough to get Kat back on track, albeit a moment too late. Stupid old story thread! She didn't have time to be distracted. "That's not necessary. I promise."

She glanced around the room, suddenly aware that the men surrounding the Gable Sizemore knockoff weren't moving like the other people in the room, with their innate sense of ease and sophistication. These were hard men, efficient and strong, and when they sidled up to her and clamped her arms into her sides, she struggled. One lifted a hand with a strange, narrow cylinder in his fingers, and Charlotte's voice rang out, curt and absolute.

"No. We're not sedating her. We don't have that kind of time."

She turned toward Kat. "You fail to understand the constraints we're dealing with here. The Arcana Council could strike again at any moment, rendering our access to this magic null and void, using it as a means to destroy."

"Let *go* of me," Kat growled. "You can't force me to work for you. That's not how this works."

Charlotte's smile turned brittle. "I don't think you're grasping your situation. Our process of working with psychics is effective, but not fully painless. You will give us the images and the story we need, and you will mark the path. With your brain in the throes of the power of suggestion, we will connect you to a network of servers capable of processing a great deal of input to extract the information. You're not the first person with this talent, Katana. Remember, you were marked for our use when you were very young. Perhaps we'll be more successful with you, preserving your mind when we're through, but I don't hold much hope."

The energy in the room shifted, and Kat's gaze darted around the table, hoping desperately for support. None of the men or women at the table offered any change of expression. They all watched her with a strange, almost avaricious intensity, as if they were reveling in her skills... and in their ability to control them.

She squinted toward the back of the room, where more men stood—and she nearly gasped. One of the men was slightly taller than the others, but still nondescript, and he stared at her with an intensity that nearly ripped the breath out of her body.

His eyes gleamed purple.

No! Kat thought, as hard as she could. *Oh my God, Hugh,*

no. Angel, demon, whatever he was, he couldn't be here. She could still work this out on her own. She had a plan, the barest scraps of a plan, anyway, and she could almost— almost!—see how it ended. But Hugh had to stay safe. The world needed him more than she ever could. Kat fought back a furious sob. If they harmed him—if they *dared*…

Katana… His cry echoed faintly in her mind, buried in the roar of chaos bearing down.

As she choked back a desire to scream, the men holding her tightened their grasp, and the Gable knockoff moved forward. He clicked open his slim black case, and Kat blinked to see the long slender syringe nestled inside.

"What the fuck is *that*?" she asked.

"A unique blend of neurotoxins with some technical amplifications," he informed her briskly. He glanced over to his support goons. "Her head, if you will."

As he pulled the syringe free, Kat glared at him with all the fury, indignation, and disdain she could muster.

"*No*."

28

*H*ugh rushed forward just as Katana lunged.

He had read the intent in her gaze loud and clear. She hadn't wanted him to interfere, not yet. There was still something she was working out about the situation. There was fear in her eyes and also mistrust. Mistrust of him? He hadn't had time to decide before the surge of motion.

He dashed forward, but instead of Katana attempting to lurch away from the man and his syringe, she wrenched herself forward, grabbing for the syringe. Her gambit seemed to work. Wrestling the needle free, she jabbed it into her arm and depressed the plunger a few millimeters, before ripping it out again and hurling it across the room to shatter against a wall. Then she wheeled around as white clouds exploded out from the ceiling.

What in the *hell*?

Smoke filled the space, dropping the humans where they stood or sat, Katana as well. Then a new group ran in, fully masked and toting guns.

Hugh had to admit, that was a pretty neat trick. The gas

cut down completely on the chaos usually associated with an attack. If Hugh hadn't been here, the Shadow Court would have been able to subdue Katana without any additional harm done, waking up all the sleepy one-percenters once the excitement was over.

Only...he *was* here.

Hugh reached Katana in three long strides and gathered her up, lifting her boneless body and rushing from the room through one of the back doors. Lasers arced after him, piercing his skin to no effect. He heard the crash in the back of the conference room as the rest of the Syx attacked, and he grinned. Katana had done her job. She'd opened up the citadel and allowed the good guys in.

Now he had to make sure she was okay.

"Wake up," he growled to her, still moving quickly. When she didn't respond, he stopped in the middle of the empty, elegantly decorated hallway, then leaned down and fit his mouth over hers. With one demonic inhale, he drew in the smoke that filled her lungs. He couldn't help anything that had already been synthesized into her bloodstream—either from the smoke or the needle—but he needed to suck out enough to wake her the fuck up.

It worked. Katana jolted in his arms, and he drew back as she gasped and coughed, her eyes lit up with urgency.

"There's a computer somewhere," she managed, twisting around in his arms. "I'm connected to it—and need to be more connected. But to get there I have to...I have to leave and come back again, a maze within a maze."

As she spoke, the walls of the corridor blurred. With no further warning, a half dozen doorways appeared, leading to alternate locations—rooms, streets, open fields—at various times of the day and night. Kat turned to the left, then back to the right.

"This," she said, and all the other portals shifted. "Then this, then this," she said in rapid succession. "Then this."

A final portal slammed open, and she threw up her hands and wheeled back. "That's not right, I didn't choose... What's going on?"

She turned wildly toward Hugh, terror skating across her face. "Does this person mean something to you?"

Hugh looked in confusion into the portal where she was pointing, then shot forward, leaping through it without hesitation.

"*Michael,*" he roared.

The archangel lay in some sort of cave. He was pinioned to a board, with dozens of thick metal nails piercing his skin, and blood coursed down his naked body. His face was tilted back, his skin burnished black from burns.

"Stay back," he yelled belatedly to Kat, but she had crashed through right next to him, skidding to a stop on the stone floor.

"I can't leave you," she gasped. "You're part of the story I'm creating. I can't see the ending if you are not *in* it."

She turned and flinched again at the archangel's ravaged face. "Is he dead?"

Hugh eyed Michael and shook his head. "He probably damn well wishes he was. But we wouldn't be here if this wasn't necessary, right? If this wasn't the right path."

Katana nodded. "We wouldn't."

She turned back to him, but her eyes lifted to fix on a space over his shoulder. "The story continues without us. There are others moving through the house. Men like you. Demons."

Hugh grimaced. "I wondered when you were going to figure that out."

"They told me, but I already knew." She smiled a little wryly. "No angel could be so good at killing."

"Oh, I wouldn't sell them short." He turned back to the archangel, grunted. "I don't know how to get him off this thing without hurting him more."

"I do." She held up a hand and made a fist. The spiked nails impaling the archangel dwindled to mere filaments, then shot free from the board, rushing toward them both before erupting into flames.

Hugh shook his head in disbelief. Unfortunately, Michael still hung in place, skewered on nothing at all.

"Why didn't it work?" he asked.

"I...I don't know." Kat looked around. "Anything is possible within the laws of this dimension, but apparently, that doesn't include freeing this man from his torment. God wouldn't constrain him so brutally, would he? I think he's doing it to himself."

"Now *that* I can believe." Hugh stalked up to Michael, fury kindling his nerves and lighting his blood as he got right up in the archangel's face, then reached beyond him to grab the edge of the wooden panel. "Look, bright boy. You will *not* fucking go off on some sabbatical of pain when we've got work to do."

He ripped the panel off the wall. The archangel's body fell forward, but didn't break free. Instead, it hung wetly, blood seeping out.

"He's still bleeding," Katana whispered.

Hugh gritted his teeth. "He's seriously hard to kill. But that's not stopping him from trying."

He shook Michael's pallet. "Do you know how *pissed* Blue is going to be if you succeed?"

That generated a reaction. The archangel's eyelids

fluttered. "She cannot know," he moaned, so faintly that Hugh barely heard him.

"What do you mean she can't know? Of course she can."

"No..." Michael coughed, blood dampening his lips. "She must lead the 144th."

Hugh's eyes nearly shot straight out of his skull as he imagined the shadowy angelic squadron that no one knew too much about—supposedly one hundred and forty four thousand rogue angels, not one of them allowed a name. "*What?* No. Those assholes are one monkey shy of a full-on circus. She'll never be able to control them."

"Nevertheless, it...it is the only path. Every weapon must be brought to bear to protect God's children." Michael sighed. "Even me."

And the ground opened beneath him, flames leaping high as both Hugh and Katana staggered back. The archangel threw back his head and howled. Then he was consumed by the fire.

"What was *that*?" Katana demanded. "Where did he go?"

Hugh could only stare as the fire winked out. "Apparently, our fearless leader has decided to sail through yet another circle of hell. But I don't have any sense of him. I wouldn't even know where to look. You?"

She focused...then slumped. "No. No—and we have to go back, like, right now. I have to—" But even as she whirled back to the portal where they'd entered, the door slammed shut. She spun around, and it was the scene in the corridor all over again. Doors, windows, holes in the ground. Opening and closing on endless repeat.

"What's happening?" Hugh gritted out.

"These people—the Shadow Court, whoever the hell they are, they have a computer," Katana said, her eyes narrowing in concentration as she tracked the flashing doorways. "I'm connected to it. I have been since the moment I stepped inside and that bitch jabbed me in the hand. I could feel it starting to map me, but didn't understand what it was doing. Now it's going deeper— tracking my thoughts, parsing my paths. It's creating stories based on what I've laid out for it, and taking the next natural step."

"Well, you've got to stop it," Hugh insisted.

"I'm *working* on that," she retorted. "I thought sucking in some of the neurotoxin would help, but it only seems to make it worse. To stop the program, I'd have to stop thinking, and if that happens..."

Hugh held up his hands, warding off that thought. "Don't stop thinking, no. It's the other way around. You need to think faster than the computer."

Now she did send him a withering glare. "That's kind of the whole point of computers, Hugh."

"You can do it, though. I've seen how your mind works. You can imagine how to make it work."

"I can't." She lifted her hands to her temples and flinched as if she'd been slapped. "You don't understand. Anything I come up with, it can come up with too, a second after me."

He chuckled. It wasn't a pleasant sound...it wasn't supposed to be. "But it can't predict what you'll *think*, Katana. It can't get out ahead of you. And it sure as hell can't predict me."

He ripped a knife free from his belt and plunged it toward her heart.

29

*K*at screamed. In one part of her mind, she couldn't believe what she was seeing, but the other part of her mind was transfixed by Hugh's gaze. It was filled with hatred, anger, everything she'd seen in the images that had been shown to her by Charlotte DuBois.

Even as her mind raced to overturn her fear, the primal human panic at seeing such a hideously ugly creature slashing toward her with curved, poison dripping talons, blanked her mind with horror. All the walls fell away again, and only one entry loomed open.

Hugh roared and scooped her up, leaping through it. They crashed onto a marble floor.

"What *now*?" he snarled, still in full-on demon mode. "Where are we?"

"The computer room," Katana gasped, taking in the computer consoles, the sensory pad she suspected served as the interface between psychic and machine. "I know this place. I saw it in my mind."

"What?" With a growling effort, Hugh dropped back into the form she'd come to think of as his. But who or what was he, really? Was he the fearsome demon, the beautiful angel, the larger-than-life man, or some mixture of all three? And what about the creature she saw in the cave that he'd called Michael...as in Michael the Archangel. How was that even possible, that the highest angel of God would be treated in such a horrific way? How did that make sense?

What was the world hurtling toward if those who were gods were so cruel and unforgiving, and those who were human were not much better?

"We have to fight it, don't we?" she whispered to the array of computers. "That's why this is happening. That's what I can do. You and me. We have to turn back the tide of power to those who wish to make their own way. You want to know what I know? You want to keep up with my mind? Then teach me what you can do."

"You're talking to computers now?" Hugh asked her in a low, strangled voice. "You're a fucking computer whisperer?"

Kat smiled, despite herself. "Shut up, my beautiful demon."

He shut up.

Straining her mind to the utmost, Kat turned to the console and imagined that she could feel the hum of the nanobots within her turning too. Part of her recoiled at the idea of connecting with a system built by those who would keep humanity beholden to the rich and the powerful. Gods by another name. But only part.

Because, as with everything, there remained some kernel of right thinking in the Shadow Court's path, some truth that had to be resolved. The Shadow Court wanted the power for themselves, but they weren't wrong about the likelihood of the common man to screw up their chance at mastering this windfall of magic. It wasn't only likely, it was probable that people would die, lives would be ruined. And

Kat wasn't a god either, to know who should be saved and who could be sacrificed. That level of thinking and computation was way above her pay grade for sure.

But not above the incredible creation of human engineering before her.

"Teach me," she said again, lifting her hands to the computer console. "What am I missing? How can we move forward without destroying ourselves? There has to be a way."

She laid her hands upon the sensor pad, then jolted as a wave of electricity burst through her, emanating from her hands and radiating through her whole body. She felt electrified, her nerve endings stretching taut, her blood practically fizzing in her veins. Around her, the screens began to crackle with imagery and noise...

And it was as if her mind was given a medium it could *finally* use to create.

Chaos descended. Visuals splashed across the monitors, thick lines slashing, curling, squaring off and jolting forward, bright primary colors bursting in violent confusion over every screen. She couldn't direct it or fully see it. She could only endure. Allowing the images to form and gain solidity before an equal and opposite force shattered them again, causing her to start over.

Over and over, she created systems for humans to master magic, paths of teaching, planning, opportunities...and over and over, she saw war lurch back into motion. Sometimes immediately, sometimes distant, but it always came. There was no peace to be had with magic filling the world. There was no utopia. She even attempted to follow the likely path that the Shadow Court had so craved, where a rarified few controlled the magic of all. But that way proved flawed as well, resulting not only in the death and destruction of people and lives, but in the gradual loss of magic altogether as it was rushed back into oblivion, and those with psychic abilities were forced once more to hide their light.

Over and over again she made the attempt, and she witnessed futures she could barely conceive. A council of sorcerers broken and bloody on a battlefield. Lightning arcing across the sky, ushering in a new rule of ancient gods. The rising up of an army of psychic warriors whose expertise was hired out to the highest bidder in countries rich enough to pay.

But in the end, there was only one outcome that assured that magic would not bring about the chaos and destruction of mankind, and that was that there be no magic in the world at all.

Which of course, wasn't possible...because magic existed in every living thing.

"I can't." She finally crumbled, unsurprised to feel Hugh's strong arms around her, cradling her close.

How long had he been holding her? How long had he stood with her and for her as she had traversed every possible computation, as she tried to save the world from itself? Tears ran down her face, her lips were dry and cracked. Her teeth chattered.

"I can't," she moaned again. "There's no way forward to peace with magic in the world. There should be, but there isn't."

"Then there isn't," Hugh said simply. "So what's the best way forward short of that goal?"

She shook her head, her eyes still clenched shut, her mind fixed on a thousand churning visions. "I was wrong on that as well. The bulk of magic must go to the few, not the many, for only the few can use it. It would be like giving a set of car keys to a camel. Not only does the camel not need the car, but it can't do anything with it, anyway. The camel needs water, and the only person who can get it is the person who knows how to drive the car to go fetch it."

"So magic *can* exist in service to others," Hugh said. "That's a start, right?"

Kat's eyes shot open, seeing it now. Seeing all of it.

"A start." She nodded, straightening, though Hugh didn't let her go. "Yeah. A start. Some people will use it that way, others will suck—exploiting the people they can, killing the ones they can't. But we'll have schools of magic to help those who want to learn. Academies devoted to marshaling this new force and giving it structure."

"An academy of magic?" Hugh sounded skeptical. "On a worldwide scale?"

"A directorate too," she said. She could see so much more. "Those who wish to learn will find ways to learn, but they must be policed and justice rendered. It'll take some time, though."

He hugged her close. "Then we'll take that time. And for as long as we need to, we will protect the Connecteds of this world as best we can."

"In the end, we can't do even that," she mumbled, her words slurred and soft. "We can only let them rise up and protect themselves—just like you told them they could, Hugh, all those years ago."

And she laid her head upon his chest and finally slept.

30

*H*ugh looked up to see the Syx at the back of the computer room. How long they'd been there, he had no idea. "What did you do with the Shadow Court?" he asked, more aware than ever of the frail human in his arms.

Warrick fielded the question. "Death brought in some doctor who does the dirty work for the Council. She removed their memories."

Hugh blinked. "She what?"

"Clean slate," Finn confirmed, not bothering to hide his glee. "Last couple of weeks are gone-zo for them, which arguably were some pretty damn important weeks if you're a megalomaniac psychic one-percenter. There are still plenty of these assholes out in the world, but at least we cut out the heart. We've also got the hard drive of the computer they were using, which was networked sixty-five ways to Sunday into the Shadow Court's mainframe. We don't have the expertise to deal with that, but somebody will. Maybe whoever runs this directorate like Katana was talking about."

Hugh winced. "You heard that?"

Warrick harrumphed. "We heard enough. It's never a good idea to let humans police themselves, but we've got other problems, according to Stefan. Some of the hell blocks are poisonous to the demons they're drawing into them."

Hugh made a face. "Poisonous in what way?"

"Not in any way you want," Warrick said. "It's turning a particularly vicious subset of the spawn into creatures that are dangerous and deadly, but killable by humans. Now these rovers have been let loose on earth, which in some ways is better than demons, but in others, worse. Because the rovers have a taste for human blood...whereas demons are just assholes unless you rile them up."

"Shit," Hugh muttered.

"My thoughts exactly." Warrick yawned with bone-cracking weariness. "So not only are the humans going to have to figure out how to handle a hell of a lot more magic than they're used to, but they're gonna need a quick course in killing mongrel demon dogs. As well as an education on how to avoid actual demons. Which means they're going to need to know a hell of a lot more about them. What's more, that miniaturist in New Jersey just posted about his warrior angel line coming to life. It's going viral."

"This keeps getting better and better," Hugh muttered.

"We'll get to him before any of the bad guys do, that's a lock. But what are we going to do with her?" Finn asked, nodding to Katana. "She looks like a long stretch of bad road."

"She needs a doctor's care, rest," Hugh said, holding her tighter to him. "Healing."

"She needs a medal," Stefan put in. "Did you see what she was doing in there in addition to playing out possible futures?"

Hugh shook his head. The connection he had with Katana did not extend to her thoughts. Those were closeted from him, even now. But the connection he had to every other part of her body had been hypersensitized. He had felt the electrical storm of power coursing through her, had sensed her anguish, learned her truths.

"It was all I could do to keep her...alive isn't the right word, but certainly awake and coherent."

"She wrote books," Raum said, his angelic voice soft and amazed. "She wrote history books for centuries as yet unlived and manuals of instruction, healing, and possibilities. In every lifetime, in every incarnation, she wrote the tools of the trades that she envisioned. And then when she reached the end and destruction rained down, she destroyed the path, but not the books of magic or the history of what now will never be. It was as if the words came to her first, the images after."

Hugh could only stare at him. "You're kidding me."

Raum shook his head. "We don't know where those books were being made, not all of them. But there are copies of them in Justice Hall now, and with the witches' covens. We can't know whether or not some of them have fallen into the hands of those who would use them to do harm."

"That's something we never could have predicted anyway," Warrick groused.

"True enough," Raum said. "And then there is the question of the archangel. We saw him again, briefly, after he left you both."

Hugh made a face. "Let me guess. He was at the bottom of the ocean practicing drowning himself over and over again. Or maybe wandering in the Himalayas trying to see how many parts of his body he could knock off with frostbite."

Raum's lips twisted. "We all know what it's like to live with a sin you never intended to commit—or worse, one that you committed in full knowledge of the consequences."

"Yeah, but we need him," Finn put in. "We can't finish our path until he stops throwing a pity party for himself."

Gregori's chuckle was low and dark. "I can assure you, if he's doing this to himself, he has lost the understanding of his original role. His mind is fragile and wants to be fully broken. By the time we recover him, he could well be mad."

"And Death?" Hugh asked.

"She's searching the database that Katana helped create," Warrick said. "The histories of all the world's possible futures. In them, she expects to find glimpses of the archangel, possibilities of where she can track him down."

Hugh nodded. It was a good idea. "Does he die in any of those futures?"

"Based on the amount of cursing we heard from the computer room, I think it's safe to say the answer to that question is yes," Warrick said. "But she keeps on looking, which makes me believe there are still possibilities as yet unexplored."

"Well, at least we've got something new to kill while she's figuring that out," Finn said. "These rovers that sucked in too much fairy dust are no joke. We're going to have a whole lot of beast mojo on our hands, mark my words. Some of the humans are going to be aces at killing them, but a whole hell of a lot are going to get chewed up like lunch meat until they get with the program."

"Will we be summoned to their aid without the archangel here?" Hugh wondered.

"Oh, I don't think we'll have any problem finding stuff to occupy our time." Finn chuckled. "It's just going to get more interesting."

Warrick looked up. "She summons us."

A moment later, they were gathered back in the hotel room in Vienna, Death studying them with bruised, haunted eyes.

"Take Katana through the ancient pathways to Dublin," she said to Hugh. "There's a healer there who knows something of the wild curative magic, which is all that's left to us until the Magician chooses to return or to seed his power into a new vessel."

Hugh was too tired to argue. "Dublin?"

"Yes. There's a reason why it's been chosen as a location for all things magic throughout the millennia. Echoes of the future gliding to the past. She will recover there, but you must keep careful watch. Her dreams and memories contain pieces of all that's possible now and evermore. It's a heavy burden. But for now, let her rest peacefully without the stench of sulfur in her nose."

Hugh stood, and when their gazes locked, he wondered when she'd slept last. Or when she might sleep again.

"Did he say anything to you?" she asked Hugh.

He squinted, trying to remember. "Yes. But they were a jumble of words, broken and in pieces. He said it wasn't finished and there was more work to do."

She narrowed her eyes at him. He wondered if she could see through him to the truth. But his very best skill was lying, and he wasn't going to tell this formidable woman that she would be forced to marshal the most maniacal subset of all of God's creations, the angels of the 144th. He wouldn't wish that fate on anyone.

Death turned away from him to glare at Raum.

"I now know your path," she said. "It appeared too many times in too many futures before they were ripped away for it to be a mistake. Which means I know your sin.

You *have* to be redeemed in order for any of this to make sense."

Raum shrugged. "We weren't pulled into this world to make sense of it. Give me my assignment, and I will do my best. But you more than anyone know how many times I have failed to achieve it."

"More than a few," she offered.

He smiled, though there was no humor in it. "More than a few," he agreed.

"But not *every* time," Finn put in brightly. "So what you're saying is, we've still got a chance."

31

*H*ugh stepped out of the brick archway as Kat came to, feeling like she was being forced to haul herself out of a very deep well.

"What is this place?" she mumbled. "What's going on?"

He squinted at the odd little violet brownstone shoved up between two equally odd looking buildings on the cobblestoned street...but in this town, he'd found buildings like this on every corner, no green smoke required. "We're in Dublin, Ireland. Have you been here before?"

"Dublin?" she echoed faintly. "No. I haven't even been to Dublin, Pennsylvania. How did we... Oh." Her brows lifted as she took in the misshapen building in front of them. "I didn't realize those would still be around. Are we supposed to go through it?"

He helped her to her feet, grateful she was willing to lean against him. "Maybe, but not yet. Right now, you're supposed to not think about anything except getting better. There's a healer in the city that Blue knows. We're supposed to look her up after a couple of days, but only after a couple of days. Until then, we're supposed to stay in the, ah,

Shamrock Bed and Breakfast." He winced. "I'm not making this up."

"For two days?" Katana asked weakly, flailing her hand until she reassured herself that she was still carrying her pack. "I guess I have my laptop, and maybe I can reconnect with that mainframe..."

Hugh snorted. "I think that sort of defeats the purpose of rest and relaxation, but either way, let's find this place. She wouldn't have sent us here without a good reason."

"Are you sure about that?" It was a reasonable question, and even more reasonable a half hour later as they stood in front of an idyllic little house tucked around the corner from a bustling park. "Is this place for real?"

"That's what the sign says." Hugh creaked open the door and ushered Kat into the tiny courtyard. A white paver walkway bisected the space, which was teeming with trees and flowers, the temperature easily twenty degrees cooler on this side of the stone wall. She stepped up onto the porch and rang the doorbell, then turned as Hugh issued a soft grunt of surprise.

"There's a note here. It's addressed to you."

Kat picked up the card from the cute wicker table as Hugh tried the door—which was unlocked. He stepped inside as she flipped the card over to read it.

Miss Midland, I understand from an old friend that you'll need some lodging for a few days. Couldn't do better than Shamrock Bed and Breakfast. Nip around to the shop when you're feeling more yourself. I'll be back in town Tuesday next, and we'll talk. I understand that you've a knack for blending things together, and that's something I did as well, once upon a long time ago.

It was signed only "T."

"Katana?" Hugh's voice from inside the house drew her attention. She stepped in, startled to see that the place was no bigger than a few rooms, all of which were visible from the front door. There was a tidy kitchen, a bedroom straight back, and the living area. All decorated and sparkling white with bits of taupe and gray, gray furniture and a grayish-taupe paneled floor. Kat pursed her lips. It looked like a doll house version of Sorcia Steele's apartment in New York. On one wall hung all her sketches from her childhood. On another hung a startlingly vivid painting of the cover of a graphic novel, showing a heroine racing toward a misshapen house of violet brick, the title *DEAD END* beneath her booted feet.

Hugh looked at her. "Have you been here before?"

"Never."

"Think hard. Did you ever imagine a space like this?"

"I don't think so..." She hesitated. So much had happened in the last few days that it was impossible to remember what she had dreamed up and what she had drawn versus what she had simply dreamed, not even in conscious wakefulness. Had she imagined this haven into being? If she did, she at least knew there was going to be coffee in the morning.

"It's just..." she said again, and wandered forward, peeking into the kitchen with its tidy little two-person table and chair setup, ducking into the bedroom and noting the bathroom off the hall. "It's so small," she said.

"I don't think so," Hugh countered, his tone making her glance over to him. "Something about these walls doesn't track right. I've felt this kind of energy before."

"What do you mean?" But she drew closer to him even as the walls shifted, the windows winking out to be replaced by long flat panels, the furniture clearing away to become gleaming white tables and humming, state-of-the-art computers. Everything white, everything possible.

"It's a *studio*," Katana gasped, excitement lighting up her blood. "She's given me a studio to work in, but...what should I make?"

"Blue said you were supposed to rest," Hugh reminded her. "This will be here when you're ready for it."

"I'm ready for it now," she protested. "Only...I don't know what I could possibly start with, after having seen so much. I can't wait to begin, though. To do something—anything. There's so much we have to do..."

But Hugh only exhaled a soft, weary sigh, drawing her focus. She froze at the expression on his face, her heart clutching with panic. She'd never seen him look so haggard, before—so sad.

"Hugh?" she whispered, suddenly uncertain.

"Before you do all that, my beautiful, powerful Katana...I need to tell you something."

Hugh closed his eyes in relief as he reached for her and Katana stepped into his arms without hesitation. She sank against him, hugging him tight, but that didn't make his job any easier. There was more he had to say to her, more forgiveness he had to ask.

"You have seen the worst. You have imagined the best," he said quietly, holding her close. "In the world...but in me too. And I, especially, did not deserve it. I'm sorry, Katana. I'm sorry I lied to you, and I'm sorry I'm not the angel you believed me to be."

"Oh, Hugh..." She pulled away, those boundless gray intent on his. "Demon or angel, you're the same to me. You saved my life. Several times over. You saved the world, for heaven's sake."

He smiled a little lopsidedly. "Only because of you. I know that I will never live up to the idea of me you have in your mind—and I've seen those pictures. I've seen the beauty you imagined me to be. I think I'm mostly sorry for that."

"Hugh, stop—"

"There's more," he said. "The Syx. We're a team of enforcers. But there's a reason we've banded together. We each have sins to redeem. The sin I told you about—it wasn't my only transgression. It was simply the one that caught up to me."

"You couldn't have known those people wouldn't prepare themselves for battle."

"I did know, though. They were humans. Some were strong, but most...most were weak. Foolish. I knew the risks, and I still let them go. I betrayed them. I shouldn't have been surprised when they betrayed me."

"So much pain," she murmured, making him blink. He refocused on her, nearly flinching back from the eerie intensity of her expression, though her gaze remained fixed on a far distant mark. Had she seen those long-ago humans then, in her mind? "But how many lives have you saved since then, Hugh? How many times have you been the answer to a prayer for humans who've strayed into danger?"

"You don't under—"

"Oh, I do," she whispered. She studied him with infinite tenderness. "I'm human, remember? Sometimes we're too stupid for our own good. No guardian angel in the world could be expected to keep up with that."

He would have stopped her, interrupted, but Katana's hands tightened on him, tears brimming over her lashes.

"And I've *always* known your worth, Hugh the Destroyer—even when I didn't know who you were. It's why it hurt me so much when you abandoned me."

He reared back. "I would *never*—"

"But you did."

She broke away from him and strode over to the wall where her hand-drawn sketches were displayed in proud lockstep. She stopped at the very first picture of the set, and unhooked the picture from the wall. It was a matter of only a few moments before she pulled the slip of paper out of the frame—and she turned it over to its back and handed it to him.

"I remembered this when I was in Sorcerer City, when I finally understood why you seemed so familiar...and why, when I dreamed up my guardian angel all those months ago, it was you—and why I was pissed at you. It just took me a while to put it all together." She smiled a little sheepishly. "I was five when I drew this, though, so cut me a break."

Curious, Hugh glanced down at the page, then froze, so startled he nearly dropped the scrap of paper. Drawn on the page in an unsteady child's hand was a creature of such paralyzing ugliness, it took his breath away. Horns extended from every surface. One arm was charred black, the other dripping with blood. Lightning bolts radiated from his kneecaps, and his feet were misshapen and knotted with claws. His arms, all four of them, were flung wide, and he roared, his mouth gaping open, flat tongues of fire coming from it. His eyes were sunken deep, and they glowed a vivid purple.

Beneath the drawing, written in a bold childhood scrawl, were the words:

I LOVE YOU.

Hugh looked up at Katana, horrified. "What is this?

Surely you didn't see me in my demon form as a child. I never saw you."

"I dreamt about you," she said simply. "Over and over again, when I was a little girl. I told my mom about the dreams only once. She listened carefully, and when I got to the part where a horrifying demon killed the other demons to save a little girl like me, you know what she told me?"

He winced. "That you needed therapy?"

"No. She told me that you couldn't always judge people from how they looked on the outside, that you didn't know their story until you looked inside. And *then* she told me I was going to therapy if I ever said anything about demons again."

Hugh chuckled, but his hands still trembled as he stared down at the picture. "Demons rarely look at themselves in mirrors. I've become adept at managing my glamour to please whatever humans I encountered as I rescued them from the worst of my kind. But sometimes humans need to be rescued from their own kind too. When that happens, I still can't kill them, for all that they deserve it. I can only scare them." His lips twisted. "The Syx are very adept at scaring humans when we need to."

"You didn't scare me," Katana said. "Not then. I wanted you to save that other little girl...but I wanted you to save me too. Maybe back then I knew what I'd become, I don't know. I only knew I needed help. I needed you. And you didn't give me a second glance."

"Katana..." Hugh whispered.

She gave him a wobbly smile. "When I saw you running toward me with the beautiful face of the guardian angel that I'd dreamed about and written into my story, I didn't make the connection. It was only when you looked at me with eyes of purple fire that I started to remember.

The joy and the pain, the hope and the loss, all mixed up together."

"Yeah, well." He met her eyes. "You can never trust a demon."

She lifted her hand, drew it along his cheek. "But I *do* trust you, Hugh. I trust you to be you—always."

The love in her voice nearly broke him. Setting the drawing down carefully, he tipped up her face and kissed her, his mind beginning to spin as she melted into his arms. They sank to the floor, and the flash of lights and color around them made him laugh as Katana shook her head. "I don't know how to make it stop," she apologized.

"You don't have to make it stop," he whispered back, brushing a kiss on her brow. "This is part of you. And so now, it's part of me. You can dream and imagine and bring into being anything your mind can conceive, and together we will find a way to learn its story. I love you, Katana. And I never knew that I could love anything, anyone, the way that I love you. Damnation itself was just my path to finding you."

He drew her to him, and time stretched and rolled, with curves and angles and jagged lines, bursts of color, streams of textures, and patterns light and dark. And later, far later, when they had made it to the bedroom and she lay wrapped in his arms, she remembered something else.

"I've never used the color purple in any of my drawings that was the exact shade of your eyes," she murmured. "I would save the crayons, markers, pastels, and colored pencils, and lock them away in a box so I didn't waste the color on anything else. And now I'll get to see it every day."

"You will," he promised her, and a greater truth he had never spoken. "For as long as I draw breath, I am yours, Katana. And for an eternity ever after."

32

A long time after that, Kat crept out of bed, and, leaving the door slightly open, stepped into the main room of their little cottage. It was an island of safety amidst the storm. She knew what she would find when she eventually reconnected with social media and the news. War and terror, climate disasters and sickness, corrupt politics and violence. Essentially the exact same issues that had faced the world prior to the events of a couple of days before.

The majority of the world didn't even know what horrors had been unleashed upon them, and didn't know the advantages and the treasures either. Magic. Real, indisputable magic. The kind that would put the charlatans of the tourist traps around the world out of business. The kind that would make believers out of any who were able to witness the possibilities.

She hugged her arms close to her body, unwilling to pick up her notepad yet. Because she knew that what she had to search for wasn't going to be a joyful kind of magic. The person she needed to find to save Hugh and his team, maybe to save them all, didn't want to be found. She'd peered into his eyes before, and what she'd seen there had gone beyond self-recriminations and doubt. It even went beyond fear.

What she'd found in the eyes of the archangel of the Lord was betrayal. And the betrayal of what? Of God, of humanity? Either were possible, but neither fit, for the same reason.

Humanity was born to fail.

As Kat herself had been forced to acknowledge, there was no solution to the recent psychic disaster that would result in a human utopia, no matter how much she wanted it. Had Michael come to the same realization? That after all these millennia of devoting his life to taking care of humanity, it was all for naught? Was that the betrayal he faced?

Or was it something entirely different? Only he could say, and he'd turned silent.

According to Hugh, it wasn't the first time this had happened.

Kat scowled, thinking of all the darkness that had reigned while the archangel had remained aloof and apart from humanity. He couldn't remain aloof now. Her lips twisted. Maybe in truth, she was the one who'd betrayed him. Maybe her deep knowledge of his possibilities was what he feared.

But she had to try to find him. His story wasn't over yet.

She'd barely pulled the pad out of her backpack when Hugh stirred. He stepped out of the bedroom, gorgeous in a pair of long flowing jersey pants and nothing else.

"You're going to look for the archangel?" he asked her, and she nodded.

"He's out there, I know he is. He's part of the path forward, but he won't show his face."

"You think he's hiding from something—or someone? He killed a human to save Death, knowing he would be punished. Did he do that because he had fallen in love with her or was there something else? Something deeper at hand?"

"I don't know," Kat said. "He's been betrayed, but who could betray the archangel other than God...and the Father wouldn't do that to one of his own. He created the pantheon of angel warriors to bow to Michael's command, except now that those angels are ready...he's not here anymore. He's been taken out of the game by his own hand."

"You mean the 144th." Hugh tilted his head. "Could that be it? Could he have been told to force Blue into action to lead those maniacs? Would that be reason enough to commit such a sin... No. After all these millennia, to strike down a human, I can't see it."

"If it was his course..." Kat countered, but her heart wasn't in it. There was simply no good reason for the archangel to have sinned in such a way.

They sat another moment in uneasy silence, then were startled by a knock at the door. Kat jolted as Hugh held out a quelling hand. He turned and strode the few steps to the door, then, preparing himself for anything, he opened it wide.

"Raum!" he blurted, and Kat gaped.

The angelic-voiced enforcer stood on the threshold—sort of. He listed a little to the right, swayed, then fell inward. His eyes were scorched black and bleeding, his skin rent with claw marks and black blood oozing in the welts.

"God's teeth, what happened to you?" Hugh demanded as Kat reached for her pad again.

"My path is open to me now," Raum groaned. "But it is impossible. I approached the gates, and the horrors awaiting me there ripped me limb from limb. I cannot pass."

"Where? Where is it you're supposed to go?" Hugh demanded, and Raum coughed up a wash of blood.

"Into the angelic realm, to call them to arms. Only they can help the humans now. We are too few."

His gaze swung to Kat. "Blue said you knew. That you had seen it."

"That the 144th would come?" Hugh asked.

"They would come if we release them, but they are forbidden to fly on their own. Their chains are too heavy. The only way to release them is to throw open the door that holds them fast and cut their chains—and to do that, we have to break through the ranks of angels. Easier said than done, as I now know."

Kat tapped her pen on her notepad. "You need Michael."

"We need Michael," Raum agreed. "Or me, or so I thought. But I can see any angel for what they truly are—I can see the sins they have not committed, but might. And so I must perish, lest anyone else learn of them. I cannot pass."

"You need a human," Kat said resolutely, and she looked down at what she was drawing, then drew her brows together in surprise. She'd sketched a fortress in the middle of the desert with lofty spires, turrets and walkways, stone and metal and glass. "I don't know this place," she murmured.

Raum squinted down at it. "I do. It was the base of the Arcana Council, but it's abandoned now. The High Priestess is hidden, the Magician gone. Justice has fled and the Fool has vanished. The members of the Arcana Council have left this place. There's no one left."

Kat pointed at the small lonely figure standing in the

shadows of the great fortress. "Someone is there," she insisted, as Raum furrowed his brow, his beautiful face worn with worry. "A woman named Lainie Grant. She was blind, but now she sees. She can help you. Go to her, and I'll make your path as straight as I can."

He looked up, and she was caught by the pain shimmering in his eyes, a pain she'd seen played out in a million futures that would never be.

Raum stood, and Kat laid down her pencil. Because this, after all, wasn't her path to walk, nor her adventure to take. It was Raum's—the most beautiful demon of the Syx...and the most haunted, for reasons that made Kat's blood run cold in her veins. She didn't envy him any of the futures she had seen for him. She only hoped there was one she'd missed.

"Go to her," she whispered.

∼

THANK YOU for reading DEMON BETRAYED!

As always, I sincerely hope you enjoyed taking the adventure with Hugh and Katana. If you did and you'd like to help other readers find them, I truly appreciate you leaving a review for the book wherever you purchased this copy!

What's next for the Demon Enforcers? Raum's tale concludes the journey of the Syx, as he works to bring a particularly unmanageable squadron of the heavenly host to Earth. The result? A showdown that will forever change the course of the war on magic.

But Raum has secrets of his own to hide, secrets no one

can know...especially not the deviously smart and dangerously reckless hired thief who crashes her way into his mission and refuses to play by anyone's rules.

Are you ready to go where angels fear to tread? Join the Syx for their newest adventure in DEMON BELOVED — now available for preorder!

BOOKS BY JENN STARK

Immortal Vegas

~complete~

Wilde Magic

Getting Wilde

Wilde Card

Born To Be Wilde

Wicked And Wilde

Aces Wilde

Forever Wilde

Wilde Child

Call of the Wilde

Running Wilde

Wilde Fire

Wilde Justice Series

~complete~

The Red King

The Lost Queen

The Hallowed Knight

The Shadow Court

The Wayward Star

The Night Witch

ABOUT JENN STARK

Jenn Stark is an award-winning author of paranormal romance and urban fantasy. She lives and writes in Ohio. . . and she definitely loves to write. In addition to her Immortal Vegas and Wilde Justice urban fantasy series and her Demon Enforcers paranormal romance series, she is also author D.D. Chance, whose fantasy romance novels are available exclusively at Amazon; Jennifer McGowan, whose Maids of Honor series of Young Adult Elizabethan spy romances are published by Simon & Schuster; and author Jennifer Chance, whose Rule Breakers series of New Adult contemporary romances are published by Random House/LoveSwept and whose modern royals series, Gowns & Crowns, is available wherever ebooks are sold.

You can find her online, follow her on Twitter, and visit her on Facebook!